AF424625

Readers' Favorite gives *The Laws of Attraction* 5 stars. *The Laws of Attraction* is "a very insightful and quirky legal thriller" where "nothing is what it seems at first." "The strange testimonies discussing the eternal soul and reincarnation, the various revelations about Susannah's past, and the way everybody's beliefs are tested all make for a page-turner." "This intelligent mystery" is a "guilty reading pleasure."

--Readers' Favorite on *The Laws of Attraction*

Howard Reiss is skilled "at making characters seem real and lovable in the space of a few pages or paragraphs."

--Readers' Favorite on *The Laws of Attraction*

Readers' Favorite calls *The Year of Soup* "a wonderfully insightful read" and recommends it to "anyone who loves mysteries, emotional fiction, and self-discovery." "Howard Reiss is able to deftly weave story into sustenance and create a plot that is beautifully original without straying too far from classic themes of this sort of genre."
The Year of Soup is "a hands-down, great read."

--Readers' Favorite on *The Year of Soup*

BookBub calls *The Year of Soup* "a heartwarming read."

--BookBub on *The Year of Soup*

"*The Year of Soup*, as with his first novel *A Family Institution*, clearly establishes Howard Reiss' credentials as an especially gifted storyteller with a knack for creating fully developed characters and original storylines that engage the readers complete attention from first page to last. *The Year of Soup* is highly recommended and thoroughly entertaining, making it an appropriate addition for community library contemporary fiction collections."

--The Midwest Book Review on *The Year of Soup*

The Year of Soup received the Silver Medal for Best Fiction in the North-East Region at the Independent Publisher Book Awards in 2013.
"*The Year of Soup*, mixes a fine stew of intelligence and wisdom, while also at times stirring in a sharp wit and a pinch of genuine, heartfelt charm and humanity."

--*IndieReader* on *The Year of Soup*

"By understanding our family history we can understand our future. A frank novel of family and what binds us all through our troubles, *A Family Institution* is a choice pick for general fiction collections."

--*The Midwest Book Review* on *A Family Institution*

"The dialogue and the physical descriptions of characters ring with truth."
"If you liked *Where We Belong* [by Emily Giffin], you'll love.... *A Family Institution* by Howard Reiss."

--*IndieReader* on *A Family Institution*

"A truly nostalgic reflection of what could have/should have been that we all question some time in life. Reiss's dialogue flows with sincere reality, making his characters very relatable . . . . The underlying themes in The Old Drive-in range from adult coming of age and self-discovery to a truly timeless romance."

--*Readers' Favorite* on *The Old Drive-in*

"Azu uses her skills in journalism to investigate the death of her high school sweetheart, unearthing truths about the man from the time she once knew him to what he became . . . . The writing is infused with both realism and humanity and the story, told in the first-person narrative, becomes very engrossing and intimate. A Lover's Secret is a beautiful and heartwarming love story that will break the reader's heart and leave them rooting for the protagonist."

--*Readers' Favorite* on *A Lover's Secret*

AFTER WOODSTOCK

by
Howard Reiss

After Woodstock
Published: October 2024
Printed in the United States of America
ISBN: 979-8-9864284-4-4

This book was published by Krance Publishing
Front cover illustration by Michael Witte
Back cover photograph by Daniel Silbert

To Ellen, my life after Woodstock

PREAMBLE

If everyone who claimed to be at Woodstock had been there, we would have been half a billion strong, not half a million. But only half a million attended, history will swear to that, and we were two of them. I still have my ticket to prove it, since they stopped collecting tickets by the time we stepped over the fence, which had been trampled down, the main gate standing alone and untouched like one of those mysterious statutes on Easter Island.

This story, however, is not about the Woodstock concert; it's about my best friend, Jackson Allen, Jacko to me back then, and how those three days changed his life, practically blindfolding him and spinning him around like a game of pin the tail on the donkey, causing him to wander far off in a very different direction which I had no doubt at the time was a terrible mistake.

Before Woodstock, I was confident we would be sharing our lives together, traveling side by side through the decades, both of us enormously successful—Jacko as a renowned mathematician and computer whiz and me as the obscenely rich go-to attorney for the biggest corporations in the Fortune 100. Inseparable friends until the end.

I imagined our families living in adjoining brownstones in Washington Square Park with vacation homes together side by side on the beach in the Hamptons, our wives best friends as well, and our kids, one boy and one girl each, growing up like siblings. We would be one big happy, extended family.

I refused to give up on that dream for the longest time.

Jacko and I, he called me Bry, short for Bryan, graduated high school two months before Woodstock, first and second in the class. Jacko was first, beating me out by a tenth of a point, but it didn't bother me all that much because I was used to finishing behind him. We both ran on the cross-country team for four years and while I would be leading at the three-quarter mark, Jacko always caught up and passed me as we rounded the final turn, and the finish line came into view.

Despite what the coach kept telling me, I always started out way too fast, insanely expecting that this time I would have the stamina to keep up my torrid pace. Jacko knew more about the art of running—about himself as well I suppose—and always kept a steady, unrelenting pace, making sure to save enough for the final sprint.

He used to describe it as running within himself.

I had no idea what he meant by that back then. It sounded like something he might have picked up from his mother who sometimes consulted the stars to help guide her through the day, although there was no denying that Jacko always had more energy than me during the final quarter mile and as a result a much faster kick.

I never seemed to learn much from one race to the next because I was stubborn and refused to believe a word Jacko or the coach had to say. All their advice ever made me want to do was start out faster the next time, determined to get far enough ahead that neither Jacko nor anyone else would be able to catch me.

Unfortunately, that never worked, at least not when it came to Jacko.

Perhaps it was something in my DNA that made me reject intangible advice like that. I needed something more concrete than "running within myself," like taking longer strides or drinking less water before the start of the race, instructions I could make sense of and easily follow.

I was the type back then, now too, who needs to see and touch something to believe in it and make it real and consequential. Would-be lawyers, as I saw myself at a very young age having religiously watched Perry Mason with my father, lived for facts and hard evidence, not abstract theories, and assumptions. John Adams once said that facts were stubborn things, unalterable by wishes and desires, no matter how passionate, and I considered life, particularly my life, to be one of those unalterable facts.

Jacko's advice, seconded by the coach, about running within myself was no different to my young teen ears than wishing and hoping. The only things that mattered in a cross-country race were my legs and lungs. As far as I was concerned, it was all about determination, and that well-accepted and well-grounded philosophy was good enough to get me named to the all-county team in my junior and senior years. Second only to Jacko who was named runner of the year both times.

There are other examples of Jacko finishing ahead of me. We both tried to teach ourselves how to play the guitar in seventh grade. He practiced and stuck to the lesson plan in Mel Bay's *Learning to Play the Guitar,* which we both bought. Jacko became good enough to read music and play some basic rock and roll songs—held back by his off-key singing voice and shyness—while I refused to follow Mel Bay's numbered lessons with the same diligence.

I got frustrated by how slowly he tried to bring me along with the first half of the book devoted to children's songs like *Twinkle Twinkle Little Star* and *London Bridge.* I grew bored and impatient and skipped ahead, eventually giving up because I was not getting anywhere, not when it came to what I really wanted, which was to learn a few contemporary rock and roll songs to impress the girls.

It did not have anything to do with more natural musical ability on Jacko's part, any more than it did when it came to running. It had to do with his approach, his patience, and his perspective. I think Jacko recognized early on that some things in life cannot be rushed and some goals can only be reached by taking small steps. Unlike me, Jacko focused more on the process, as opposed to the outcome, and he never allowed himself to be distracted by fantasies, the television, the Yankees, or girls, the way that I did.

If you think that by the end of this story, six decades later, I would have changed my approach to life by learning how to stay within myself, focusing more on the moment, and embracing those intangible, unseen forces to help guide my way, you would be wrong. I am still easily distracted and measure most activities by how quickly I can accomplish them and move onto something else. I still run from one moment to the next, eyes straight ahead, rarely looking from side to side, as if I am racing toward the finish line, except the finish line these days is not the one I want to cross ahead of anyone else.

Jacko used to warn me about this in his letters.

I confess as I sit here today, I can't help but agree with much of what Jack wrote over the years, although saying it is very different from living it. It's like I used to advise my clients during our corporate takeover battles, don't listen to what they say, watch what they do because that's where the truth lies.

It was not easy to make the kind of changes in my personality and outlook on life that Jacko did. I've come to believe that for most people, who you are at eighteen is pretty much who you are at seventy-eight with some minor adjustments to account for life experiences and those bits of wisdom you pick up along the way, at least the ones that manage to stick like Velcro despite your best efforts to brush them off.

Jacko was one of the exceptions to that rule. He was very different when he died from whom he was in high school. Almost totally unrecognizable in my opinion.

There are many other examples of my finishing behind Jacko. I remember I was taller than him in elementary school and middle school, but he shot past me in ninth grade and hit six-two by graduation, while I missed the six-foot mark by a quarter of an inch. I always weighed more than him if coming out first on that metric can be considered an accomplishment, instead of the result of the meat and potato diet that was one of the tenets of my mother's religion.

Jacko was always easier on himself when it came to his failings, which included his shyness with girls—being one of the original math nerds in high school—and his general awkwardness when it came to small talk and social situations. He was much more introspective, more sentient, and always thinking about the bigger picture—the meaning of life and his place in it—while I was generally focused on my immediate gratification like most of my classmates.

Jacko always had inciteful things to say in class, particularly in English when we were discussing the latest classic novel we were reading. He was able to put feelings into words that often remained inchoate in my brain and come up with observations and issues I had not noticed or if I did, gave little thought to. It didn't bother me because I was much funnier and could always crack up the class, including the teacher, with my little witticisms.

Despite the differences, which turned out to be significant in terms of the paths we wound up following as adults, and the good-natured competition, we remained inseparable from the day we first met at age two in Preschool Playhouse. That kind of bond is unbreakable, at least it seemed that way to me when we tossed our graduation caps into the air on June 20, 1969, screaming and hugging like a couple of battle-weary soldiers grateful to have survived the war.

Jacko and I vowed earlier that spring—when we both turned eighteen—to spend every second of our final high school summer together. He was going to an avantgarde college in rural New England, his choice because he did get into Harvard. While I didn't, I was going to another ivy league school in New York City.

We both knew our summers would be very different once we left home and we vowed to make this last summer of our youth—we considered high school students to be boys and college students to be men—memorable, if not lifechanging.

Little did we know how lifechanging it would be, at least for one of us.

We took an evening job together at the local drive-in theater so our days would be free. Jacko had access to his mother's car since she was working on a cookbook that summer about creative ways to turn leftovers into gourmet dinners, although like all the others she started over the years it was never finished. We spent a lot of our days at the Jersey shore trying unsuccessfully to meet girls and in Greenwich Village prowling the streets looking for something neither one of us could have articulated if our lives depended on it.

The summer of 1969 was eventful, not just for me and Jacko but for the entire world. It started in early June with the last episode of Star Trek—we were both obsessed with the travels of the Enterprise—during which Captain Kirk's former lover steals his body. It was the only television show Jacko still watched and it had taken me quite a while to get him into it.

The Stonewall Riots in New York City were next. It was the first time I can recall being aware that there was another group of people fighting for their civil rights. Jacko talked a lot that summer about the inequalities that permeated our country which included racial, sexual, economic, environmental, educational, and religious. Even some permutations of God, Jacko pointed out, were considered second-class, putting it in the mathematical terms he was most comfortable with.

I was sure he was hearing about it at home. His parents were way out there politically. They got their news from the New York Times and Channel Thirteen, the local public broadcasting station. They were always discussing national events around the kitchen table when I ate over, which might explain why Jacko was more politically aware and principled than I was.

The end of June brought our high school graduation. Jacko and I both gave speeches. I gave mine first as salutatorian concerning our responsibilities as the future leaders of America to work as hard as our parents to protect democracy and to grow our economy, so we could remain the envy of the world. It was based on an article I had read in one of my father's accounting magazines.

Jacko gave his valedictory speech on our generation's responsibilities as well. While mine was all about taking the torch from our parents and carrying it further down the road, building on the progress they had fought two wars to achieve, Jacko's was about the need for our generation to reject society the way it was—filled as it were with discrimination, inequality, and war—and to begin the process of radically changing things for the better.

Jacko had originally written that we needed to burn down many of our existing institutions so we could rebuild them from scratch. The New York Times, which Jacko often read as well, was always finding fault with something or other going on in the country and writing editorials in support of those protesting.

My father was a New York Post man, a more conservative evening paper, the only one he ever read and the only one I regularly looked at until I became a business lawyer and started every morning with the Wall Street Journal. The Post barely covered world and national events. It avoided the more controversial issues and always featured a pretty girl on page five. It was the first page I turned to when my father was done with it, after which I flipped to the back pages for the sports. The Post had a much better sports section than the Times.

Jacko wanted a disarmed world that would use the money saved on armies and weapons to educate everyone and eradicate hunger and disease. He didn't believe we needed bigger warships, faster fighter jets, and more apocalyptic bombs. It was all utopia-talk as far as I was concerned, and I told Jacko that while some people might agree with him on a theoretical basis, most of them would recognize it was way too idealistic to ever come true.

I considered myself the realist in our relationship.

Jacko wanted people to take better care of the planet and the animals who shared it because he believed they had the same right to it as we did. He wanted a society that provided free healthcare for everyone, along with clean air and water, and above all he hated war. It's not that I wasn't okay with his ideas, who wouldn't be, but I had to call them for what they were—pipe dreams.

Jacko was ahead of his time when it came to the things that he thought were important and which I would eventually come to believe in as well for the most part, although never with the same fervor he did. I was the lawyer-type from a young age, meaning a defender of the status quo and the laws already on the books. I was a man of rhetoric more than action, happy to tweak things, but fearful of radical change.

The school principal had to review our speeches in advance and while he had a few minor comments on mine, he took the red pencil to Jacko's speech. All the burning down language became improving, all the issues we needed to address that were being ignored became age-old problems we had to continue working on just as our parents had and their parents before them.

The principal drew the line when it came to Jacko saying anything negative about war, particularly the Vietnam War. He struck his suggestion that the United States should eliminate combat as a tool of foreign policy and commit to unilateral disarmament. He wasn't going to let Jacko blame our parents or our politicians—past or present—for the lines they had to draw, the wars they had to fight when they were crossed, and the tribalism and nationalism that had been around since the dawn of civilization.

"It's a graduation," he told Jacko. "Families are here to applaud and beam with pride, not to be lectured by some snot-nosed eighteen-year-old kid who wants to blame them for all the world's problems."

What Jacko was allowed to read was nothing like his original speech. It had been stripped of all its urgency, and he read it quickly in a monotone like he was reciting the multiplication tables. It was supposed to last fifteen minutes, but Jacko finished it in under ten.

July overshadowed June in terms of making the summer of '69 special because America landed on the moon. It was July 20, and Jacko and I were glued to the television set along with everyone else watching Neil Armstrong take his first step onto the dusty lunar surface. I remember looking into Jacko's eyes, which were as big as the recent supermoon—I knew mine must have looked the same way—as we promised each other that once they started taking space tourists up to visit, we would make the trip together.

We were both scheduled to report for freshman orientation the last week of August so when I heard about a three-day rock concert taking place in upstate New York beginning on August 15 it sounded like the perfect last hurrah. We ran out and bought tickets. They were eighteen dollars for three days, a lot at the time, but not too much to splurge on for our sendoff into the real world which to my thinking meant college, grad school, work, financial success, and families, the parallel paths we had long discussed taking.

Practically every band we knew would be performing with some major exceptions like Bob Dylan, the Beatles, and the Rolling Stones, although our new favorite, the Who, would be playing songs from the Tommy Album, a rock opera that Jacko and I had been listening to nonstop since it came out two months earlier.

We borrowed a tent and some sleeping bags from someone my father knew who was in the Army Reserves and planned to arrive early and stay until the end, no matter the weather, and despite my parents' misgivings, notwithstanding that I had turned eighteen earlier in the spring and was now legally in charge of my own life. The way I figured it, decisions about where I wanted to go and what I wanted to do were now totally mine.

That's how I explained it to my parents—it was more an emotional outburst than an explanation—when they said they were reluctant to let me go. I reminded them I was going away to college a little more than week after the concert where I could stay up as late as I wanted, go wherever I wanted, and do whatever I wanted without them ever knowing.

"If you don't trust me to go camping in the Catskills with my best friend to listen to three days of music with thousands of other kids," I added, whined would be a more accurate way to describe it, "how can you trust me to go to college."

It was a winning argument I practiced on Jacko first. His parents, not surprisingly, did not raise any objections. They just nodded and went back to whatever it was they were doing. They were different from the other parents in our conservative suburban enclave. In addition to reading the New York Times and watching Channel Thirteen, they attended the opera and ballet at Lincoln Center, and talked about movies that never played at any of our local theaters.

They hardly ever watched television, certainly not while I was around. Perhaps because Jacko's father spent so much time during the day at his store surrounded by televisions. There usually were a half dozen of them turned on for display purposes and they were not always tuned to the same channel.

Jacko's parents were always busy with their own hobbies. His father liked to read about Medieval history, study books about birds, and analyze the tricks of old magicians. His mother liked to read poetry, paint landscapes that looked nothing like any landscape I had ever seen and cook foreign-sounding dishes with exotic ingredients like snails, goat, and octopus. She had a whole shelf filled with cookbooks and was always working on one of her own. They even liked some of our rock and roll music, while my parents and their friends could never get passed Frank Sinatra, Steve Lawrence and Eydie Gorme.

Jacko wasn't much of a television watcher either. He preferred to stay in his room reading, doing math problems, or drawing colorful geometric shapes with those special markers his uncle had given him one Christmas. His drawings all looked the same to me, although Jacko would always point out the subtle differences in the shapes and colors which he said reflected his thoughts and moods. I could never tell the difference between his happy red octagon and his concerned one.

Jacko did not have the rules and curfews the rest of us had. His parents never screamed up to him to turn off the light and go to sleep. It was up to him when he was tired and ready for bed. He didn't have a list of things he couldn't do without asking, calls he was required to make when he wasn't home by a certain time, and he didn't have to present himself for inspection whenever he was getting ready to leave the house. They let Jacko make his own choices and take responsibility for raising himself. That's what they told him, word for word, often in my presence.

I never heard them reprimand him for anything he did or said. In fact, I can't remember them yelling at Jacko about anything. They always talked to him in their serious adult voices, reminding him that he was old enough to make his own mistakes and learn from them.

His mother liked to tell Jacko to listen to his "inner voice" when he had any doubts. I took that to mean listening to his heart instead of his head, which I thought was the same thing as his conscience, but Jacko told me it was more than that. He said his mother once described it as the "music of his soul."

"What music?" I remember asking with a chuckle thinking Jacko was making one of his rare jokes.

But he was serious when he answered, "the music that connects us to the universe."

I tried not to chuckle, but I couldn't help myself.

"Is that like a God thing?" I asked.

"I suppose."

I think I shrugged in response and changed the subject. That was the extent of my curiosity back then.

Neither of Jacko's parents seemed the least bit religious. His mother had books on astrology mixed in with her sacred cookbooks, which I thought the church frowned upon, and neither one of them ever went to church, not even on the holidays, although Jacko agreed to attend Sunday School with me when my parents forced me to attend because he thought it would be an interesting experience.

I wasn't nearly as intellectually curious as Jacko, there was no question about that, even if I was just as smart. I didn't believe in any of that spiritual stuff, and I didn't think Jacko did either. Most of what they talked about in Sunday School made me roll my eyes at Jacko who rolled his right back at me. We spent a lot of time there doodling and passing notes.

After what happened at Woodstock, I wondered if Jacko's mother regretted telling him to listen to his inner voice because I figured it had to be that inner voice—which I decided after that wild weekend had to be connected more to his hormones than the universe—that told him to drop out of college before starting and become a hippie.

They called it the Woodstock Concert or simply Woodstock because it was originally scheduled to take place in the Catskill town by that name. It didn't because at the last minute the Woodstock town fathers got cold feet, revoked the permit, and the concert was moved to a farm thirty miles away by White Lake in the tiny village of Bethel.

Since the posters and tickets had already been printed, they kept the name, otherwise history might be calling it the Bethel Concert or the White Lake Concert, neither of which would have resonated as well in the history books, at least in my opinion.

The promoters originally predicted 30,000 to 40,000 kids would attend and then a few days before the concert revised that estimate upward based on ticket sales to 100,000. As everyone knows, 500,000 showed up and for three days we were the second largest city in New York State. The amount of garbage I saw strewn about after the concert was ample proof of that.

It's worth remembering what the world looked like back then, at least to Jacko and to some extent to me as well. It looked like a big blue and green balloon that was about to pop. There was chaos everywhere. The cold war was still raging, along with an arms race that had moved from atomic bombs to hydrogen bombs, as if focusing on one element from the Periodic Chart would make mass destruction more potent and more palatable.

The generals called it a gamechanger.

Jacko and I had both lived through the Cuban Missile Crisis earlier in the decade when we went to bed thinking the morning might bring the nuclear Armageddon that they had been warning about and for which we had been drilling for by hiding under our desks at school.

There was also a more conventional war going on in Vietnam which the politicians assured everyone was necessary to prevent the Communists from taking over the world one country after another, and a growing draft that was plucking kids from their homes and shipping them to the other side of the world to kill other kids or be killed themselves by people they didn't know and who didn't know them for reasons that didn't make much sense, certainly not to Jacko, and at times not even to me.

Charlie Manson and his followers had just committed a massacre in the heart of America's fantasy heartland, Hollywood. On the other side of the continent, John Lennon and Yoko Ono were having a bed-in for peace in Montreal because our government said it would throw him in jail if he stepped foot into the United States, like he was an international terrorist instead of a convicted marijuana user. So, he stayed in Canada and wrote a song—*Give Peace a Chance*—which our government probably found just as subversive.

The tragedies surrounding the Kennedy family which started with the assassination of JFK continued. The year before it was the assassination of Robert Kennedy in California immediately after he won its presidential primary. Then Edward Kennedy drove his car off the Chappaquiddick bridge killing the young woman he was with and failed to report it for ten hours.

Our current President, who we liked to call Tricky Dick, made it clear he didn't trust anyone under thirty—the feeling being mutual—and it seemed as if he hated college students most of all.

In addition, there were growing concerns about overpopulation, hunger, and pollution.

The whole planet seemed in danger.

By the summer of 1969, Jacko was sure that it was up to our generation to save the Earth. I remember him talking about it one hot afternoon at the end of July. We were sitting on a blanket at Jones Beach broiling under the sun, Jacko talking about what we needed to do to save the planet, while I watched some girls in bikinis chase the tide out and scream as it chased them back in.

"How do we do that?" I asked without taking my eyes off the show.

Out of the corner of my eye, I caught a glimpse of Jacko rubbing his chin while he thought it over.

"We have to stand up and scream at the top of our lungs," Jacko said. "There are a lot of us baby boomers and we all need to be heard."

"Great," I said, still distracted, "more protests and more chanting. It's a waste of time. It hasn't stopped the Vietnam War."

"I'm not talking about marching with signs. We need to do something different. There are other ways to get people's attention and change minds."

"Such as?"

"Not reporting for induction and going to jail instead."

"They're already doing that. There was a story in the New York Post the other day about the draft dodgers. You're going to have to come up with something better."

Jacko thought it over.

"Look at that girl in the yellow bikini," I said. "I think they're about to pop out."

She was jumping over the waves, and it seemed as if her breasts were trying to jump even higher. It looked as if they wanted to break free.

Jacko looked up for a moment before staring back down at the sand and drawing circles with his finger while he thought it over.

"You going to need something different to start your revolution," I said with a chuckle, thinking I had him stumped.

Jacko thought about the world a lot more than I did and on a higher philosophical level, which is why I suppose he often took his time answering. I knew he wouldn't suggest anything violent like blowing up the factories making the bombs and chemicals we were dropping on Vietnam. That was too radical for Jacko, and inconsistent with his pacifist philosophy.

"There are other ways that might work," he said.

"Such as?"

"Music, poetry, flowers . . . and love."

I turned away from the yellow bikini girl in response to that crazy answer. I thought it was the funniest thing Jacko had said in a long time, but he wasn't joking. He looked serious like he was in class instead of on the beach.

"How is rock music and free love going to save the world?" I asked, laying back to soak up some rays since the yellow bikini girl and her friends were heading back to their blanket. Those were the days before sunscreen when I wanted to get as tan as possible to impress the girls.

"By taking it to places where it's never been before."

"Like the Enterprise in Star Trek?"

"By defying all their rules and expectations. By refusing to work in their industrial military complex. By taking over parks and filling them with music and love."

"You've been reading the Village Voice again."

It was a newspaper that Jacko's parents had subscribed to that was unlike any newspaper I had ever seen before.

"And by living a simpler life closer to the land, one that's not devoted to conspicuous consumption."

"Conspicuous consumption? Jesus Jacko, you sound like you've been reading the Communist Manifesto."

"You're missing the point. Love, flowers, poetry and music are contagious, they appeal to everyone . . . young and old . . . much more than guns and bombs. Martin Luther King said that love always trumps hate. Love is the way to bring the change we need to save the planet."

I let Jacko ramble on while I lay there feeling the sun scrubbing at the few pimples that still popped out from time to time. He went on to explain how music and love were a universal language that spoke to everyone everywhere and could help bring the world together and end war.

"You know what we have to do," Jacko said, laying down alongside me to soak up some rays as well.

"Meet that girl in the yellow bikini and her friends?"

"We need to live the rest of our lives somehow differently. Not the way we've been told to for the last eighteen years. We need to live differently from our parents . . . focus more on the planet and less on ourselves . . . and we need to be kinder to each other."

"You want us all to become monks?"

"No, more like Johnny Appleseed."

I told Jacko that I had no intention of living my life wandering the country planting seeds and the conversation petered out after that. A couple of pretty girls sat down in front of us and there was no way I wanted to continue talking about the earth after that.

During the week leading up to the concert, Jacko began talking about how he thought Woodstock would turn out to be more than just a music festival, but a turning point in American history. He thought it would wake up our generation to the challenges ahead and plant the seeds necessary for the radical change the world needed, the kind of burning down and rebuilding he had written about in the original draft of his valedictory speech.

Jacko thought it was possible, indeed likely that a new political party would arise from Woodstock, one fueled by young voters in tune with the Earth, intolerant of the prejudices that focused on a person's birth and color instead of their merit and heart and disgusted with the vast inequalities in our society.

"A party," he said, "with a platform much closer to what the hippies stand for than the Republicans and the Democrats."

"Which is what?" I asked, chuckling as I often did that summer in response to Jacko's grand statements because all I knew about the hippies was what I saw on television and read in the New York Post. They had long dirty hair, ragged tie-dyed clothes, and liked living in parks, begging for handouts, and worshipping psychedelic music and drugs. They wanted everyone to make love instead of war, as if three thousand years of history had not taught them how easy it was to do both.

Of course, I welcomed the free love part, but it didn't seem like much of a political platform to me.

Jacko told me that I shouldn't believe all the nonsense I heard on television or read in the Post because hippies stood for much more than music, drugs, and free love.

"The health of the planet for one thing."

I could agree with keeping the oceans and air clean and preserving the forests. What kid my age couldn't? Still, I was old enough to recognize that one man's pollution was another man's economic progress.

"That's it?" I responded. "Pretty small platform."

Jacko didn't have to think twice. Perhaps he had been reading the hippie manifesto in the Village Voice or listening to his parents talk about them.

"Hippies are spiritual seekers of truth who practice the one true religion."

"Which is?"

"Kindness."

'Isn't that part of every religion."

"They also renounce wealth and greed."

"You mean ambition?"

"I mean the materialistic pursuits that have become the evil master of the soul of this country."

Now I knew he had to have read it somewhere because Jacko never talked like that before.

"Jesus, Jacko," I responded, "are you planning on anointing the hippies as saints?"

"No, far from it, they're just ordinary people who are seeking a more meaningful life of peace and self-sufficiency."

"Then why do they always walk around with their hands out?"

"Because it's difficult to bring about that kind of change, it takes time."

"I thought you believed in burning down institutions," I said, reminding Jacko of the part of his valedictory that the principle was quick to cross out.

"That was a figure of speech. The problem with the past generations is that they didn't worry about the world nearly as much as they worried about their place in it. Hippies are different, they're less for themselves and their own creature comforts and more for the greater good. They look at things through the eyes of the planet."

I scoffed in response to that grandiose pronouncement that gave the Earth eyes to see with and turned our parents and grandparents into selfish sinners.

"Hippies don't follow expectations like sheep. They're not desperate for fame and fortune in this life to pay for some eternal reward in the next. They're all about creating heaven right here, right now, by sharing and being kind to everyone and everything."

There was no point in arguing with Jacko when he got like this. I had nothing against kindness. You could have a successful career, make tons of money, and still be kind. In fact, the way I saw it, achieving the American dream enabled you to be kinder and more charitable. Look at Carnegie and Rockefeller, both captains of industry whose charitable activities were praised in all our history books.

Having a nice home, money in the bank, and a good life was what everyone wanted. It was not a dream our parents invented. It went back thousands of years. It was basic human nature. Why should I want anything different?

A couple of days later, Jacko read me an excerpt from either the Rolling Stone or the Village Voice, I can't remember which, that identified the most notable influences on the hippies as Buddha, Jesus, St. Francis of Assisi, Henry David Thoreau, Gandhi, and Tolkien.

"Pretty good company," Jacko pointed out. "No mention of drugs or handouts."

"I suppose that makes me a kind of hippie," I replied with a smirk since Jacko knew I was a big fan of Tolkien.

He sighed in response to my little joke. Of course, I had moved on from *The Hobbit* and the trilogy by senior year when I started talking incessantly about my plans to ace college, get into a top law school, get a job at a large firm, become a partner in record time, marry a beautiful young associate, and make enough money to buy a Penthouse in the city, a summer place on the beach, and send my kids to the best private school.

"Hippies are Hobbit fans for a different reason, Bry, because it's about good triumphing over evil, light over darkness, not because they fantasize about slaying dragons."

Now it was my turn to sigh.

Jacko said that he was going to read up on the Buddha, St. Francis, Thoreau, and Gandhi, which I'm sure he eventually did, Jacko being one of those guys who usually meant what he said. We did not get to talk much more about it since the summer of '69 was ending, and after Woodstock we would be off on our own.

Looking back on it now, Jacko was clearly acting a little odd that summer, even if it didn't seem significant to me at the time because Jacko had always been a bit of a contrarian. He didn't follow trends or play fashion games, and it never bothered him when I called his ideas ridiculous or unrealistic. He had thick skin when it came to who he was and wanted to be.

I didn't think much about it despite Jacko's occasional diatribes that summer against the status quo and our expectations because he still loved the Who, ate sausage pizza with me at Volante's and looked like the old Jacko, my best friend for the past sixteen years. He still wore his hair short like me, not the flattops we had in elementary school, but well within the length proscribed by our high school which required a boy's hair to be at least one inch above his shirt collar in back and above his eye in front.

He still wore khaki pants and collared shirts most of the time, the same as me, our high school outfit for the last four years. We both started wearing jeans and T-shirts more often that summer, including the nights we worked at the drive-in because it was dirty work, and we knew it was the uniform of most college students. Jeans were not allowed in our high school back then, except on Fridays.

We were both free of facial hair largely because our attempts at growing moustaches after graduation had been futile. We thought it would make us look older and attract girls, but they looked more like something we had drawn on for Halloween.

Near the end of July, Jacko's mother took him clothes shopping for college, and they discovered a small store called Om that sold tie-dyed shirts and hippie clothes. It was on a side street in a seedier town on the other side of the county. He bought two tie-dyed T-shirts and started wearing them to work at the drive-in.

He took me there and I brought one as well, but I didn't have the nerve to wear it to the drive-in, not after the manager started calling Jacko "Stardust" the first time he showed up wearing one. Strangely enough, Jacko liked the nickname and introduced himself as Stardust to the girls passing by his snack bar station during intermission who commented on it.

It never worked as a pickup line, but the girls would always chuckle before moving down the line.

In early August, Jacko stopped talking about the math courses he was going to take in college and how he wanted to invent a faster and smaller computer, one that could think for itself and answer questions. His father was gung-ho about the future of computers having had a front row seat to the demise of the vacuum tube and the miniaturization of everything electronic. He said that one day we would be watching computers instead of televisions and they would fit into the palm of our hand.

His father was sure that one day computers would run the world.

Instead, Jacko started talking about becoming a civil engineer so he could join the Peace Corp and help bring clean water to third world countries. He talked about living in Greenwich Village after he returned so he could discover new poets, listen to folk music, and watch art films in theaters the size of a living room until he met the right girl. Then they would move to a farm upstate where they would grow everything they needed to live.

I called him delusional and promised Jacko he could come visit me in Manhattan any time he craved a real hamburger or at my beach house whenever he needed to see the life he was missing.

The week before Woodstock, while I continued talking about my plans to become a lawyer and buy a house twice as big as my parents with a built-in pool and a game room in the basement larger than our local pizza place and an Aston Martin in the garage like the one James Bond drove, Jacko was musing about ways he could live the rest of his life somehow differently.

"Different from what?" I remember asking him.

His answer was simple . . . my father.

I didn't think that was such a big deal since I wanted to be different from my father as well. I didn't want to commute two and one-half hours a day to and from a nine to five job in the city working for a big company where I would have bosses on top of bosses. I wanted to be a managing partner at a large law firm making an obscene amount of money, so I wouldn't come home every night and complain to my wife about the tedious work, the salary too low to afford the vacations they always talked about taking to Paris and Rome, or how one of his bosses told him in front of everyone that day to get his shoes shined.

I would never have to worry about paying my bills on time or putting off buying a new car when the old one started to fall apart. I would take expensive vacations anywhere I wanted, and I wouldn't have to worry about snow or lawns because I'd live in a doorman building on Park Avenue where I would be close enough to walk to work or take a taxi.

And no one would ever dare to tell me to get a new tie or shine my shoes.

It turned out that Jacko wanted to live differently not just from his father, but from me and everyone else.

THE BEGINNING

CHAPTER ONE

I first met Jacko at Preschool Playhouse. We were about two-and-a-half-years old, so neither one of us remembered it. Still, we heard about it often enough from our mothers every time we ate over each other's house that it seemed as if we did. I don't remember much about those early years, but I have vague memories of racing Jacko to the swings and up the monkey bars.

He used to win all the time back then as well, although he never seemed to care as much as I did, which might have been the secret to Jacko's success. He didn't want to win as much as I did and never felt the pressure. He ran within himself even in preschool.

I remember when our kindergarten teacher announced to the class that both Jacko and I had become big brothers over the summer, and we looked at each other and rolled our eyes. Now that we had little sisters, it meant we had to depend on each other to play cowboy and Indian and soldier games. In first grade, we swore an oath as blood brothers to remain best friends forever, although we used ketchup instead of our own blood.

Jacko and I had a lot in common. Neither of our mothers worked. They called themselves housewives or homemakers back then. Both our fathers had served in the Navy during World War II, although neither of them shot a gun except in training. My father never left the states. He flew in the back of a reconnaissance plane up and down the New England coast peering out of binoculars looking for U-boats. Jacko's father spent two years in North Africa servicing this new device they called radar which was being installed on all the Navy planes.

My father went to college after the war on the GI bill and became an accountant. He worked for a large corporation in New York City. He started in accounts payable and worked his way up to become one of a dozen assistant controllers. He specialized in accounts receivable. He commuted in and out of New York City for almost forty years and liked to joke that he spent one-fifth of his life sitting in traffic.

Since fixing radar in airplanes meant testing and replacing defective vacuum tubes, Jack's father decided to open a television repair shop when he returned from the war. Back then televisions were filled with vacuum tubes, and they were not disposable like they are now. When a television set broke, you either brought it in for repair or paid extra for him to come to your house with his big toolbox filled with vacuum tubes to identify the one that needed to be replaced.

Jacko's father said he liked fixing things and being his own boss. He eventually expanded from repairing televisions to selling them, and then expanded even further to selling stereos and other small appliances. He liked working fifteen minutes from home so he could return for lunch whenever he wanted to taste whatever Jacko's mother, a gourmet cook, was experimenting with. She always had a cookbook open in the kitchen whenever I was there and was always working on some strange new recipe.

It was always late when my father came home from the city. My mother, my sister and I would have already eaten, and he'd have dinner with the New York Post while my mother straightened up the kitchen and filled him in on our day. Afterward he would watch television or play poker. He had a regular game on Friday nights that lasted into the early morning hours and another one every other Tuesday night that always ended at midnight.

Most weekday nights he fell asleep in front of the television and my mother had to call him from their bedroom to come upstairs. On weekends he liked to watch old movies at night and sports during the day. He always found a reason to root for one of the teams that was playing, even if he was not a fan of either one.

Jacko's father was unusual when it came to that. He didn't watch much television, probably because he was around them all day, and he didn't care for sports. He always came home early enough to shower and change before dinner and Jacko's family always ate together. I ate there often enough to know; way more often than Jacko ate at my house.

Dinner was no big deal at my house. My mother's dinners were always ordinary—meatloaf, hamburgers, hot dogs, meat balls and spaghetti, roast chicken, or fish sticks. Steak on Saturday nights if my parents were not going out.

I never knew what to expect when I ate at Jacko's house, but it was not likely to be anything I had ever seen before. His mother was always experimenting with new ingredients like raw chop meat, octopus, snails, and something she called speck which was a kind of pork fat. I rarely recognized the dishes she put down on the table and they often had strange-sounding names. They were usually edible, but if I couldn't hold my nose and get it down, she never pushed me to eat it, just as she never did Jacko or his sister.

Both his parents were very lackadaisical about things like that, unlike mine.

After dinner, Jacko's father usually retired to the small room off the garage which he called his office where he would read or work on his hobbies: magic and birds. Jacko's father liked to study the tricks of the old masters and to look through bird books. He said there were fewer and fewer species to see in our suburban neighborhood because we kept cutting down trees to make room for more houses and strip malls.

His father even tried his hand at carving and painting birds. Jacko and I would watch him sometimes. He had an incredibly steady hand when he was working with those razor-sharp knives and there was a stillness and patience about him when he was painting with those small, thin brushes that I found mesmerizing.

He was different from my father who could never sit still whether he was sitting at the kitchen table drinking a cup of coffee or lying back in his recliner in front of the television. His legs were always twitching or bouncing up and down. If not, his fingers were drumming against the table or the arm of the chair. Sometimes when he was watching a movie and the commercials came on, he would jump up and run into the kitchen for a snack or out into the garage for a smoke, although he always made sure he was back in time for the show.

Jacko had no interest in magic or birds, although he did teach himself—and me—to juggle three balls. We got pretty good at it after a while and even talked about moving up to four balls, although we never did. Once we got into high school there were too many other demands on our time.

I wonder if I could still juggle now. It's been a long time since I tried.

While our parents were friendly, they never became friends. They never went out together for dinner and a movie. His father never came over to watch a football game like the other poker players, and I never heard my mother talking to Jacko's mother on the telephone for hours at a time like she did with her other friends.

Jacko and I played little league baseball together through elementary and middle school, both outfielders with weak arms, but decent hitters. When we got to high school, Jacko decided to go out for cross country instead because he loved running, and I followed suit because hanging out with my good friend after school seemed like the right thing to do. I loved baseball, but I knew I was not good enough to make the high school team, especially since I had trouble hitting the curve. I could never see the spin the way the better players said they could.

As we got older, Jacko and I liked to call ourselves brothers from different mothers because we had so much in common. We were both lefties, both tall and thin with dark hair and brown eyes, and we both did exceptionally well in school. We were quick studies, natural test takers, and never got the least bit anxious about exams.

We even took best friends to the junior homecoming dance and the senior prom— Sherri and Carol. I was sure at that point I would marry Carol and Jacko would marry Sherri and we would live next to each other and raise our kids who in turn would become best friends.

But Jacko and I were also very different in fundamental ways, even if I didn't appreciate how significant those differences were until after Woodstock. Jacko was ahead of me in terms of puberty. He started growing hair in all the appropriate places about six months before I did. He was also way more political than I was. He announced that he was against the Vietnam War early on in high school, while I continued parroting my father's argument about the "domino" intent of communism and a more subtle version of his "love it or leave it" refrain.

Jacko talked about the civil right protests, and while I agreed with him one hundred percent, he did something about it by attending marches in the city with his parents. They invited me on a couple of occasions, but my parent's would never let me go, not because they did not believe in equality but because they had seen the protests on television, and sometimes they got out of hand. I never pushed hard against their decision, not nearly as hard as I did when it came to curfews and their other rules that impinged on my social life.

Jacko was ahead of me in terms of music as well. While I remained devoted to the Beach Boys and the Beatles, he branched out to the Blues Project, Iron Butterfly, and the Jefferson Airplane. His go-to songs senior year were Sympathy for the Devil by the Rolling Stones, a song and title that my father found repugnant, and In-A-Gadda-Da-Vida, by Iron Butterfly, which I hated the first time I heard it, the primary reason being that it was seventeen minutes long. It was considered one of the first heavy metal songs and had a drum solo in the middle that lasted twice as long as any of the pop songs I liked listening to on my transistor radio.

Jacko explained to me that In-A-Gadda-Da-Vida meant in the Garden of Eden and was intended to be a love song from Adam to Eve, which didn't make a difference to me because I still found it way too long and repetitious.

"How long can it possibly take to say I love you?" I remember asking him.

It turned out the composer was drunk when he wrote the song, which might account for its length and slurred title.

Jacko did not like sitting around doing nothing—he considered reading, drawing, and writing to be doing something—while I liked coming home from school and having a catch with myself by throwing the ball up in the air and settling under it like I was playing centerfield at Yankee Stadium. I also enjoyed spending a few mindless hours at night in front of the television.

I had been doing that since I was a little kid. I watched all the Saturday morning cartoons in elementary school, while Jacko found them boring. As we got older, I switched my allegiance to sitcoms like My Three Sons, F-Troop and Bewitched. Aside from Star Trek, the Twilight Zone and watching the news with his parents on the Public Broadcasting Station, Jacko did not watch much television.

Jacko read more than I did, and he was always taking books out of the library that were not on our reading list. Science fiction was his favorite when we were in middle school and early high school like "Stranger in a Strange Land" by Heinlein and anything by Issac Asimov or Herbert Clarke. When we became upper classmen, it was books by Carson McCullers, Faulkner, and Dostoyevsky.

I kept my youthful infatuation with science fiction even as a senior and loved fantasies like Tolkien's trilogy and Herbert's Dune. I read the trilogy twice. I figured that I got all the classics I needed from our high school English classes where we read books by Orwell, Melville, Steinbeck, Dickens, Hemmingway, and Twain.

During the summer of sixty-eight, Jacko read *The Catcher in the Rye* by Salinger twice and pronounced it the best book ever written. I did not read it until my freshman year at college when I picked it up hoping it might help me understand Jacko's strange behavior. It did if I assumed he had similar feelings of angst and alienation over the superficiality of society.

All teenagers feel alienated from society to some extent, but I had no idea how much deeper it ran in Jacko. He didn't talk much about it, and I didn't ask. For a lot of teenagers back then, no doubt today as well, it was difficult hearing much over the din of their own thoughts. My younger sister used to complain to my parents that I never listened to anything she had to say, which I thought at the time was largely a younger sister thing, as opposed to a teenage thing.

In truth, I was not a good listener.

Jacko had a far more poetic soul than I did, there was no denying that. He would spend hours looking at his father's old issues of National Geographics—he saved every one of them—and then write a story based on one of the more interesting photographs. He liked to imagine himself living in the photo. He spent a week once talking about what it would be like growing up in one of the lost tribes they had discovered in the Amazon.

Jacko also liked to look through his mother's Life Magazines and show me the more striking photographs, thinking that they might inspire me to become a photographer, which he thought was one of my dreams. He got that impression because I said on more than one occasion that it might be fun being a travel photographer. It was not something I really aspired to do, but I said it sometimes when I was with other classmates, particularly with the arty girls, to demonstrate that I had other interests besides the law and money.

Jacko also wrote poems and short stories which he didn't show to anyone but me. Poetry was never my thing, and he would get frustrated sometimes when I didn't get what he was trying to say and he had to explain it to me. His poems frequently contained images of birds and clouds. Often the clouds were dark and sometimes the birds were lying dead on the ground. What I did get was that a lot of his poems dealt with the fragility of life and the inevitability of death, depressing subjects I preferred not to think about, let alone discuss.

I always raved about his short stories, even though I did not care much for them either, in part because they were easier to understand. I knew I had to try to be supportive of my best friend's interests, and I always looked for something to praise in his stories like one of the characters or the twist at the end.

In truth, Jacko's stories never had much of a plot, certainly not enough for me. They were mostly words and ideas, detailed descriptions of places and things that always sounded overdone, odd, or out of place, and the dialogue never made much sense because no one I knew talked the way he wrote. His stories were nothing like the plot-driven fantasies and mysteries I preferred.

Jacko liked to draw as well, but he was not very good at it, certainly not compared to the painting of the sailboat that hung in our living room or the street scene in Paris behind our dining room table, both of which looked as if they might have been copied from photographs. Jacko's drawings were always abstract, filled with geometric shapes and lines that often ran off the page, as if his ideas and feelings were too big for the paper.

I exercised my artistic muscles with my Kodak camera which is another reason why Jacko was always showing me interesting photographs from his parents' magazines and encouraging me to take pictures of flowers, butterflies, and animals. The camera was a Christmas gift from my parents, not one I had asked for, but which I still had to use and pretend to like for their sake. Unfortunately, it required money to buy and develop the film which meant I had to save it for special occasions like family gatherings when my father would pay for the film and its development.

Neither one of us touched drugs during high school and that included marijuana. Beer was our lubricant of choice. We didn't turn eighteen until the spring of senior year, the drinking age back then, but it was easy enough to get, and acceptable to most parents provided you didn't abuse it. It was the kind of thing fathers turned a blind eye to since most of them had done the same thing when they were our age.

In 1968 and 1969, there was a "pothead" school on the other side of the county where a lot of parents worked in the theater and wrote for magazines, and the students smoked grass which they called reefer, railed against the Vietnam War, and drew peace signs on their book covers.

Jacko didn't despise them the way the rest of us did.

For the longest time, I wondered if Jacko's parents blamed me for what happened since Woodstock was originally my idea, as if I should have known something about Jacko they didn't, like how fragile he was, and realized that marijuana, endless rock and roll, and a free-loving hippie girl would be enough to crack him wide open.

About fifteen years later, his parents died one day apart after being seriously injured in a car accident and I got to speak to Jack for the first time since Woodstock. It was not in person but over the telephone. I hadn't seen or talked to him since the day he informed me over a slice of pizza that he was returning to Woodstock to be with Astra, instead of starting college. We had communicated over the prior fifteen years but only sporadically through letters.

I was at his childhood home after the funeral along with the other mourners, a funeral Jack did not attend. I had just offered my condolences to his sister when the telephone rang. I answered because his sister was busy and motioned for me to get it since I was closer to the phone.

I collapsed down onto the couch; the same one I had sat on many times growing up as soon as I recognized Jack's voice. He sounded the same as he did in high school and for an instant I was transported back there, as if Jack was calling to make plans to meet up later.

He didn't want me to interrupt his sister's conversation.

"Just tell her I called," Jack said like it was just another other day. "I'll call back when things quiet down."

"Quiet down?"

I thought that was an odd choice of words.

"How was the funeral?" Jack asked instead of explaining what he meant.

The question dumbfounded me.

"How do you expect? It was a funeral . . . really, really, sad. Accidents are always sudden and unexpected. It's not like an illness; you can prepare for an illness; you get a chance to say goodbye. And both at the same time, what a tragedy."

I sighed. I am sure I sounded angrier than sad. I couldn't understand Jack not attending his own parents' funeral.

I told Jack that all the old neighbors were there, including my parents, and some friends and relatives I didn't know, as well as his sister and her family. I said that everyone had been asking about him and wondering where he was.

I listened to my own breathing for a bit before asking straight out.

"Why didn't you come, Jack? You live one hundred miles away. It was the least you could do."

The old Jacko might have apologized and mumbled something about how hard it was to come back after all these years. His sister had confirmed with me earlier that Jack hadn't seen his parents since he took the bus back to Woodstock, rarely wrote, and hadn't called more than a half dozen times.

"It has nothing to do with the distance, Bry, not the way you think about it in terms of time and space," Jack explained, although without any of the emotion I would have expected during a conversation like this.

"Then what was it? Did you forget? Lose track of the date?"

I heard Jack clear his throat while he thought it over. I half expected him to hang up.

"I don't attend traditional funerals as a matter of principle."

"There's a principle for that?" When Jack didn't respond, I kept talking. "Well, I do as a matter of respect. Christ, Jack, they were your parents."

"We had a celebration in the forest this morning to honor their lives." Jack didn't sound the least bit put off by my tone of voice.

"Who did?"

"Kai and Harmony, our friends were there as well. We are all a big family here."

"But your parents were being buried down here, Jack, not in the forest."

I said that a little louder than my normal phone voice and a few people standing nearby looked over.

"That wasn't my parents, Bry. They left their bodies the moment they took their last breath."

Jack's sister caught my eye and raised her eyebrows. I shrugged in response.

"What does that mean?"

"They returned to the stars. They are part of the endless flow of time and the infinity of space now."

I started coughing in response.

"They are part of the circle again ."

"What circle?"

"The circle that encompasses the past, present and future. They have rejoined the cosmos. They are everywhere, as much here in the forest with us as down there with you . . . which means we can celebrate their most recent life wherever we are and whenever we want."

I almost said Hari Krishna in response to that New Age bullshit, the Sanskrit mantra that a group of devotees chanted most afternoons outside Columbia Law School during the three years I attended in the mid-seventies, but I thought better of it and remained silent.

This was not the time or place to argue about religion or philosophy.

How could I be surprised at this point that Jack was a spiritual outlier, the same as he was when it came to his lifestyle and politics.

"Funerals are a capitalistic concept," Jack said, as if he thought my silence was the perfect moment to push his agenda. "They're another means of transferring wealth from the poor to the rich. It's the same at birth. Babies can be born at home, delivered by midwives. It happens all the time up here, like it did with Harmony, yet society expects people to use doctors and hospitals. Can't you see what they're doing?"

Jack paused as if we were back in high school, and I was being called on for the correct answer.

"Yeah, reducing the infant mortality rate."

"It's all about their profits, Bry. They make money on you when you're born, they make money on you when you follow the path that they've laid out for you, and they want to make one final sale on your way out."

His remark made me angry, but I was in a room filled with mourners, so I put on my lawyer's hat and stayed calm.

"Maybe so, Jack, but this was the path your parents were on, and it would have been nice for you to be there at the end to acknowledge it and say goodbye in the house where they raised you and lived together for forty years. It's a gesture of respect. It wouldn't have cost you very much, barely a day, very little considering all the time and effort they spent on you."

Jack didn't reply.

"And it would have been nice for people to see you, friends and family who haven't seen or heard from you in fifteen years. Not everyone is as enlightened as you are."

"You've got a point, Bry."

"It's Ryan now."

"Right, well, you've got a point, Ryan, which you honored by attending, but that was right for who you are and what you believe. My view on life and death is very different and to remain true to myself I honored my parents in my own way."

"Your view on death!" I said, but Jack didn't hear the exclamation point I put at the end, he heard a question mark instead.

"Yes, there's a lot more to life and death than you think, and they taught us in Sunday school."

"Like?"

"Like, I don't accept your concept of death."

I sighed so loudly Jack's sister looked over again.

"It's more than a concept, Jack," I whispered. "Lives end and people disappear forever. You don't get to see them or talk with them again. It's as final as final gets. It's the end of the road, and it's only natural that friends, neighbors, and family should want to share these moments of grief and say goodbye. It's basic human nature."

"I disagree. That's the way you and most everyone else in this country have been programmed to think. Our society puts way too much emphasis on endings."

"Because endings are significant," I countered, shrugging in response to the fisheye I was getting from Jack's sister, "none more so than death."

"It's not as significant as you think, and they want you to believe. We are all part of the whole, Ryan, part of the cosmos. We may experience ourselves, our thoughts, and feelings as separate from everything else, but as Einstein said, it's just an optical delusion of our consciousness. We are all one with the universe and the universe never ends. Nothing ever ends and that includes us. We don't need our bodies to exist."

That was a lot to take in over the phone and pure nonsense as far as I was concerned. Back then I believed the law codified all the rules I needed to live by, and the concepts handed down by the church over the past two thousand years were all I needed to die by. History and tradition had to have way more correct answers than Jack could possibly have come up with during his decade and a half as a dropout.

"I suppose death is another capitalistic concept."

I could hear Jack sigh softly.

"Is this some new age religion popular with the hippies?" I asked.

It's not as if this was coming completely out of the blue. I already knew a lot of what Jack believed from his letters, but none of that mattered now. I was a lawyer arguing my case before a room full of mourners who were not paying any attention and a heavenly jury that I imagined was, and Jack's defense was without merit.

There was no excuse for him not attending his parents' funeral, none whatsoever.

"Nothing ever ends my friend," Jack said, repeating those words calmly and with considered intention just the way they sounded in his letters. The same way I would hear them in my head over the next thirty-five years, his conviction unchanged even on his deathbed.

"Consciousness is not required for existence, Ryan."

"It is for me."

"That's a hard way to go through this life."

"Tell me about it."

"We are all made up of the same stuff," Jack continued, his voice softening so I had to strain to hear him. "People, trees, rocks, clouds . . . every law book you've ever read."

"Carbon," I said, recalling what Mr. Eiben used to tell us during high school chemistry.

"No," Jack replied, "stardust. The stars were born from hydrogen and helium atoms. Everything in the universe comes from the stars . . . and everything returns to them."

It made me chuckle to think how appropriate the drive-in manager's nickname for Jack was now.

"That was your nickname back at the drive-in, remember, stardust."

"Ironic, isn't it?"

"I never realized how spiritual dust could be."

"It has nothing to do with spirituality. The problem with our society is that it confuses spirituality with thinking about God while peeling potatoes."

"That's not spirituality?"

"No, spirituality is the act of peeling the potatoes and being in the moment. The thinking and the prayers have nothing to do with it."

"Like yoga," I said.

One of my recent girlfriends had dragged me to her yoga class hoping that focusing on my breathing would help me stop acting like a lawyer twenty-four-seven. One class was enough for me and the relationship.

"Exactly, breathing is spirituality, much more so than praying."

"Then I guess I'm a spiritual person because I breathe all the time."

"Conscious breathing," Jack countered, "mindful breathing . . . that's spirituality."

Jack was no longer a student of math and science. He had not been for a long time; I knew that from his letters. Woodstock had turned him into something abstract—like one of those amorphous shapes in his school drawings—connecting him to some invisible force in the cosmos that only he and the other hippies could feel.

It made me chuckle for a moment because it reminded me of that television show I once watched as a kid, *My Mother the Car,* where the main character got to talk with his late mother who had been reincarnated as a car. Her voice came out of the radio, except he was the only one who could hear her.

"Spirituality is being aware and living in the moment." Jack added when I didn't respond.

The Jacko I remembered was a boy of few words. He was most comfortable cloaked in silence. This Jack was different, he had an answer for everything, he was never at a loss for words. Ironically, I, the lawyer, needed a moment of silence to catch my breath.

I handed the phone to Jack's sister who had walked over to find out what was going on and left.

It was the mid-eighties when Jack's parents died, but it seemed to me he was still living back in the seventies in the mystical Age of Aquarius, which offered him the meaning and logic he had once found in math.

WOODSTOCK

CHAPTER TWO

We left home at dawn on Friday, although the first performer was not scheduled to take the stage until five in the afternoon. Jacko insisted we leave early to beat the crowds. I thought he was nuts since Bethel was less than an hour and a half away. I didn't care if the promoter was predicting one hundred thousand kids, I could not imagine that many people would be willing to drive up to a small town in the Catskills to sit outside in the sun and rain for three days, even if the music was great, but Jacko said he had a funny feeling about it.

I did not argue because I didn't mind getting an early start considering this would be our last hurrah together before college started us on our separate, albeit parallel paths. More importantly, getting there early might offer us a better opportunity to meet some girls our age before the college guys swooped in and gobbled them all up.

I wondered afterwards if Jacko's mother had read his horoscope for the weekend and warned him about the traffic and the crowds, and the changes it portended. I always thought Jacko found them as silly as I did when she read them to us, but on the ride up he talked about Woodstock as if he already knew it would turn out to be a life-altering experience.

Looking back on it now from high up the actuarial hill I've spent over five and a half decades climbing, it seems to me that the Woodstock concert was the big fork in the road Jacko had been looking for—the one less traveled—that offered him the opportunity to live the rest of his life "somehow differently,"

He had been preparing for it all summer, becoming more outspoken about his opposition to the war, more enamored with the hippies, and reading books like *On the Road* by Kerouac, *One Flew Over the Cuckoo's Nest* by Kesey, and the *Doors of Perception* by Huxley.

I remember this strange conversation we had a little more than a week after the moon landing.

We were sitting by Forty-Foot, a fishing hole where we sometimes went to skip stones and talk. It got its name because it was supposed to be forty feet deep at the center. We used to fish there when we were younger, but Jacko stopped fishing in eighth grade when he decided it was cruel to catch fish on a barbed hook, even though my father assured him that they did not feel a thing.

"How can your father know that for sure?" Jacko asked me. "They certainly look terrified when we reel them in, and they fight like hell to get free."

"Because they don't want to leave the water," I said, defending my father, "not because they're in pain."

I was not going to fish by myself, but we continued going to Forty-Foot when we wanted to get away from everything. We were lying on our backs getting some sun after spending an hour skipping stones, watching the birds and clouds pass overhead, and making mindless conversation about the Drive-in, when Jacko told me he had been doing some research about the moon in the town library.

"It's the summer, Jacko," I said, as if the library should be closed for vacation as well. "You'll be busting your ass soon enough in the college library."

"A lot of ancient cultures viewed the moon as a deity," Jacko said, ignoring my sarcasm.

"Why," I chuckled, "because of its smiling face?"

"Because of its influence on the rhythmic life of our planet."

"The tides, big deal."

"It's more than that. They recognized that the moon's phases could affect people as well."

"Let me know the next time you see a werewolf."

I sat up and shook my head to clear away the drowsiness.

"They believed the moon had a subtle effect on everyone."

"Everyone?"

"Because of its connection to the cosmos."

"Huh?"

I think that might have been the first time I heard Jacko use the word cosmos and I wasn't exactly sure what he meant by it. The universe I understood. It was everything that existed, all matter and energy, including the galaxies, the stars, and the planets. Even the vacuum of space was part of the universe.

The cosmos seemed less defined. It was invisible, like a thought, more akin to the harmonious and orderly systems that created the universe and continued to govern it. For most people that might meant a deity of some sort, but for scientists, people like Jacko with his mathematical mind, and me, more agnostic than anything else, it meant the complex, invisible, often impossible to understand natural laws that governed all things.

At least I think that's the way I understood it back then.

Mr. Call, our physics teacher in high school, used to tell us that humans had yet to discover most of the laws of nature, which he also called the laws of physics.

I would eventually come to understand from Jacko's letters that the hippies used the cosmos to suggest something less organized and more spiritual that kept the universe in working order. It was not God in the traditional sense, defined as a sentient, all powerful being, but a kind of omnipresent force like Mother Nature charged with keeping time, space and all of life flowing together in harmony and, most importantly, in circles.

"The cyclical process of the moon's disappearance and reappearance," Jacko continued, still lying on his back while he talked up at the clouds, "suggested to the ancients that the moon was the place where souls ascended after death to wait to be reborn."

"You got that from a library book?"

"I did."

I remember thinking that was interesting, but so what. The ancients also believed that staring too long at the moon would drive you crazy and that the earth was the center of the universe. I knew Jacko did not believe everything he read. Indeed, he had become more and more skeptical over the last couple of years about what we read in our social studies and economic textbooks, so I wasn't sure what he was getting at.

"Are you suggesting we start praying to the moon?"

Jacko chuckled.

"No, of course not, but I don't think it's a good idea to colonize the moon the way they're talking about, and if they do start taking tourists, I'm not going to be one of them."

Now it was my turn to laugh.

"Well, I'm going if I get the chance. Are you afraid it might be haunted?"

"There are better things we should be spending our time and energy on."

"What about Star Trek and going places where no one has ever gone before?"

Jacko stood up and skipped a stone across the pond.

"Eight," he said.

I could never skip a stone as many times as he could.

"Star Trek was a television show, Bry."

"And a damn good one."

Jacko nodded and picked up another stone.

I asked a few more questions, but the best answer I got was that if the ancients considered the moon a sacred place, we ought to respect their belief.

"There are more than enough places to explore down here," Jacko added, pointing at the pond, "like the ocean bottom."

These days I wonder if the bad feelings and doubts he was having back then were not about exploring the moon as much as they were about the technological leaps that were taking us there and what they might mean for the future.

Perhaps Jacko foresaw new and more lethal weapons, as well as the new levels of alienation and discord the computers and the internet would bring and had doubts that he could fit into a world like that. I did not figure Jacko to be an old-fashioned type of guy, his parents weren't, but perhaps I had been too close to him for too long to notice the cracks that had begun to appear.

We took his mother's car to Woodstock, a Volkswagen Beetle, along with a small tent, two sleeping bags, our tickets and a knapsack filled with peanut butter and jelly sandwiches, cookies, and water. We did not even bring a change of clothes, at least I don't think we did because I don't remember ever changing.

I do remember we had about forty dollars between us which included a ten-dollar bill Jacko's mother gave him and one my mother gave me to buy something to eat when we ran out of sandwiches. By the time we did, it didn't matter since there was nothing to buy, everything was free. I even volunteered to ride around on the back of a farm truck handing out sandwiches flown in by helicopter since nothing could get through the clogged roads, not even the performers.

It didn't take long for me to realize that Jacko's premonition was right. There was so much traffic on the New York State Thruway at seven in the morning that we never got above thirty miles per hour, and once we got onto Route 17, we slowed to a crawl. By the time we got to the Bethel exit, we could have walked the final five miles to the concert site faster than driving it.

About three miles from the concert, we turned off in frustration onto a side road and found a bungalow colony where some enterprising families were collecting ten dollars to park your car on their softball field. It took us another couple of hours walking with the crowd before we finally came to the main gate which, as I described earlier, stood like a sculpture rising above the trampled fencing on either side of it.

I was beginning to feel a bit apprehensive. Could the concert go forward under these conditions and if not would the crowd riot? This was too big a crowd to control, especially since there were so few police and security guards around.

When I mentioned my concerns to Jacko, he laughed and pushed ahead. This was the opposite of the way things usually went down. I was always the one willing to take risks, tightrope walking across the railing on the bridge over the parkway and climbing onto the roof of the high school to look for lost balls. Jacko was always the cautious one pointing out the danger and asking one of his favorite questions—is it worth it?

Jacko was not one to take a risk for risk's sake. It had to be for something worthwhile. Finding a few lost balls on the roof was not worth it, nor was bragging about walking across the railing over the parkway. Woodstock, however, and the revolution it was going to bring to his life and the world was a different story.

Almost fifty years later, as Jack lay dying, a smile on his face, he told me he had a calling that day—I assume from the cosmos, I didn't ask—suggesting it was not a concert we were was attending as much as a door he was meant to walk through.

"A door to what?" I asked.

I had just turned sixty-eight, same as Jack, and thought myself wise and experienced, although I knew my wisdom and experience was hugely different from his and exaggerated in the eyes of most people by my legal and financial success.

"A door to the stars," Jack said, which I took to mean the infinite and unknowable.

It's a door I suppose we all get to walk through eventually. I just didn't think it opened at eighteen or offered much of anything on the other side when it did.

On the Friday of the concert, Jacko walked through the gate without any apprehension, although when I first brought up going to Woodstock, he was not all that excited since he didn't like the idea of sleeping in a tent for three days. He was fastidious when it came to keeping clean. Also, Jacko was not a fan of big crowds and used to complain when we had to sit shoulder to shoulder in the packed stands during the high school football games. Now, he was eager to cram together for three days with a half million other dirty and smelly kids, and I was the one nervous about all the things that could go wrong.

The stage was at the bottom of a giant hill that curved around it in a semi-circle. It looked big enough to hold tens of thousands, perhaps one hundred thousand screaming kids, but half a million was beyond my imagination. We set up our tent at the top of what everyone was calling the bowl.

We made instant friends with our neighbors who were older than us. Some were in college, some had already graduated, and some had never been. A lot of them were genuine hippies with torn jeans, tie-dyed shirts, beads around their necks, flowers painted on their faces, headbands, and ponytails.

Boy or girl, it didn't matter, they all had the same look.

Their joints were our joints. I took little puffs at first as they passed them around, barely inhaling. Jacko sucked them down like he had been smoking his entire life. Small talk with strangers was generally hard for Jacko, especially when it came to girls, but the pot and the carnival atmosphere loosened him up.

The next three days passed by like a dream. The concert ran into Monday morning, and we stayed for every minute. We had already quit our summer jobs at the drive-in because we had to report to our freshman orientations the following week and we needed time to pack and make our goodbyes.

My parents ran out of the house the moment Jack dropped me off and examined me from head to toe looking for any injuries or subtle changes they feared Woodstock might have wrought. They found nothing and my mother wiped away tears of relief when she told me how sick she had been with worry. They had been watching the television news all weekend and she said it looked like a disaster area, at least from the news helicopters.

They were both shocked I hadn't come home right away or at least called and I explained it was impossible to leave since all the roads were closed and there was no way to call. There were no pay phones anywhere and we were decades away from cell phones. I assured my parents that while the news may have painted a dire picture of dirty, starving kids, Woodstock was nothing like that.

I described it as a giant party.

"The music was fantastic, there was plenty of free food, and everyone was super-friendly."

"Somebody died," my mother countered.

"It was an accident. A water truck ran over his sleeping bag."

I knew that because I passed the scene just after it happened. I was on my way somewhere; I can't remember where. It was early in the morning, perhaps I was on my way to the lake.

I listened to a lot of the music, I remember that, although I don't remember much of it and not simply because it was over fifty years ago, but because I spent most of my time getting stoned with different people, including a lot of girls, unlike Jacko who spent all three days getting stoned with the same one.

I remember The Who playing songs from the Tommy Album at dawn with the sun rising and the psychedelic Joshua light show being projected on the giant screen behind them. I don't know who I was standing with at the time, but it was someone I had been sharing a joint with who suggested that I burn that moment into my brain because life wouldn't get any better than this.

I did burn it in my brain, and it did turn out to be one of the highlights of my life, although it took me most of my life to realize it.

I remember Joe Cocker's great rendition of the Beatles' song "I Get High with a Little Help from My Friends," and everything about the opening act, Richie Havens. I had never heard of him before Woodstock but his album, Mixed Bag, would become a big part of the soundtrack for my college years. I can still close my eyes and hear Jimi Hendrix playing the Star-Spangled Banner to close the concert, his guitar sounding like the bombs being dropped on Vietnam.

I went to the lake half a dozen times, maybe more, I'm not sure, to cool off and clean up. Jacko barely left the tent area and the girl he had met moments before the music began, except when I dragged him with me after they asked for volunteers to help distribute sandwiches.

However, this is not about Woodstock. Hundreds of books have been written about that weekend—I've read quite a few of them—and I have nothing new to add. This is about Jacko and how Woodstock radically changed his life. Perhaps something else would have come along if there hadn't been a Woodstock to knock him off his trajectory, perhaps something or someone during his first year in college who would have changed everything for Jacko the way Woodstock did, but there is no way to know for sure because he never made it there.

Before I get to what happened after Woodstock—and Jacko's quick return—I need to introduce Astra.

Just before Richie Haven took the stage, a couple camping somewhere in the woods sat down with us. The guy liked our view of the stage. He looked to be in his mid-twenties, tall, sandy blonde hair down past his shoulder, and sky-blue eyes, the kind that were difficult to look away from because they seemed too blue to be real. He looked as if he belonged in a surfer movie.

The girl was also blonde with blue eyes, although her hair was duller, more straw-colored than yellow, and her eyes were a paler, less gripping blue. She was shorter and younger, but still a couple of years older than us. I guessed she had to be in her early twenties. Jacko and I seemed like kids in comparison.

While he was movie-star handsome, she was simply cute. While he was sinewy and loud, she was softer, fuller, and quieter. She spoke in whispers, and I had to strain to hear her words, particularly with all the background noise around us. She sat as still as Forty-Foot which never had a ripple in it unless we skipped a stone, while he was in constant motion, rubbing his hands together or slapping them down against his thighs. It seemed clear to me that he played the lead role in their boyfriend/girlfriend relationship, and she was the supporting actress.

They were certified hippies with matching red headbands, painted flowers on their cheeks, beads strung around their necks, his hanging down to his chest and hers snuggly wrapped around her neck, embroidered jeans, colorful cloth belts and tie-dyed shirts. His was a T-shirt, hers was a blouse with a low scoop neck with nothing for support underneath that played havoc with my imagination.

He took a joint out of the leather bag he had tied around his waist and lit it. They each took a slow, deep hit like it was their morning coffee before passing it onto Jacko and me. Jacko did just fine, but when I tried to inhale it the way he did, I had a coughing fit.

The guy laughed before explaining to me why he wasn't surprised.

"You've never had anything like this, man, it's way stronger than any other grass you've had before. It's purer, the best you can buy."

I didn't tell him that it was also the first grass I had ever taken that deeply into my lungs.

He told us that he and a good friend grew it on his friend's family farm without any pesticides or chemicals.

"All-natural, handpicked at the perfect moment and sun dried. No stems or seeds, just pure weed."

He offered me an ounce for ten dollars. I thanked him but declined.

"I know," he said, "seems like a lot, but just look at it." He took a baggie of grass out of his belly pack and tossed it to me. "You'll never see a cleaner ounce. Look through it, you won't find a twig or a seed."

I told him it looked great even though I had no idea what an ounce of pot was supposed to look like. I handed it back and told him I didn't have the bread.

Meanwhile his girlfriend continued talking in whispers with Jacko like they were trading secrets. I tried to listen in, but I couldn't make out what either one of them was saying.

It turned out they were not a couple—some of the couples in school used to look a little alike, as if they had been attracted to their own reflection—but brother and sister and while he was twenty-four, she was twenty. They had spent the last three days traveling to Woodstock from Buffalo, stopping along the way to camp at this giant gorge he had heard about near Ithaca.

His name was Frederick, but everybody called him Rick. Her name was Astra. I didn't know if that was her real name or her name for the concert like the way Jacko—after first introducing himself as Jack—told her to call him Stardust because it was what everyone had called him over the summer at the drive-in.

She laughed for the longest time after he told her that.

After a while, I heard her say she thought Stardust was a "perfect" nickname for him. I didn't think so since Jacko still looked nerdy with his smooth baby face, thick black glasses, and short dark hair, at least compared to everyone else at Woodstock. The only star-dusty thing about Jacko was his tie-dyed shirt and the look in his eyes as he sat there staring at Astra.

The closer I looked at her, out of the corner of my eye so as not to be too obvious, the more angelic she looked. Maybe it was the way the sun lit up her face and illuminated the little fuzzy blonde hairs on her arms and legs. She seemed content sitting there talking to Jacko, leaning closer and closer to him, as if she had come to Woodstock to meet him, not to listen to the music.

I remember noticing how smooth and clear her skin was and thinking how round her face looked. Her features were perfectly centered almost as if she had started out as a child's drawing. I'm sure it was the grass, but those were the memories of Astra I carried away with me and still have to this day.

I nodded as Rick kept talking to me about the advantages of growing grass naturally, but I was not really listening because I was still trying to eavesdrop on Jacko's conversation and wishing that Astra had sat down next to me instead of him. I used to wonder sometimes if my life would have turned out differently if she had, although I can't imagine it. I would never have abandoned my dreams or my parents' expectations, not the way Jacko did.

I do wonder these days if there was indeed a cosmic force that drew her to him—and Jacko to her—as opposed to it being completely random. I tended to believe in the randomness of life back then, as I did for most of my life. I still do to a certain extent, although much less these days.

Before Woodstock, Jacko thought everything could be explained by a mathematical equation or the laws of physics. After Astra came into his life, he came to believe in inexplicable molecular and cosmic forces that connected all of us and have no beginning or end.

I watched Astra out of the corner of my eye as she took out her own joint and lit it. She and Jacko smoked it together, passing it back and forth like it was some hippie mating ritual. Rick lit another one for he and I to share while we listened to Richie Haven and the band that followed. I cannot remember who that was.

Rick never stopped talking and I gave up trying to eavesdrop on Jacko's conversation. Rick explained how hard it was to cultivate marijuana plants up in Buffalo where the winters were brutal and how he and his friend had to hide them not only from the police but from his friend's family. I got more and more stoned while Rick continued to talk about his pot business, his plans to expand into other drugs, his van, and his dream about taking it on a trip across the country. He talked about dozens of other things that I can't remember all these years later.

When there was a break after the second band, Rick dragged me into the woods to see the hog farm. He said the food there was free and I needed to know where it was. When we got back, Jacko and Astra were in the tent going at it. Rick smiled and walked off.

Looking back on it now, I wonder if Rick was gay and thought I might be as well since my hair was relatively short, my clothes clean—my mother always liked to iron my shirts, even my t-shirts—and I didn't make a play for his sister. The walk in the woods might have made it clear to him that I wasn't interested—I was too stoned to remember any of the conversation—because he disappeared shortly after that leaving Astra alone to hang out with Jacko for the rest of Woodstock. At least that was one of the theories I came up with over the years and I had dozens of them.

I never saw Rick again. When we packed up at the end of the concert, it was Astra who lingered beside Jacko until we were ready to leave, at which point she went looking for Rick. When I asked Jacko if she was worried, he assured me she was not because Rick was always wandering off and disappearing. Jacko sounded as if he already knew everything he needed to know about Astra and her brother.

I asked Jacko if he wanted to wait with Astra until Rick showed up, but he didn't. He was in a hurry to get home. I thought it was because he was tired and dirty, and eager to talk about the best weekend of his life, not because he had arranged to meet Astra in the town of Woodstock in a couple of days and wanted to get home to pack some things.

I did not spend much time with Jacko at Woodstock. When he wasn't in the tent with Astra, he was sitting with her at the top of the hill listening to the performers. I listened to the music as well, but rarely near the tent. I did not want to intrude on their privacy, so I wandered around. I even climbed the speaker towers at one point and sat there for a while watching half a million kids below gyrate and copulate to the music.

When the thunderstorms approached, they made us climb down.

I spent time at the lake watching the skinny dippers. I could never have imagined seeing so many naked women in one place and I never would again. I spent Saturday afternoon sitting on the bank of the lake talking to a young woman in her mid-twenties. She had driven to the concert from Iowa with two girlfriends who she hadn't seen since they arrived.

We took hits from joints that occasionally made their way past us. We wound up taking off our clothes and going for a swim together in the lake. It was the first and only time I had sex with someone in a large body of water. It was memorable, fantastic really, and I can still picture it sometimes late at night when I close my eyes.

I looked for the same girl the next day but couldn't find her. I was not even sure I knew what she looked like. I found someone else instead and someone after that. I got passed around in a way like a joint, at least that's the way I remember it.

I stuck to pot avoiding the pills offered to me since they were always warning us from the stage to stay away from certain colored pills and I could never remember which colors were supposed to be dangerous.

I got stoned a lot over the next four years at college, but always at night and on weekends, never in the morning or afternoon, and I never stayed stoned the way I did at Woodstock for days at a time.

Jacko was quiet on the ride back, speaking only in response to my questions.

What did you wind up eating?" I asked.

"Whatever the hog farm was serving."

"I never saw you there."

"We never ate it there; we took it back to the tent or down by the lake."

It was generally a bland mixture of overcooked rice, beans, and vegetables. Still, it was free and plentiful, so I wasn't complaining.

"You liked it?"

Jacko smiled to himself as he shook his head yes.

"I don't know how that's possible," I murmured thinking how accustomed Jacko was to his mother's flavorful, gourmet concoctions.

"Pot makes everything taste better."

I nodded since I had learned that as well at Woodstock.

"I don't know about you," I said, "but I can't wait to have a hamburger, a hot dog, and a large order of fries, and wash them all down with a cold Pepsi."

The smile vanished from Jacko's face.

"I'm done with meat. Astra is a vegetarian; we talked a lot about it. It's a much healthier way to live. There are a lot of contaminants in meat and it's way more ethical. Do you have any idea what they do to the animals? How they raise them, one on top of the other, and the way they slaughter them?"

I didn't, but it was not something I wanted to discuss.

"We've been eating burgers and dogs since we were in preschool."

"Things change, Bry. Life offers you different choices along the way . . . almost as many choices as numbers have permutations."

I look over at Jacko like he was a stranger. This couldn't be the same guy I went through junior high and high school with. The one who ate whatever his mother put on the table which often came from weird parts of various animals and would eat two hot dogs whenever we went to Yankee Stadium.

"Well, at least you're still a math nerd," I said, trying to be funny.

Jacko didn't respond, he looked lost in thought.

We didn't talk much after that because we were both tired and dirty and needed to sleep in our own beds for a while to help process what we had experienced. I didn't see Jacko the next day. He said he had packing to do which I assumed was for college. I hung around at home as well to begin assembling what I needed to take with me for freshman year.

My mother kept asking me about Woodstock like she was suspicious I was hiding something traumatic that I was afraid to tell her. I kept assuring her the music had been great, and the audience well behaved. I even talked about the rain and the free food, but I didn't say a word about the pot or the girls in the lake.

"You can't believe how many kids were there. It took me an hour to walk from one side of the stage to the other. There were people everywhere . . . sitting, standing, sleeping. You had to step over them, go around them, and squeeze through them. It was slow going."

She gave me a little smile and a sigh of relief as she checked off the next item on the list of things the college suggested I bring. She called it my college trousseau.

Jacko and I met at Volante's Pizzeria for lunch the next day. While I got mine with sausage, as always, Jacko switched his order to mushrooms.

"Looks awful," I said.

"Mushrooms are healthy."

"And exceptionally smelly."

After talking about the music, the pot, and the girls, with me doing most of the talking, Jacko leaned forward and whispered, "I'm in love with Astra."

"I figured."

"I mean really in love."

"You know what they say, the first cut's the deepest."

It was a line from a Cat Stevens song we were both fond of.

He smiled to himself and nodded.

"Sometimes it's the only cut you ever need . . . or want," Jacko added, speaking as much to himself as to me.

"They'll be plenty of cute girls at college, some of them math nerds like you."

Jacko looked confused, like he wasn't sure what I was getting at.

"Buffalo is not that far from Vermont," I added. "Maybe she'll come for a visit."

"She's not going back with her brother."

"What's she going to do?"

"She's waiting for me up at Woodstock."

"The concert's over."

I was not quick at grasping the obvious back then.

"Not the concert, the town."

"She's almost twenty-one, Jacko" I reminded him as if two-plus years at our age—more than ten percent of our lives—was an impossible divide.

"Meaningless, three percent difference over the span of the average lifetime," Jacko responded as if he had already done the math a dozen times. "I'll be in my twenties in nineteen months."

"Is she going to wait four years for you to graduate or follow you up to college?"

I was being facetious. I knew neither one was likely.

I still didn't get it. I assumed Jacko was talking about a short detour to the Catskills for another wild couple of days before heading off to college to get his math degree and become a rich computer geek. As far as I was concerned, he and Astra were incompatible long term because one of the first things she said after she and her brother sat down with us in response to one of my questions—I assumed everyone her age was attending college somewhere—was that she had dropped out after her first semester at the University of Buffalo because she wanted to get on with her life.

Her brother added that he didn't even make it through the first month.

"College is high school converted to a sleepaway camp." he said. Astra took a hit while she nodded in agreement. "You can learn a lot more out in the real world."

I wasn't going to argue with them or try to defend college. I was enjoying the pot, as well as the non-stop parade of girls walking by, all of them without bras.

I eventually learned that after Astra dropped out of college, she started earning her own bread embroidering jeans and making beaded necklaces and that Rick was doing well selling pot.

"I'm going up to Woodstock tomorrow morning," Jacko said, snapping me out of my revery. "I'm taking the bus."

"Where will you stay?"

"Astra has a room in a house outside of town. Her brother took the van and went back to Buffalo."

"You don't have much time before orientation. Why doesn't she visit you in college? I'm sure she could make a fortune selling embroidered jeans and beaded necklaces to the freshmen."

Jacko didn't smile. He looked puzzled again as if I had missed the answer to the simplest math problem.

"I'm not going to college, Bry, I'm dropping out."

"How can you drop out; you haven't even started."

"Okay, I'm not enrolling. I'm moving to Woodstock."

"Jacko, be serious. You finally fall in love with some random girl and you're going to jump off a cliff with her?"

"More like jump into the water and yes, it feels fine."

"Think about what you're throwing away. What about everything your father's been saying about the future of computers. He thinks they'll be everywhere in ten years, and they'll all need math. You'll be rich, even famous . . . maybe before me, although I'm not sure that's possible."

I waited for Jacko to laugh or even smile, but his lips remained snapped shut, as securely as the clasp on my mother's Saturday night purse.

"What about everything we spent the last four years working for and talking about?"

I thought maybe I had hit home with that argument because Jacko's head shook slightly, almost like a nod, but I couldn't be sure, and then he started rubbing his chin.

"Astra is more important than any of that."

"More important than what? An education? A career? A future?"

"I've already got an education."

"High school? What can you do with that? Nothing. You can fix televisions."

It was a low blow, I knew it, but I was desperate to save Jacko from himself.

He stared at me, his eyes registering both disappointment and determination. I suppose he expected his best friend to be a little more understanding and supportive.

"A college degree doesn't define a person, Bry," Jacko finally said, "nor does his wealth or the kind of work he does."

"I didn't mean it like that, everyone needs to work to live, I get that, and whatever you do is important to a well-run society," I added trying to channel Mr. Mendelsohn, our economics teacher senior year, "but you've got a great math mind. Why waste it? Getting a college education will be fun and give you a thousand more choices."

"I don't need a thousand more choices. All I need is the right one, and that's what I'm making. I'll find something I like to do while I start living the life I want now."

"Not with computers."

"With Astra. College isn't for everyone. Neither is fame and fortune."

This argument wasn't getting anywhere, and I took a bite of my pizza while I thought it over. I was one hundred percent certain this moment of insanity was brought on by Jacko's sudden and explosive sexual awakening with an older woman who knew what she was doing.

I could not believe Jacko would really blow off all his dreams like that. I figured that after a few days stuck in a tiny room in a little mountain town with someone he hardly knew, the opposite of the three wild days of music and dope surrounded by half a million screaming kids—the backdrop for Jacko's great awakening—and the path she was offering would lose its luster. I was sure Jacko would come to his senses after a few more days of nonstop sex.

Perhaps it was some weird kind of post-traumatic syndrome, the trauma not the result of a battle, but a weekend of ear-splitting music and non-stop love. Jacko was a naïve eighteen-year-old, fragile as an eggshell in some ways, easily cracked by the counterculture war dance he had just experienced filled with drugs, hippies, and free love.

It might not have been bombs and bullets, but Woodstock could be just as traumatic to someone as shy and risk adverse as Jacko.

I considered Woodstock a once in a lifetime experience, but I often wondered how many other attendees tried to find a way to keep it going and hit the road, making the mistake of trying to measure their short, uneventful lives against those three days at the greatest concert and wildest party in history. For someone like Jacko, whose road had been quiet, cerebral, and paved with numbers, a new fork leading in an entirely different direction must have looked look like the yellow brick road.

Unfortunately, the timing was terrible, Jacko had less than a week to get Astra out of his system, put Woodstock in its proper perspective, and get up to college. He could be late for orientation, but not for the first day of classes.

"Okay, Jacko," I said, "I get it, endings are hard. Take a few days, go up to Woodstock to say goodbye, make plans for some wild weekends in Vermont, and a trip to Buffalo, but then come home and get up to school. You don't have a lot of time."

Jacko stared past me as if he had already left.

I could not imagine how his parents must have reacted when Jacko told them, particularly his father, who had said on more than one occasion that his biggest regret in life was not going to college. You don't spend your life repairing televisions and selling appliances so that your son can run off on a whim after a weekend of marijuana-enhanced sex.

"Why not attend the first semester to see how you feel, you know, just to make sure. Give college a chance, see if it measures up. I'm sure Astra can wait four months. I'll bet you anything you meet someone up there you'll like even more. There will be hundreds of girls to choose from, a lot of them math nerds like you, just think of the possibilities . . . no, the probabilities. You'll have a lot more in common with them than you do with her, and you'll all be the same age."

"You keep bringing up the age thing," Jacko snapped back. "The difference is meaningless, mathematically, and otherwise. Look at the age difference between your parents and mine."

He had a point, my mother was two and half years younger than my father and Jacko's mother was two years younger than his father, but one big difference was that they both waited until their early twenties to marry. They didn't elope when they were eighteen. Of course, the war might have had something to do with it, and in both cases our mothers were younger than our fathers, not older, which seemed an enormous difference to me at that moment. When I pointed that out to Jacko, he looked at me like I'd lost my mind.

I realized that I should have known better than to argue with Jacko about numbers, so I asked Jacko what his parents said when he told them. I couldn't imagine something this radical would get

the typical response I had heard so many times over the years—
"it's your life, you decide."

He cleared his throat in response and looked down at his
hands.

"I can't believe it," I said as soon as it dawned on me, "you
haven't told them yet."

"I'll leave a note and call after I get there. It'll be a lot easier
that way."

"They'll call the police."

"To say what, that I've decided not to go to college, and have
a girlfriend? I'm over eighteen, it's my life."

My words were gone, I didn't have any left, and I sat there
wondering what happened to the old Jacko, the one from a month
earlier, even a week ago, the one who refused to make any major
decisions without first weighing all the risks and possible
outcomes and then discussing them with me at length.

I had picked up Jacko on the way to the pizza place and when
I pulled over in front of his house to let him out, he stared at me,
his expression as serious as I could ever recall. I was expecting
something maudlin like a final goodbye, which it would be in a
way since I wouldn't see Jacko in person again for a long time, but
it wasn't.

"Remember our pledge," Jacko said, sticking his hand out for
me to shake as if to seal the deal. In sixteen years, I couldn't recall
ever shaking his hand. We'd punch each other in the arm, push
each other, throw our arms across each other's shoulder, even give
manly hugs from time to time like the way the baseball players did
sometimes on TV, but I couldn't recall ever just shaking his hand.

Now it was my turn to nod. I knew what Jacko was referring
to, a second pledge we made in middle school when we were both
complaining about our sisters tattling to our parents about
everything we said and did, a pledge we sealed this time with
actual blood by pricking our fingers with a pin. We swore never to

divulge our personal secrets to anyone, not to a classmate, not to our sisters, and especially not to our parents.

That meant I couldn't tell my parents, who would have immediately called his parents. Maybe they would have been able to stop Jacko before he got on the bus. It's much easier stopping someone from leaving than it is bringing them back after they're gone.

His mother did contact me after Jacko called her from Woodstock to confirm he wasn't going to college and moving in with someone he'd met at the concert. She asked me what I knew about his decision and the girl. I told her about Astra and what had happened between them during the three days that they were together, at least a more sanitized version of it.

She asked me if Jacko had taken a lot of drugs. I told her he had smoked some marijuana like everyone, but nothing else that I knew of.

"Mostly it made us act a little silly and get very hungry," I added.

"I know what marijuana does," she said as harshly as I could recall her ever speaking to me. "What about LSD? The papers said it was everywhere."

"No, we stayed away from pills. I'd have known if he had taken anything like that."

"Then why?" she asked. "Why is he throwing away everything over a girl he just met?"

I told her I tried to talk him out of it, but he wouldn't listen. Jacko's mother had tried as well, but it was harder to do over the telephone. He didn't want to hear it and after listening to her for a little while she told me that he hung up.

"I was telling him there would be other girls and that eighteen is not the time to make a life-changing decision like this."

It felt as if she were talking more to Jacko's father than me.

"He'll come back," I said, "just give him time."

Two days later his mother called the school to tell them that Jack would miss orientation and might be late for the beginning of classes, but the admissions office confirmed he had already called to withdraw his acceptance, and his spot had been given to someone on the waiting list. They assured her that Jack could reapply next year if he changed his mind.

She called me the next day to tell me what he had done. She did not sound overwrought, not the way I imagined my mother would be. She sounded tired and disappointed, like he'd made his decision and there was nothing more she could do about it. I wondered whether she had read Jacko's horoscope and it revealed that everything would turn out alright in the end.

Jacko's mother asked me to call her when I heard from him, assuming it would be soon. I promised I would, except I didn't speak with Jacko again until we talked briefly over the telephone at his parents' funeral almost fifteen years later.

The only contact I had with Jacko before that was by mail. People wrote letters back then instead of calling. Long-distance calls were expensive, and you could say things in a letter that you might be reluctant to in person or over the telephone. You had the luxury of thinking a lot more before speaking when you were sitting alone with a pen in hand.

No one gets annoyed and hangs up while reading a letter.

If you ask me, later generations lost a lot when they stopped corresponding and started relying exclusively on the telephone. They lost even more when they stopped speaking over the telephone and reduced their communications to emails dashed off in an emotional fog and cryptic texts thought up with the help of their thumbs.

During the four years I was in college, Jack's letters never contained a return address. I suppose it was Jack's way of making it clear he didn't want to hear any more arguments from me about why he was throwing his life away. They all had Woodstock postmarks, but I couldn't simply send him a return letter care of the post office, or maybe I could have but I wasn't willing to try. If he didn't want to hear from me, I was not going to force myself on him. Besides, I was angry at Jack for abandoning the plans we had made to journey through life together, plans that went back to kindergarten.

As predictable as my college life was, it was still engaging and fun. I was determined to move on from the past, the same as Jack, although in a much more time-honored and acceptable way. There was plenty of free love available in the early seventies to make sure I was not the least bit envious of Jack in that regard.

I did spend some pot-infused moments freshman year trying to understand how one long weekend, even a momentous one like Woodstock, and one cute, uninhibited hippie girl could change the arc of Jack's existence, and not for the better in my opinion.

The first letter I got from Jack arrived in my college mailbox in the spring of freshman year. I had almost given up on hearing from him, figuring he was too embarrassed and might wait until graduation, so he didn't have to hear about all the fun I was having. I know if it were me who had rejected the world and run off, I would have been writing to him at least once a month.

I still have the first letter, I saved it to this day, as I did most of the others.

Hi Bry,

Hi Jack, I remember whispering. I could no longer think of him as Jacko. Somehow, he had stepped across a great divide in terms of age and maturity when he went off on his own, ditching his parents and their support, abandoning me, and rejecting college, along with all the other norms and expectations we had absorbed growing up.

Hitting the books or just playing around? Pick a new girl to replace Carol? What's college like? I imagine it's a lot like high school except without any parents looking over your shoulder. Still chasing those good grades, I bet. We thought we would be done when we graduated high school, at least that's what they wanted us to believe, but they always have another hoop for you to jump through. In high school it was all about getting into a good college, now I suppose it's about getting into a good law school.

You will never be done with their expectations, not if you keep placing them above your own instincts and desires.

I didn't know what Jack was talking about since "their expectations" were my expectations—my instincts and desires—just as they were once his. I wondered if Jack was beginning to sense his mistake and trying to rationalize it away, hoping that by trying to convince me, he could convince himself as well.

The truth was that I was doing fine in college and enjoying it immensely. I liked the courses and my classmates, particularly the females, and I was not troubled by any expectations, theirs or mine. I was doing exactly what I had always said I would do. I was attending an ivy league college and building a foundation for my future as a rich, successful lawyer.

Unfortunately, I could not write any of that back to Jack. I could not give him my opinion of his new philosophy of life or say anything to bring him back to his senses, not without a return address.

After law school, it will be about getting one of those coveted associate positions at a big firm so you can work ten hours a day seven days a week and make partner, so you can work twelve hours a day seven days a week for an obscene amount of money that you will never have the time to spend or enjoy.

*In high school we were like rabbits chasing a carrot
on a stick that they never let us catch up to. You'll never
stop chasing their unreachable carrot until you get off
the merry-go-round and follow your heart.*

Wrong, I thought, reading it again almost sixty years later. It
was six days a week after I was made partner, not seven, although
twelve-hour days did sound about right. He was correct about the
money; I couldn't put a dent in it. Every year my net worth grew
exponentially.

He was also right about the carrot because after partner, there
was department head, then a seat on the management committee,
and finally head of the firm. No matter how obscene my
distributions grew, every step up the ladder meant even more
money, more prestige, and more power.

Now that I am retired and inching closer to the abyss or the
next turn of the circle as Jack liked to think of it, I have no idea
what to do with all the money I've accumulated. I was never a
shopper; I never had the time. I don't wear suits anymore the way
I once did. Retirement wardrobes in Florida tended to be simpler,
even if everyone in our privileged gated community still notices
the labels.

I have no real desire to travel. I spent forty years traveling for
work, mostly around the United States and occasionally to Europe,
South America, and Asia, and it feels as if I have spent more than
half my life living in hotels. I would like to see more of the world,
the parts outside the big cities, but doing it alone or as part of some
senior singles group does not hold much of an attraction.

I do like sports cars, and I have a classic Porsche convertible,
but I don't drive it all that often. I prefer to have a driver take me
to doctors' appointments or when I have someplace to go more
than thirty minutes away. I drive it mostly to the supermarket.

In my will, half of my assets goes to Jack's daughter—won't
she be surprised when she finds herself instantly rich—thirty

percent goes to my sister and her kids, and the rest to charity. The Earth was always dear to Jack's heart, so I have picked three charities focused on saving the planet.

Hopefully, it is not too late.

> *I can't wait to hear one day about all the things you accumulate. The penthouse in the clouds, the country house with a horse barn and Koi Pond, and the one you used to talk about more than anything else senior year, the beach house with the long dock out into the ocean that will be the envy of every tourist and fishermen who sails by.*
>
> *I remember you once saying that even the seagulls would get jealous.*
>
> *I'm sure the wife will be a former model or cover girl—the centerfold is probably too hot to handle—the kids tutored in everything to guaranty their rise to the top of the class, both stars on the tennis team having grown up with their own court and a personal instructor, and a couple of pedigree pooches raised largely by your maid, nanny, and butler.*

I know Jack was making fun, but it wasn't far from the way I pictured it back then. Those were the things I saw when I closed my eyes at night and tried to look past the horizon. I could never accept the hippie way of looking at possessions and life the way Jack did.

> *Maybe if you're lucky, you'll be able to buy the Yankees.*

That was one of my more fanciful dreams, not one I really took seriously. It was more a pipe dream like playing first base for them or writing a best seller. I preferred dwelling on the more reasonable and obtainable dreams; the ones I knew money could buy.

> *Our future will be more modest, not surprisingly, focusing on what we need, and what's sustainable in terms of the Earth's resources. We will try to be good stewards to ensure that we pass on a healthy and vibrant planet to the next generation, while working at the same time for peace and equality. We may not accumulate much in terms of assets and possessions, but we'll accumulate a lot in terms of personal satisfaction which we will be able to take with us when it's our turn to join the stars.*
>
> *I can't ask for more than that.*

Jack was wrong about the wife, the kids, and the houses. I settled on a luxury coop in Manhattan, six thousand square feet, river to river views, but it was one floor below the penthouse. The penthouse never came up for sale. And I never got around to buying the beach house or the country estate. I did not have the time to look or the inclination to buy them, not after I reached my forties. I was too busy practicing law, representing big corporations in their quest to take over smaller ones, and flying around the country to argue their cases in court.

The one marriage I had was to another lawyer. I thought Gayle was the prettiest lawyer I had ever met, especially when she smiled, which turned out to be rare outside of business hours. But I also liked that about her, her seriousness and determination, particularly when it came to her ambition. She also loved being a lawyer and saw it as a way of getting the keys to the kingdom.

She was not at my firm, that would have been a mistake; she was at a smaller boutique firm that specialized in the tax implications of mergers and acquisitions. I met her when we were on the same side of a big pharmaceutical deal. We were both ambitious, midlevel associates on partnership tracks. We worked long hours together in Chicago working on behalf of the acquirer. It was a contentious, complicated takeover that required many months of intensive work which made for a quick intimacy that neither one of us had experienced before.

After the marriage, we continued working long hours except we never worked on the same transaction again, either on the same or opposing sides. The firms made certain of that. There would have been ethical issues if we worked on the same matter for opposing parties and neither the clients nor the partners wanted husbands and wives on the same team. It wasn't conducive to the sexual tension needed to fuel the all-nighters, the same sexual tension which had originally drawn Gayle and me together.

We were often apart for weeks at a time working in different cities on unrelated matters. It was better for our careers, we both knew that, but the time we did get to spend together, late nights and Sundays when we both happened to be in town began to feel awkward, as if we were supposed to be someplace else.

She once described it as living "alone together."

We couldn't talk about what we were working on because of attorney/client confidentiality, and we eventually realized that we didn't have much else to talk about. Having work in common was not a strong enough glue to hold two ambitious people together for very long.

Gayle decided to move out to the west coast when she got an offer she couldn't refuse, a partnership in a big land use firm that was starting its own tax department. I didn't care, not really. We had been married for about two years and I hated feeling guilty about being away so often working on big oil and gas deals.

To be truthful, I was a little relieved when she told me she was moving to California because I would not have agreed to slow down and stop traveling if she had suggested we both needed to do that to save the marriage. I was intent on becoming the youngest partner at my firm and I was on track to do it. Unfortunately, it was not easy to accomplish while working on a relationship at the same time, evidenced by the fact that most of the partners in my firm were already on their second and third wives, and the others enjoyed being rich divorced men about town.

I forgot to mention the Olympic-size pool, the big collection of sports cars, and the extended vacations to Europe. Isn't that what you said you needed to die a happy man? Those were your exact words junior year.

Jack was right about that, but a lot of our classmates made similar grandiose statements back then, at least those of us who were more business-oriented and big fans of the American dream. I remember one of our classmates had his eye on the presidency and was always talking about which cabinet posts Jacko and I were going to fill.

Did you sign up for pre-law the first day of college? Are you going to classes in a suit and tie?

Just joking, old friend. being facetious as Mr. Pollard used to call it in English class.

I don't see you as a lawyer in my imagination, despite how you see yourself. I see you teaching Social Studies in junior high school or writing science fiction or perhaps becoming a photographer for Life Magazine. Wouldn't that be groovy. No house on the beach, no Playboy model for a wife, but the deep satisfaction of doing something meaningful for love, as opposed to financial gain.

There's a lot more to life than accumulating things. You know what they say, you can't take them with you. I suspect you will realize that someday. I just hope that day doesn't come too late.

It does for most people. Why should I be any different?

Wishing now that I had given photography a chance is a total waste of time and energy which I have a dwindling supply of these days. No one can go back and change their past, so why sit around and dwell on the what-ifs.

If I do get another life and another trip around the circle, as Jack truly believed, would I do it any differently? How do I bring what I've learned in this life to the next one if I can't recall it? Perhaps your karma changes or you knowledge gets sub-atomically imprinted into your new DNA, somehow incorporating those prior life experiences into your new subconscious.

If only I could be sure, then maybe I would be as calm and content as Jack when my time comes.

> *One thing I've learned over the past year from Astra and our friends is that the only person you need to satisfy is yourself, and by that, I mean who you are at this very moment. You don't need to prove anything to who you once were, especially as a teenager, or who you think you might be in the future.*
>
> *Your past and future selves will be fine, so long as you take care of the present you.*
>
> *Does that make any sense to a lawyer wannabe like you?*

I'm sure I thought "not really" when I first read the letter. My response today would be more like "no kidding." At seventy-eight, all that really matters is the "you" now, the one you can see and feel, no other "you" matters.

It's not like you have much of a choice because if you live in the past, you dwell in obscurity, in a time and place that's difficult to understand since most of the context and details are impossible to remember. It's a place filled with regrets and longings, at least in my case. Focusing on the future, particularly at my age, is guaranteed to awaken an existential angst that will turn you into an insomniac, which leaves one place for a guy like me to live, most anyone really, and that's the present.

People my age should always try to be fully in the time and place where they reside. It's the best way to avoid depression.

Jack's letter didn't move me. I had set goals when I was young, and I was not the type to quit on them. I remained focused and driven. I was not interested in asking myself every morning if this was what I still wanted. I thought it was more important to keep moving forward and to stay the course because "he who hesitates is lost."

I have always been a big fan of cliches, even if I don't always use them appropriately.

A lot of us were like that back then, we had absorbed our parents' expectations and relied on them for the momentum to keep moving forward from high school to college and out into the real world. No one else I knew from our small suburban high school graduating class abandoned them and changed direction as suddenly and completely as Jack did. I never heard another story quite like his.

I can't deny that being a photographer would have been fun, teaching as well, but neither offered the kind of lifestyle I had heard my parents extol and dream about, the one I saw pictured in every magazine lying around the house and fantasized about for so many nights in bed. A lifestyle that would make me the envy of everyone, especially my younger self. I had envisioned that kind of life for so long it had become an addiction as much as a dream.

Not everyone in college talked about becoming rich and successful though many did. The others talked about doing something that was relevant and meaningful, as if a successful lawyer or businessman could do neither.

It is important to remember that this was the late sixties and early seventies, a time when the anti-establishment types—like the hippies—were telling us, screaming at us really, that ambition was evil, that capitalism and the military-industrial complex were fueling the wars, destroying the planet, and keeping most of the world in poverty by forcing people to slave away at a minimum wage.

To them, being relevant and doing something meaningful meant living differently from our parents, rejecting war and conspicuous consumption, being kinder to the earth, living a simpler life and leaving a smaller footprint, and working to provide equal opportunities for everyone, as if those things were entirely within each of our control.

It sounded more like communism to me than the American way of life. In any event, they were pipe dreams. If you didn't take whatever you could, someone else would.

Meaningful and relevant also meant following your heart, another definition Jack was fond of, although I could never figure out what was so smart about the heart. Mine had never done much for me. I am sure Jack would say that was because I never listened to it. I once read that the heart's whispers can best be heard in moments of stillness and silence, and I generally avoided those.

The way I saw it, my heart was more connected to the me below the waist than to the me above the neck, at least in high school and college. So, instead of sitting cross-legged staring at the sunset like some of my artier college classmates and allowing the moment to fill my heart with all that sensory joy they raved about, particularly when they were stoned, I focused on the course work to get the good grades I needed to get into a big-time law school.

I suppose it was easier to strive toward that goal with my heart under lock and key.

That didn't mean I wasn't having a blast in college—partying, smoking pot and sleeping around—because I was and that offered more than enough meaning and relevance for me back then. I didn't give a moment's thought to how I might feel looking back on it at seventy-eight. How many twenty-year-olds do.

I'm happier now than I've ever been, Bry. I hope you can say that as well, I really do. Perhaps one day.

I feel truly free. I wake up every morning and sit there with Astra watching the sunrise and listening to the birds. Do you know they start calling out the dawn before the sun appears? Many mornings we go on long walks in the woods looking for edible plants. I've read quite a bit about which plants are safe to eat and which are not, and we have yet to get sick.

When I'm ready, I'll do something a little more remunerative, something I really want to do, and I'll do it until I grow tired of it and then move onto something else. It won't matter what my parents think, what society thinks, or you for that matter. I won't measure anything by its monetary reward, and, most importantly, I've got someone to share every moment with, someone who shares the same desire for a mindful and meaningful life.

There was that magic talisman again . . . meaningful. In a little more than six months, Jack had convinced himself that doing nothing or doing only what he wanted—which I imagined included skimming rocks for hours at a time—was the pinnacle of existence, the holy grail that his hippie girlfriend and her hippie friends had convinced him was the one and only path to eternal joy.

Not only was my best friend in need of a higher education, to my thinking he was also in need of a psychologist, an exorcist, and a good historian to explain to him how all the prior attempts at utopia had turned out.

Every day should be lived as if it were a lifetime without worrying about the past or the future, and certainly not fame and fortune. The moment is all that matters. I never close my eyes and dream about being

*someplace else riding around in an Austin Martin . . .
sound familiar?*

It certainly did. I talked about owning one, but Jack forgets
he was a lot like me in high school. He dreamt about starting his
own computer company and one day—along with the perfect
woman, another mathematician—touring the country in his
Corvette convertible.

We both had big dreams back then. A year later I still had my
dreams which I could feel inching closer, while Jack had given up
on his except for the one about finding a woman, albeit the one he
found was clearly not destined for a career in math. I felt sorry for
Jack and still believed he would come to his senses in a year or
two, after he grew tired of the smallness and aimlessness of his
life—as well as her—and found his way back to college.

At least this way I would finally finish ahead of him, even if it
was only in terms of earning my B.A.

*Enjoy each day's journey, my friend, because every
day is its own simple pleasure. Be thankful for whatever
it brings and whatever you have. Don't obsess about the
things you don't have and want. I think you'll find that
you don't really need them. Those feelings of entitlement,
desire and disappointment are easier to put aside if you
let go of everyone else's expectations.*

I'm guessing you find that hard to believe.

I did; it sounded like a lot of nonsense. Why should living
everyday prevent me from having a dream and working towards a
goal? They were not mutually exclusive. If life was a journey,
wasn't each day a step along the way? Can't you enjoy the flowers
as they go by while at the same time keeping an eye on the horizon
to make sure you're headed in the right direction?

That was my thinking back then. Being ambitious and having fun were two sides of the same coin.

I can assure you that I am happy with my choice. I feel as if I have been reborn into a world that is much closer to nature and more in harmony with the universe, a world that's very different from the claustrophobic, lockstep world we grew up in . . . the result of birth, not choice.

It seemed to me that Jack was reading from some hippie manifesto. He had a good life growing up. He had a lot fewer rules and curfews than the rest of us. He had a variety of interests and more than his share of accomplishments, being named all-country in cross-country two years in a row and finishing first in our class. It did not seem to me like he—or we—grew up in a claustrophobic, lockstep world.

I suppose you want to hear some more details now that I've hopefully made it clear I'm not coming back to ride your capitalistic merry-go-round, so here it goes. First, Astra refused to call me Jacko or Jack, and she felt I deserved something more personal than Stardust.

While she thought it over, she started calling me J, that's it, just the letter J. She said it was a spiritual letter being the tenth in the alphabet, and ten being a complete and perfect number. She said it signified responsibility and completeness, which is why there were ten plagues and ten commandments.

I never realized how integral math was to spiritual matters, but it makes sense. Math is basic and elemental; it was there at the very beginning. It's found everywhere in the universe so why not in the Bible. There is so much more we have to discover, especially in this new age of Aquarius.

Astra has a way of finding the commonality in things that connect us to the cosmos, as well as to each other.

I remember rolling my eyes at the ceiling of my dorm room after reading that bit of Aquarius magic. Here was someone who once talked about programming computers and solving great mathematical problems, who one day might have helped create the world's first humanoid robot, as well as spaceships able to travel to faster than the speed of light, now talking about math as if it were a mystical life force.

Astra felt we both needed new names since we were both being born anew. Astra picked Bodhi for me, it's a Sanskrit word which means awakened. Very appropriate considering where I was before and where I am now, don't you think?

"I don't," I replied to Jack's letter which he had decorated along the margins with stars and peace signs instead of the geometric shapes he used to draw when we were growing up.

I thought it was a dumb name, maybe not for a Buddhist monk, but certainly for someone who spent much of his senior year dreaming about finding a girl in college who loved numbers as much as he did and would sleep with him for that reason alone.

I got to pick Astra's new name. Astra had originally picked her name from the Latin word for stars—her birth name was Sarah meaning princess. I picked Kai, Hawaiian for the sea. From the stars to the sea, a long journey made in a single breath.

It feels as if we have already traveled far together, and I don't mean in terms of space and time, not as we typically understand it. I'm talking about a connection that began at creation and which will never end . . . like my favorite number, pi.

I could not help wondering if Jack had moved on to some harder drugs. I chuckled at the fact that he considered his trip to the town of Woodstock, barely one hundred miles from where we grew up, to be a long journey.

Traveling in one's head was not nearly the same as traveling somewhere, at least that was the way I looked at it back then. Still, I thought the crazier Jack sounded, the closer he was to hitting bottom, which meant it might not be too much longer before his new name and new relationship would begin to recede in the distance like the stars.

How much longer could Jack keep wallowing in this hippie mumbo jumbo?

It turned out I was wrong because Jack and Astra—Bodhi and Kai—would not leave each other or the Catskills over the next five decades. Their relationship would last a lifetime, two lifetimes to be more precise, and beyond those two into the infinite realm of mathematical possibilities, if I am to believe what Jack wrote in his subsequent letters, which I do sometimes late at night when sleep deserts me.

We are going to change our names legally if we can figure out how. No lawyers buddy, sorry. Guess that means a trip to the library.

We have a room in a house, a commune really, with five other couples. We share food and household responsibilities. Kai bakes cookies, she's a great baker, which she loves doing and she sells them to some of the local restaurants and believe it or not I have been working part-time on the town's maintenance crew helping to maintain the roads. You get a lot of potholes up here in the mountains, particularly after a freeze. They need young backs and I know you won't believe it, but I find the physical labor very rewarding.

We need to earn some extra bread because we want to buy a piece of land to build a cabin and grow our own food. The days of staking a claim and farming it to make it your own have been relegated to our old high school textbooks.

I couldn't imagine Jack as a farmer or working on a road crew. He was not a fan of physical labor when we were growing up. There was nothing he hated more than mowing the lawn or shoveling the snow off the driveway. Of course, he was working for himself now instead of his parents, and I figured that made a difference.

Still, it seemed out of character.

Physical labor feels good at the end of the day. We have been given muscles for a reason and you would be surprised at how defined mine are becoming. It's nothing like the way I felt when we were working at the drive-in and I'd come home every night feeling dirty and used, as if they'd found a way to prick a hole in my soul and suck a little bit out of it.

A little dramatic Jack, I remember thinking after I read that. We were kids earning minimum wage, gorging ourselves on snacks, trying to meet girls, and watching great moments from whatever movie was playing. What if our boss was a screamer; working at a place like that was one of those teenage rituals everyone goes through. Work doesn't start sucking the life out of you until much later and then it does it slowly over a lifetime.

I really wished Jack was in the room or on the phone, I would have given him a piece of my mind about his new philosophy of life. What he needed in my opinion was a good friend to slap his face and tell him the truth, instead of listening to the candy-land fantasy words of his hippie girlfriend and their commune friends.

I would have been satisfied with a return address so I could write back to him. I suppose that was why he didn't provide me with one.

Still, I don't plan on doing it much longer, working for the man as one of our housemates put it is a sellout. I don't want to work for anyone else, especially not the government, no matter how small and local. Kai and I prefer to live off the grid and working on the books keeps us way too visible. We don't want taxes taken out of our paychecks to support the war or the great American bureaucracy, and I do not intend to file any income tax returns assuming I ever make enough to have to.

We can barter for what we need and in our small way help create a cashless society.

Good luck with that I muttered to my empty dorm room. Let's see him build his own car. Was he going to study medicine or find some local witch doctor to proscribe herbal remedies in exchange for a load of firewood? It sounded like the frequent sex had burned out Jack's logic circuit.

We are close friends with another couple, Bear and Rainbow, I know it sounds funny, but he really is like a bear, big, round, and hairy, and she always dresses like a rainbow with brightly colored clothes. I love her originality and freedom of expression. Can you imagine anyone coming into high school dressed like that? She'd have been escorted to the principal's office the moment she walked through the front door and sent home.

I wish we had been more rebellious in high school and listened to our own hearts instead of their words.

How could Jack's heart be telling him that caused him to disown his parents, his best friend, and the world we'd grown up in while mine—having grown up right alongside him—was saying the opposite? My heart whispered to me to follow the well-worn path laid out by my parents and their parents and the generations that came before them, and to work hard to uphold the law, protect society's institutions, and help grow the businesses that had fueled our capitalist economy for centuries and made us the envy of the world.

I saw nothing wrong with growing my bank account while fighting for the rights of my clients. Indeed, it was the American way. Back then I was a fervent believer in the power and integrity of big business. Keeping our economy resilient and strong was essential to the American way of life because big business was the backbone of our democracy. As hard as it might be for someone like Jack to appreciate, big business could only succeed by keeping the best interests of the country and its citizens at heart.

A half century later, having seen firsthand what big businesses are really like, I can tell you in no uncertain terms that their hearts beat for one thing and one thing only—profits and share price. Corporate earnings are the only oxygen they need, and without strict laws and their active enforcement, most big businesses would eagerly stray from the straight and narrow.

The four of us are planning to open a new age store in town to sell local handmade clothes and art, as well as spiritual and meditative objects. We're going to call it the Age of Aquarius.

Kai will sell her beaded necklaces and embroidered jeans and shirts, and I am taking responsibility for the crystal section of the store. I am sure your eyes are glazed over by now. What do I mean by crystals? Not the fancy drinking glasses my mother and yours kept in the breakfront.

I'm talking about real crystals, the ones found in nature. They're everywhere and people have been digging them up and using them for healing since ancient times. They work best where real healing always begins . . . in the mind. The mind has the most potent healing power in the human body; few western trained doctors appreciate that.

Crystals stimulate mindfulness, reflection, and acceptance. Mindfulness brings calm and calm promotes healing. Clear quartz is considered the master healer because it amplifies energy and helps balance the body. Rose quartz helps restore trust in the body and its natural processes, essential to better health. There can never be true healing without being calm and trusting.

I know it must all sound strange to you growing up as we did in a community that relied on pills and shots, but it's true. I can feel the energy emanating from the crystals, as surely as I once felt the lapping of the waves at the beach against my feet. Math and science, it turns out, address only half the universe. The other half can't be seen or touched. There are no formulas for it, it can't be converted into a mathematical equation, or broken down into elements of the Periodic Table. There are no premises or proofs to explain it, as Western logic would suggest, which is why it's so difficult for people to accept.

Disbelief doesn't make those unseen and unfelt forces any less real.

It sounded to me like Jack's brain had been washed and hung out to dry; the mathematical deductive reasoning he was once so proud of having been replaced by images of giant crystals that in my imagination looked as if they had been plucked from a chandelier.

> *Crystals have all kinds of benefits. Jasper absorbs negative vibes and promotes courage, deep thinking, and confidence. Obsidian is protective and promotes clarity and compassion. It also aids in digestion and helps alleviate pain.*

Now Jack sounded like a traveling salesman trying to sell me some snake oil guaranteed to cure everything with one teaspoon a day.

> *I could go on and on because there are dozens of different crystals: citrine, turquoise, tiger's eye, amethyst, bloodstone, sapphire, and ruby, among others. My favorite, not surprisingly, is moonstone which is good for new beginnings because it encourages inner growth and inspires the heart.*
> *It was the first gift Kai gave me and I always carry it with me.*
> *I am writing a book about crystals, and we intend to carry a wide variety of them.*
> *We will also be selling crafts from third-world countries like handmade dolls and cloth from Thailand and Africa, as well as stone keepsake boxes from India. We plan on having a library corner with books about meditation and mindfulness, including books for children. All for sale, but welcome to be read while you sip some of Rainbow's herbal tea and enjoy one of Kai's cookies.*

"What about rolling paper and pipes?" I asked. Jack answered me as if he had been anticipating my question.

Bear knows where to get some beautiful pipes carved from stone which we will also be selling, along with some glass blown water pipes made locally. I can't begin to tell you how much fun this is and what an education I'm getting. A real education in living and sharing with Kai, with friends, and with the entire community, not words out of a textbook.

I feel as if I am finally getting started with life, as opposed to spending four more years being lectured at while I wait for permission to climb to the next rung of society's ladder of acceptance. It's a useful and mindful way to live—sharing a life with someone in a small community where I can find my completeness every day and start anew the next—instead of being reeled in like a fish on society's barbed-hook.

I had to laugh at that metaphor. I didn't quite see how Jack's opposition to fishing related to his dropping out of society.

I am also working on a book called "Letting Go." It's about the art of releasing, which is a way of freeing ourselves from the unseen forces that weigh us down. Think about it, we are weighed down with heavy expectations as children and they only get heavier in high school and college.

We need to be more aware of expectations, theirs and ours, the obvious ones and the subtle ones, and we need to learn strategies to let them go, along with the paralyzing fears and worries that accompany them. The dreams of fame and wealth they dangle in front of you will never be satisfying in the long run because all they do is create an unquenchable thirst for more.

There are always more dreams, more fame, and more wealth to be had, if that's all you can see. Those dreams and expectations are theirs; they shouldn't be ours, and holding tight to them inevitably leads to emptiness, loneliness, and profound disappointment. Releasing is the art of letting them go.

I probably laughed when I read that as well, I don't remember. It certainly sounded like Jack was willing to condemn me to hell because I was still focused on becoming a successful lawyer with all the trappings of wealth and comfort that came with it.

Since when was everyone in the world required to want the same thing or very little in Jack's case? We had evolved beyond an agrarian society long ago and if he preferred to live in the past and spend his life tilling the land and sitting in the sunshine that was his choice.

I do remember thinking that his expectations were just as unreasonable and demanding, if not more so. Hoping to achieve some sort of spiritual nirvana sounded just as time consuming and even more futile, condemning him to greater disappointment and failure than a life striving for something concrete and attainable like business success and financial security.

All these years later, I would have to admit Jack had a point. While I did achieve my dream of becoming the managing partner at one of the largest law firms in the country and accumulating more money than I could ever spend, I sit here most nights thinking about the things my money could never buy, not the least of which was love and a lifetime companion.

I never did get the family, which was always on my to do list, albeit lower down than it should have been. I always envisioned one like the kind I grew up watching on the television sitcoms with a devoted wife waiting at the front door for me to come home from work, an apron tied around her waist, a contented smile on her face, a drink in her hand, and a list of funny things to tell me about her day. Behind her would come the children, a boy, and a girl, who would greet me with a dozen questions and requests, followed by a large hyperactive sheepdog who would squeeze through to drool over my expensive hand-sewn leather shoes.

It's not that I was alone all those years. I have always had company when I wanted it. You can always find companionship when you have money. There were always people around at work or in the luxury high rise where I lived who were eager to join me for dinner or drinks, especially when I was treating. There were always colleagues and clients, and later clubhouse people and neighbors, happy to get together for cocktails or a stroll around our manmade lake to bring me up to date on their children and grandchildren.

Pleasant enough, but not nearly what I had in mind or what Jack had.

Those casual relationships and encounters grew tiresome over the years. Even though the Florida neighbors and clubhouse members were new, their stories and questions were pretty much the same.

Don't get me wrong, I am happy to have made it to old age with a stellar legal reputation and an obese bank account, just unhappy to have arrived here alone. If this had all been a dream, a preview so to speak, and I was still twenty-two, I like to think I would choose a different path. It wouldn't be the same as Jack's, not by a longshot, but it would be a lot closer to his than mine.

Unfortunately, you don't get do-overs in life, at least not in this one.

I kept telling myself it was more bad luck than anything else. I kept hoping to find the right woman, intending to make more of an effort when I found her, but time is the ultimate optical illusion, it tricks you into seeing things that aren't there like an endless road ahead filled with endless opportunities.

Time lulls you to sleep when you're young, convincing you that it moves slowly, and that the horizon never gets much closer. Then time picks up its pace in middle age, but you're too busy to notice it, like a race where you begin to coast because you think you have an insurmountable lead. Then old age arrives, and you realize you've been tricked, and time has blown past you with a breathtaking kick just as the finish line comes into view.

The path I took—and stayed on—was my choice. Following it to the end was also my choice, just as Jack's road was his.

I will be sure to send you one of the first copies of my books.

Yours in Peace and Awareness,
Bodhi

"Thanks," I whispered before sticking Jack's letter at the bottom of the shoebox I kept in my dorm closet.

I felt sorry for Jack, I really did. In my mind, he was a casualty of war, except in his case it was not the Vietnam War that had blown his mind, it was Woodstock and the war raged by the Quixotic counterculture.

I never did get a copy of either book because Jack never finished them. There were already plenty of books about crystals for the store to carry, and he didn't get far on his "Letting Go" book. Somewhere along the way he decided that writing was an "ego-trip" and egos, along with expectations, dreams, and ambitions, were a one-way road to disappointment and despair.

I still found it hard to believe back then that someone like Jack could walk away from his life after three days of rock music, pot, and sex. There had to be more to it. There had to be things about Jack I had not noticed when we were growing up that might offer some additional clues.

I would have to admit I was not the most sensitive kid on the block back then, nor the most observant. Like a lot of teenagers—no doubt it's much the same these days—I made very little effort to see things through anyone else's eyes other than my own. I was too busy with my own life and my own thoughts and concerns to pay much attention to anyone else's, including Jacko's.

Observing and learning was another thing Jacko was much better at than me.

NOTHING IS CRYSTAL CLEAR

CHAPTER THREE

At thirteen, Jack experienced something I never had, and would not until my mid-twenties when my Aunt Sarah, my mother's unmarried sister, died from cancer. Until then, death kept a respectful distance, confining itself to the movies, the television, and the news. It never felt all that real to me, or even possible when it came to my world.

Jack's mother was an only child, but his father had a younger brother, Francis, who they always called by his full name, never Frank or Fran. Francis was too young to have fought in World War II and he avoided the Korean War by qualifying for one of the first college student deferments.

I met Francis three or four times at Jacko's house. What I remember most about him was his appearance.

Jacko's father was always in slacks and a collar shirt, not the dress kind my father wore, but more casual and both often specked with grease and paint from working in the store or painting his birds. His hair always seemed unruly, sticking up in back and in disarray in front, except on Saturday nights when Jacko's parents often went into the city, and it was slicked back, although even then he looked as if he needed a shave.

My father, on the other hand, shaved every morning whether it was a weekday or a weekend. When he left for work, he always wore a suit and a tie which he called the company uniform. It was the way office workers in big corporations were expected to dress.

Except for the tie being loose and the suit being a bit rumpled, he came home at night the same way he left in the morning. On weekends my father wore his "comfortable clothes" which consisted of his clean and neatly pressed slacks and an open collar button down ironed sport shirt.

Uncle Francis was different. He always looked as if he had just come from the barbershop, his hair neatly trimmed and his face clean-shaven, even on the weekends, which was the only time I ever saw him. He always smelled like a leather couch sitting in a field of flowers. I knew it had to be his cologne, but it was very different from the one my father splashed on his face which smelled vaguely of soap and dry cedar.

The times I saw Francis he was wearing stylish, tailored suits, not the business blues and grays my father wore to work, but the night out on the town kind—pinstriped and very snug. He looked as if he had stepped out of a fashion magazine which made sense since Francis worked for one. I think it was Woman's World Daily, but it might have been Vogue since Jacko's mother always had issues of both lying around the house.

Francis was not married and never showed up with a girl on his arm. According to Jacko, when Francis was around, he talked mostly about baseball, his favorite sport, and his latest vacation. Francis was always taking trips to exotic places in the Caribbean and "on the continent," which meant France and Italy.

In addition to taking Jacko to Yankee Stadium every year, he took Jacko to the city every spring to see a Broadway show. He took him to see Mame, Hello Dolly, and The Sound of Music. One Christmas he took Jacko to see the Rockettes at Radio City and they went backstage afterward to meet one of the dancers who was a friend of his.

Francis always brought him extravagant birthday gifts. One year it was a beautiful hand carved chess set, another year it was an old-fashioned bicycle with a basket in front and a horn instead of a bell. It was in perfect condition, although Jacko never rode it when I was around, not after I told him it looked like a girl's bike. Once he gave Jacko a collection of leatherbound classics that Francis told him he had inherited from a close friend.

Francis called Jacko the last Sunday of every month to say hello and to ask about school. He always asked about the novel he was reading in English class and Francis was always familiar with it. Jacko said his uncle was very well read, the best listener in the family, and never judged anything he said. His only reaction to anything out of the ordinary that Jacko might bring up—his nutty ideas as I sometimes called them—was to say "interesting."

Then one of those calling Sundays, a month or two after Jacko had turned thirteen for which Francis had bought him a portable record player and a stack of 45s, Francis didn't call. It turned out Francis had been out late Saturday night drinking at a bar in Greenwich Village and the police found him beaten to death the next morning.

They did not have a funeral, just a burial. Francis did not have a plot, but they were able to get him one next to the plots Jacko's parents had. He said there were a lot of men at the cemetery, all of them dressed in black, and all of them reminding him a little bit of his uncle.

I realize now that Francis was gay and likely killed because of it. His parents had to be aware of that; if Jacko knew he never said a word. It was not the kind of thing you talked about back then in our conservative, suburban community. I don't recall if I was even aware as a teenager that there were men who liked other men more than women. It was certainly not anything my parents discussed, or I read about in the New York Post

At that time, I remember thinking that Francis was incredibly unlucky to be walking in the wrong place at the wrong time.

I knew Jacko took his uncle's death hard, even if we hardly talked about it, because I could see it in his eyes for the longest time and hear it in his voice. I wasn't that obtuse, but I did avoid bringing the subject up for his sake, as well as mine. I remember mentioning something about it once to my mother who told me to give Jacko a little more time and space because sadness, even one as deep as that, eventually passes, adding that it usually passes quicker at our young age.

My mother was right because a couple of months later Jacko decided to go out for the cross-country team which appeared to snap him out of it. He was back to his old self as far as I was concerned, all forgotten, although as we come to know when we grow older, sadness like that never completely disappears. It may not remain visible from the outside looking in like a scar or a burn, but it's always visible from the inside looking out.

I can't help but wonder if Francis' sudden, violent death might have sparked Jacko's first doubts about whether he wanted to put off living for another four years of college, two years of grad school, and the ten years it might take afterward to climb the academic or corporate ladder of success, since at any turn of the corner he could also find himself lying dead in the gutter.

There are a million different reasons why something like that could happen to you at any time, in any place, and not all of them are manmade. Perhaps Francis' death convinced Jacko that life was too fragile and unpredictable to put off which meant coming up with an alternative to the long, slow path we had been laying out for ourselves.

It took a lot of years for me to appreciate Jacko's life choice from that perspective.

Maybe Jacko began thinking about a way to honor his uncle and over time decided the best way to do that would be to live his own life differently, just as Francis had. His first chance to do that came after we were emancipated at eighteen and when Jacko saw the opportunity at Woodstock, he took it.

Jacko might have avoided talking to me about what he was thinking because he knew how I would react being a strong advocate and true believer in the well-worn path laid out by our parents and their parents before them. He knew how much I needed the comfort of those expectations and rules even as a child, which might explain my attraction to the law at an early age.

Or perhaps it was something unconscious like a DNA switch that belatedly turned on a gene Jacko could not resist. I would have felt better if that were the case because it would have meant I had nothing to do with Jacko's sudden turn away from everyone and everything. It would have meant that even if I had talked with him about Francis' death and not suggested going to the Woodstock Concert, something else would have come along to knock him off course.

The next time I heard from Jack a/k/a Bodhi was about a year later. It was the end of my sophomore year and I had just returned from a semester study abroad program in Spain. I had taken enough Spanish in high school which when added to the language course I was required to take freshman year qualified me to go.

I had no desire to continue studying Spanish or to become fluent in a foreign language. I didn't see any monetary value in that, but it was an opportunity to see Europe and experience another culture that would be interesting when I talked about my college experience with whatever woman I might be courting. It would also look good on my resume when I applied to law school and for a job at one of the big law firms. They would notice that I'd had an opportunity to get any wanderlust out of my system.

I also figured it would be my only chance to make this kind of aimless trip abroad since I planned to go straight to law school after graduation, clerk in Federal Court immediately after that, then find a good job at a big firm and settle down into the life I had talked about when Jack was Jacko, making a ton of money, and eventually marrying someone perfect for the long haul, perhaps someone like my mother.

Jack sent the letter to my house because he must have figured I would be home by then working at a summer job to make money for my junior year. I did find a job that summer working at the local New York State welfare office. I found it at the last minute when I walked in to see if there were any openings and was told they needed someone who spoke Spanish to do home visits. After four months in Spain, my Spanish was good enough for that.

> *Hi Bry,*
>
> *Halfway to the next goal, I hope college is all that you dreamt it would be. Are the girls like flowers there for the picking, isn't that how you once described it? I suppose we were all guilty of objectifying women back then. It's not like that here. We are all equal, all the same, all seen and heard, all respected, and all sharing equally in the labor and responsibilities.*
>
> *If you ask me, women are the stronger sex because real strength has very little to do with muscles. It's about intelligence, temperament, determination. and heart. I find Kai and the other women here to be much more even-tempered. They don't get annoyed over insignificant things the way the men often do; they never lose sight of the bigger picture and what's most important.*
>
> *It's not always about winning for them. Men are way too competitive about everything.*
>
> *I doubt we'd be at war in Vietnam or have an arsenal of nuclear weapons sufficient to destroy every living creature on the earth a dozen times over if the world were run by women.*
>
> *They have more patience and understanding, compassion as well, which to me makes them stronger.*
>
> *I'm sure you don't agree, but I doubt we would agree on much these days.*

I certainly did not agree. Women hated conflict. but sometimes conflict was necessary and inevitable. Look at what happened with appeasement before World War II. Government leaders are required to make hard choices sometimes and the biggest mistake they can make is to take force off the table. War must always be an option if we are to secure a lasting peace.

At least that was what I believed back then.

As far as I could tell—and my father fervently believed—it was our nuclear arsenal that had helped us avoid another world war by keeping disputes localized in places like Vietnam and limiting those wars to conventional weapons.

I was certainly changing my thinking when it came to some things, how I looked at women for example, although there was no way for Jack to know that. When we were teenage boys driven by our new raging hormones, we thought and talked about them in ways we shouldn't have. I had become more enlightened in college. The coeds I met were freer with their bodies, but they also demanded respect since they were just as accomplished and smart as any of us, if not more so.

Women's lib took front and center in the late sixties and early seventies, along with the struggle for civil rights, and I did not see how you could believe in one and not the other. All people should be free to define their individual identities and roles in society. Their destinies should depend on their own efforts and desires, not some accident of birth.

I certainly agreed with Jack when it came to that. People should not be pigeon-holed or subject to baseless historical prejudices, although I recognized that getting rid of those was easier said than done.

Are you taking any interesting English or Philosophy courses or just focusing on Government and Economics? I assume that's the approved path for a pre-law student. You shouldn't limit yourself, old buddy. You should take courses outside your comfort zone in areas like psychology, sociology, art, and religion. Far Eastern religions have a lot to offer in terms of contentment and enlightenment. It will make you a better lawyer in the long run.

Perhaps you could become one of those lawyers who help conscientious objectors or work with non-profits to protect the environment. I'm guessing there's not enough money to make either one attractive enough, but still worth thinking about or volunteering for from time to time. Don't let dollar signs limit your reach or your vision.

I got the put down, but I didn't care. Accumulating money has always been and would always be an accepted goal in American life. Even if some people considered it evil, it was one of those necessary evils. Once I had the money, there would be plenty of ways to use some of it for good.

I know you must be wondering why I haven't given you our address to write back. It's because Kai and I decided the first day we moved in together that it was important to start fresh and the best way to do that was to cut our ties with the past. We needed to start all over and live completely in the moment which meant freeing ourselves from who we once were and the demands and expectations that came along with that.

The past—and the voices from the past—will hold you down if you let them, which is why both Kai and I agreed we needed a clean break to distance ourselves from the old and make ourselves anew.

Make yourselves anew? I remember reading that and thinking it was up there with relevance and meaningfulness in terms of unintelligible gibberish.

Kai doesn't write to anyone, not even her brother, and no one knows our address, not even my parents. Except for a couple of notes that I have sent them to let them know I'm okay, you are the only one I have written to on a regular basis.

Once a year was hardly on a regular basis.

Kai knows that I do; we have no secrets.

Letters to you feel different, it's almost as if I'm writing to myself since there is no response which I like. We grew up like brothers, ketchup brothers, so I don't think of writing to you as holding too tightly to the past, it's more like opening a window to let it go and give the present more air to breathe. This way you get to better understand the path I'm on and perhaps think more about the one you still feel compelled to follow.

Kai understands and agrees.

I thought it was more about Jack proselytizing to win me over to his new hippie lifestyle, the one Timothy Leary defined as turning on, tuning in, and dropping out.

Living in the moment is our mantra. As Kai likes to say, it may look like an eternity at our age particularly if you're staring out in the distance the way they encouraged us to do when we were growing up, but it's not. It's really a short trip in this body, which means you should treat every moment as if it's the entire world and all of life. In another year or two, when we have completely shaken off the past, "let it go" as Kai likes to say, I will send you our address so you can write back . . . if you want.

I will understand if you don't.

I had to chuckle when Jack said to treat each moment as if it were the entire world and all of life. It sounded very small minded and self-absorbed to me because the entire world—my entire world—had yet to arrive, and college was far from all of life. The life I wanted was still laid out in front of me, yes, in the distance, and I continued moving toward it.

I would have been very disappointed if this moment in college was my entire world.

There were plenty of moments in college to enjoy, but I considered those moments to be transitory. There were moments to study, moments to reflect, moments to party, moments to linger in and moments to pass through as quickly as possible. The point was to keep my eyes straight and make sure I was always heading in the right direction.

A test would be a good example. I certainly didn't want to treat that moment as if it were my entire world. The point of that moment was to keep calm and get a good grade. It was just another hurdle to jump over on the way to the better and more lasting moments ahead. That was my thinking back then.

Obviously, I didn't get it.

I did not have that breadth of vision that Jack had, I realize that now. I was a conventional twenty-year-old who was not the least bit concerned about time since it appeared to be endless from where I stood; the horizon was always way off in the distance and never seemed to get any closer.

Having awakened this morning in the eighth decade of my life, I realize time misled me with its infinite promises in my youth and fooled me again with its elusiveness in middle age. Now that I am confronted with the truth about its preciousness, I have a much better appreciation of what Jack meant when he wrote about the importance of conscious breathing and living in the moment.

Since every life is a collection of past experiences and the present moment, living fully in that present moment is the only way to go, particularly at my age. It is certainly the best way to slow time down and enjoy what's left of this life. The past may never leave us as all the poets say, but trying to live inside it or in the future is a total waste of time.

Present moments are what you want to have deposited in the bank when you're approaching eighty. Unfortunately, every time I check the balance, I realize it's much less than I would like. There is no such thing as having enough time and no place to buy any more, no matter how much money you may have accumulated.

The big question I ask myself these days is this: am I spending the dwindling present moments I have left on the right things?

Kai and I have moved to a smaller house further outside of town that we share with Bear and Rainbow. The day-to-day chores are easier with just four people. We opened our small business. The name on the door is Crystal Clear, but Kai likes to call it the Community Center. You pay what you can afford or make a trade for a lot of our items, particularly the ones we make; there are minimum prices on the things we buy from others. It's a popular place to hang out because there's always a pot of herbal tea brewing and a plate of fresh cookies.

We don't need to earn much to live. We've started growing some of what we eat and making clothes to wear. The library helps with our continuing education and provides us with the opportunity to travel the world, while the clear, starry mountain nights keep us connected to the cosmos.

There are other things besides pot that can help expand your vision and understanding. I wonder if you have tried any of them. I doubt it.

Jack was right. I smoked pot in college, took an upper on occasion when I needed to pull an all-nighter, but I stayed away from the psychedelic drugs out of fear I might turn out to be an eggshell like Jacko and crack too easily.

> *The book is still a work in progress. It's now called The Art of Releasing and it's a joint effort with Kai. She illustrates and I write the words. She drew a great picture of a hand holding a pencil and then another letting it go . . . releasing it . . . so it falls to the ground. Internalize that muscle releasing technique, find a mental way to perform the same movement in your mind and you can train yourself to let go of the everyday stresses and worries caused by expectations and disappointments and live a happier, more mindful life.*
>
> *I'll send you the first copy. Hopefully, it will work with lawyers, although I'm not sure since you guys train your whole life not to let go. You are programmed to hold tight to convention and defend the status quo at all costs, even when it comes to an unjust war.*
>
> *I will tell you something else, but it stays between us. A pledge is a pledge whatever road you choose and however old you get, remember that. There is a group of us, Kai included, determined to throw a monkey wrench into the military industrial complex that runs this country, at least to the extent we can do it from our neck of the woods.*
>
> *We started small, squeezing some glue into the lock at the local army recruiting office. That caused quite a stir, but nothing like when we poured water into the gas tanks of a couple of military vehicles parked outside the armory. Despite what you might have heard, it works much better than sugar.*

I had never heard anything about pouring sugar or water into gas tanks since it was not something I ever considered doing. In those days it was easier to get away with mischief like that because there weren't cameras everywhere.

I don't know if you heard about Mayday. I'm sure you were too busy with your finals. It was the largest mass direct action in American history, the motivation being that if the government won't stop the war, we, the people, will stop the government. A half-million concerned citizens traveled to DC, just like Woodstock, to sit-in at the Selective Service Agency and to bring the government to a temporary halt.

We didn't go, but some of our friends did. They called themselves the Mayday Tribe and said the sit-ins were amazing. The intent was to bring the government to its senses, if not to its knees, and they weren't planning just sit-ins. The organizers had this elaborate tactical manual that detailed 21 bridges and traffic circles to block the next day to disrupt the city. It came with instructions on how to do it by using stalled vehicles, barricades, and their own bodies. Unfortunately, it didn't work all that well because the police had gotten a copy as well and were waiting for them.

Still, Mayday was a big success in terms of getting the public's attention and turning sentiment even more against the war. Think about it, they had to mobilize 14,000 police and National Guard troops to arrest 13,000 people, many of whom turned out to be innocent bystanders. I can't imagine anything more delegitimizing to a government than having the whole world watch it conduct the largest sweep arrests in history, turning the everyday bustle of the capital into a televised scene of martial law.

It was the largest mass action of civil disobedience ever, larger than any organized by Gandhi or Martin Luther King.

I wished we could have gone, but we didn't sit on our hands. We did what we could from up here in Woodstock. I'll tell you about one thing we did.

I remember Mayday, not that I participated in it, but it did make all the newspapers. A caravan of buses left the campus before dawn to journey down to DC and while there were quite a few students from our dorm who went, I told everyone I couldn't go because I had an important paper due on Monday. In truth, it was about done, I just wasn't interested; I was still not very political.

I have always been one of those devil-you-know-is-better-than-the-devil-you-don't kind of guys. Who knows how worse off the world might be now if we hadn't gone to war in Vietnam? No one knows the answer to that question. It's certainly possible that dozens of smaller neighboring countries could have fallen like dominoes to the communists. What if China and Russia wound up controlling all of Asia and took over Africa as well? What would the world be like now?

Mayday took place one year after Nixon invaded Cambodia and the National Guard fired into a crowd of protesters at Kent State killing four students and wounding nine. I did attend the candle lit vigil on campus in their memory and announced my opposition to the war to my dormmates and girlfriend at the time. And I wasn't pretending, I had finally come around and turned against it; my passions, however, remained on my studies.

I remember reading an article a few years later, after Nixon's resignation, detailing how much the Mayday protest unnerved him and his administration. The author said it was one of the reasons he sped up his efforts to find a way to end the war that would not be too damaging politically.

By the end of May 1971, the newspapers were reporting that more than half of the country's students were against the war and a quarter of them were actively protesting in one way or another, no matter how unsuccessful those protests appeared to be in terms of ending the bombing and deforestation, and no matter how many of them were getting arrested. They refused to give up. They continued to burn draft cards, to refuse induction, and to march in mass to block traffic and stop commerce. The more radical protesters stopped troop trains, destroyed troop transports, and bombed government buildings.

There was no way an aspiring attorney could get involved in anything like that because it could jeopardize his or her admission to the bar. It would only take one arrest or some other black mark on my record for the character committee to decide I was not a proper candidate to practice law.

There is a small army base nearby that the National Guard uses for training. One of the guys we know was in Vietnam and learned how to work with explosives. We talked about blowing up the warehouse where they stored some of the ammunition and defoliants destined for Vietnam, but Kai thought it was too dangerous and could injure someone or result in a forest fire.

So, we decided instead to damage this large troop transport plane that was being used to ferry soldiers and supplies to Vietnam. We blew it up, one of the wings anyway—yes, it's true, even if you find it hard to believe—and the newspaper said it was a total loss. There was a big blowback for a while from the love it or leave it warmongers around the county who blamed anyone with long hair, but the police couldn't find the perpetrators and the papers eventually blamed it on outside agitators.

The love it or leave crowd are in the minority around here. There are too many of us "dirty, long-hairs" as they like to call us, and other honorable and religious people who can't stand to watch the war on the news any longer and listen to them recite the body counts like they were baseball scores.

Most of the Catskillers are coming around. What mother wants to send her son to the other side of the world to kill some other boys she doesn't know for reasons she can't understand. When it comes down to it, if you win the hearts of the mothers, the country will have to follow.

I hope you are politically aware and active, at least more than you were in high school, and as an aspiring attorney I expect you to continue to honor our pledge.

Jack was right, I should have done more. Instead of feeling guilty, I remember being shocked by Jack's admission and seriously considered breaking our pledge by reporting what Jack and his comrades had done to the New York State Police.

What if they were planning to bomb a building and accidentally did kill someone? People might die despite their best efforts to avoid it. Didn't I have a moral duty to turn them in, not to mention a legal obligation as an aspiring lawyer now that I had been made aware of their criminal conspiracy?

I thought about it, but I knew I could never turn Jack in, although I did wish I could pick up the phone and try to talk him out of doing anything else unlawful and dangerous. Jack had recently turned twenty, the same as me, but in my mind, we were both still teenagers.

He needed someone with a cooler head, someone more detached from the situation and well-grounded, someone who believed in the law and the social contracts that make society work to dissuade him from doing anything stupid that might land him in jail and ruin his life forever.

Despite my concern, I made no effort to contact Jack. I thought about driving up to Woodstock to look for him. How many hippies like Jack and Kai or Bear and Rainbow could there be running around Woodstock? How hard would it be to find their store?

The truth was I didn't want to get involved or be associated in any way with violent protesters. What if Jack and Kai were already under surveillance? What if there was some FBI agent taking photographs of them through a telephoto lens and I appeared in a couple of them. I could not afford to be on the wrong kind of government list. I had to keep at arm's length from anything like that if I wanted to be admitted to the bar, obtain a clerkship with a federal judge, and become a partner in a national law firm.

As far as I was concerned, Jack was on his own. As my father often liked to remind me when I was growing up, "when you make your own bed, you have to lie in it."

> *I am now 100 percent vegetarian if you can believe that. I feel so much better, lighter, less dense if that makes sense, and I have way more energy. No more soda, no more unnecessary sugar, or sweets, except for Kai's cookies which we sell at the CC. She sweetens them with honey from Bear's hive. Unprocessed food is the only way to go.*
>
> *Grains and vegetables. There is a world of things you can do with them. I wouldn't be surprised if one day they learn how to make hamburgers and hot dogs out of vegetables so we can stop killing animals. No more meat for me, just what we can grow. It's more humane and sustainable than slaughtering our animal friends and neighbors.*
>
> *Peace and Love,*
> *Bohdi*

From a little boy with his face covered in ketchup and mustard to a revolutionary living on vegetables and love, how strange Jack's life had become in such a short period of time.

I had no way of confirming whether Jack and his angry group of pranksters committed any more felonies in Woodstock. There was no internet back then to check and none of the protests or disruptive actions in the Catskills, whatever they were, made it into the national newspapers.

The news was filled with protests and attacks on recruiting stations and military installations, but mostly in big cities and large college towns. Students were burning draft cards and lying down in front of troop transports. Protesters were blocking the ROTC reps from recruiting on campuses and even Vietnam Vets were marching down Pennsylvania Avenue in opposition to the war. They did not get any more respect from the government than the college protesters did.

The next winter I did get a book in the mail from Jack, but it was not about crystals or the art of releasing. It was something called *The Whole Earth Catalog*. It was very different from the Sears catalogue and the other catalogues I had seen growing up.

Jack put me on their mailing list because he thought I should "check it out." He called it "the first meaningful catalogue of our generation." He said it was filled with all kinds of neat tools that were "earth-friendly and intended for constructive, not destructive purposes." The catalogue didn't even sell the tools, it was intended to educate the readers about their existence. The writers did the research, found the tools, and provided the information on where to buy them.

I figured the vendors must have paid to be included in the catalogue or kicked back a portion of their sales because otherwise I didn't see how the catalogue could have made money.

Jack suggested I go through it slowly, page by page, "as if it were a classic novel" because it offered more than just things to buy. He said it offered clarity and an understanding about the kinds of products we needed to preserve the environment, to cultivate the land more respectfully, and to learn how to better share the planet with others.

Jack made it sound more like a religion than a business. He made the catalogue sound like the new hippie bible, almost as if it were the new New Testament.

I think I got a half dozen of the Whole Earth Catalogs in the mail before it went out of business in 1972 or 1973. I did find them interesting and spent hours going through each one, although I never bought anything because there was nothing I needed. Steve Jobs called it the first Google because it was "idealistic and overflowing with great notions and neat tools." I still remember the final issue and the recommendation printed inside by the publisher: "Stay hungry. Stay foolish."

There had to be other events growing up besides the violent death of Uncle Francis that might help explain Jacko's radical transformation into Bodhi, and I racked my brain over the years trying to figure out what I missed.

Jack had to have felt out of place in our small suburban community because his parents were rather odd compared to the other parents. They hardly ever watched television, except for the news, even though Jack's father repaired them and sold them at his shop. They read a lot instead, magazines they didn't sell at our local stationery store devoted to art and architecture that were as thick as paperbacks, and hardcover books that they took out of the library with serious titles by authors I never heard of. They never read the bestsellers and murder mysteries that my mother and her friends did.

Jack's parents also had strange hobbies. As I said earlier, his father liked to study the tricks of the old magicians. He was also into bird watching, as well as carving and painting rare birds. His mother loved experimenting with unusual new foods and finding strange new ways to cook the familiar ones.

They raised Jacko very differently from the rest of us. They trusted him to make his own decisions and take responsibility for his own actions. They weren't always second guessing him or demanding he explain why he did or didn't do something. Not that my parents didn't trust me, but I often got called on the carpet to explain my choices, and they were quick to override my decision or plans if they thought them unwise or unnecessary.

Even at a young age, Jacko did not have all the rules the rest of us had like a drop-dead time to be home, no matter what we were doing or how much fun we were having, a list of the things he could eat and when he could eat them, and the exact minute he had to turn out the lights and go to bed.

I never heard Jacko reprimanded for speaking out or giving his opinion and I spent a lot of time at his house. In fact, I don't remember his parents ever disciplining him or raising their voices. They didn't ask him how much homework he had to do when he came home or require that he finish all of it before doing anything else. They trusted him to get it done on his own schedule.

Jacko did not have limits on how much television he could watch, although he wouldn't have cared since he preferred to read, write, and draw. His parents were not always reprimanding him for eating with his hands. Indeed, some of the foods his mother served were supposed to be eaten with your hands. I never heard them once tell Jacko to comb his hair, wash his face, or change his shirt because it looked dirty.

He was never required to finish anything on his plate, a familiar command at my house that was usually followed by a guilt trip about all the starving children around the world or reminded that children should be seen and not heard, one of my father's favorite expressions whenever my sister or I were making too much noise.

I never heard Jacko's parents warn him to turn down the radio or they'd take it away, yell at him for forgetting to turn out the light or order him back upstairs because he left a wet towel on the floor. I don't know for sure, but I bet his mother didn't stick her head into the bathroom while he was showering to remind Jacko to wash behind his ears and to use the washcloth that she had put out for him on his private parts.

Jacko's parents were the first ones to go out at night and let him babysit for his sister. He was barely ten when his parents started doing that and it wasn't just a trip to the local movie theater, they went to concerts and lectures in the city. Sometimes they did not return until well after midnight.

They let Jacko make his own decisions, right or wrong, and learn from his own mistakes. That was their mantra. His father liked to say that Jacko would learn more from trial and error than he would ever learn from a lecture. His mother always encouraged Jacko to follow his own path and never let himself be pressured to follow the crowd.

I doubt she had in mind the path he wound up taking.

While I had a strict bedtime through eighth grade, Jacko was free to keep his lights burning until he was ready to turn in. He liked to take books out of the library, books we had not been assigned to read, and he often stayed up late reading them. Sometimes he came to school bleary-eyed, but eager to tell me about the book that had kept him up. He never got hooked on the sitcoms the way I did, as well as most of the other kids in school, except for Star Trek and the Twilight Zone which I forced him to start watching and he grew to like.

When we were in elementary school I used to draw the same pictures, suburban homes with trees and rope swings or rockets flying through outer space. Jacko drew landscapes with birds and clouds, no two ever the same, not one of them looking much like anyplace I had ever seen, until he got older and switched to geometric shapes mixed in with amorphous ones that looked like the amoebas in our biology textbook.

I do not know what any of that might signify, if anything, in terms of Jacko's sharp left turn after Woodstock, except it might suggest that since he had a lot more freedom growing up, he developed a bigger, more vivid imagination than the rest of us, particularly when it came to his future, along with a healthy skepticism about rules and expectations the rest of us absorbed from our parents.

In middle school, I became interested in girls before Jacko and that took up more of my thinking than I thought possible. He never found the ease in making small talk with girls like I did. Jacko did not talk about them nearly as much, nor I suspect did he think about them as often. His thoughts were more focused on books, clouds, and math than tight sweaters and the short shorts the girls wore in gym class. He did not have a real date until I set him up with Sherri, Carol's best friend, for the homecoming dance junior year.

There can be no disputing that I was more outgoing and sociable, and Jacko was more introspective, but how does that explain anything? Maybe if I added up all the little differences in our upbringing and personalities, the total would cross some threshold that might help explain why Woodstock and Astra changed everything. Or perhaps none of those differences really mattered because Jacko was the proverbial eggshell destined to be cracked by the first wild experience to rock his world.

It's all speculation, I realize that. There are no simple answers. No obvious cause and effect. There is no line graph to follow Jacko from pre-school to high school that would lead inevitably to his transformation at Woodstock. Some outcomes will always be surprising and unexplainable whether they are life or the law.

Some things have to be chalked up to serendipity.

If it was something in Jacko's DNA, his sister did not inherit the same variation because she went on to live a normal life. She went to college, studied biology, became a schoolteacher, married an engineer, moved out west, and had two boys, one who became a dentist and the other an accountant. As far as I know, she had very little contact with Jack over the years, certainly much less than I did.

I was the one at Jack's bedside with his daughter when he took his last breath, a breath he considered meaningless since he did not believe conscious breathing, essential to this life, was necessary for the next, at least on a molecular and spiritual level. Indeed, he was excited to join Kai who had died almost three years earlier.

I did look on the internet from time to time but could never find anyone who had done a study to determine how many lives had dramatically changed as the result of Woodstock.

THE DRAFT

CHAPTER FOUR

I got another letter from Jack at the end of my junior year. He stopped dating his letters at this point, as if he couldn't bring himself to mark time in such a traditional manner. The easiest way for me to know the order of the ones I still have—thinking crazily I was saving them for Jack to laugh over one day—is from the postmarks.

This one is postmarked May 11, 1972.

Hi Bry,

Did I ever tell you how Kai was waiting for me when I got off the bus at Woodstock, even though I hadn't told her the day or time I would be returning, and I had no way to reach her by telephone. I don't know how she knew but she said she did. I found it hard to believe at first, but I've learned over the past three years never to doubt her intuition.

She always seems to know what I'm thinking. She often knows what I'm going to say and do before I say and do it. But it's more impressive than that, sometimes she knows what's about to happen, not just with the weather like one of those old souls who can feel the rain coming in their bones, but when someone is about to come knocking at our door with something interesting to

*say or when we should wake up early because the sunrise
is going to be spectacular.*

*It is equally remarkable the way she can talk to
babies and dogs, calm them down in an instant, and
approach birds without scaring them away. She says it's
because she is tuned into the cosmos. If that's the case, I
must be like a television set with a broken antenna
because I'm not getting anywhere near that kind of
reception.*

It was one of Jack's rare jokes and I had to smile. I was
always the one making jokes and trying to get him to laugh. At
least he was loosening up a bit which was a good thing, although
believing that Kai could see into the future and talk to animals like
Doctor Dolittle was something else.

*I've learned that not everything in life can be
reduced to a mathematical equation—a premise to which
you apply deductive reasoning to reach the one and only
logical conclusion—despite what we were taught in high
school. Not everything in the universe is governed by
physical laws like the law of gravity and the law of
motion.*

*Do you remember Physics class? Remember how
Mr. Call used to tell us that the laws of nature were the
only true deductive system? That some of the laws were
simple and weak, and others complicated and strong, and
that education, experimentation and time would help us
discover more of the unknown laws out there. He used to
say that all the laws worked together to sustain the
universe and keep it from collapse. Mr. Call believed
that science and math were the lens through which we
would eventually come to understand the architecture of
the universe.*

I always thought that meant math was the key to making sense of life, as well as the universe. Now, I realize it's not true. The universe is not always logical, and life is not purely deductive. They are also organic, molecular, and instinctive. They are both endless and not everything can be explained by science and math, certainly not when it comes to life.

I had no idea what Jack was talking about. Of course, I didn't remember much from physics class. Whatever I memorized to get the good grades I coveted flew out of my head the moment I finished the final exam. I never liked physics or chemistry and it was never as important for me to retain what I had memorized for the test as it was for Jack.

There aren't laws for everything. Why isn't a matter-less and law-less universe also possible, at least in some respects? I'm sure your eyes are glazing over by now. I've seen that look before when you lost interest in class. What I'm trying to say is that I can't explain Kai's intuition any more than I can explain the compelling attraction between us when we first met at Woodstock.

Science and math cannot explain everything . . . or close to everything.

You can call it love at first sight if you want, but that would be an oversimplification. I think it goes beyond that or should I say before that. If you ask me, we have a connection that reaches deep down to the subatomic level, while at the same time extending up to the stars. It's elemental and infinite at the same time, impossible to define or understand with any mathematical equation or physical law.

You might call it fate or kismet, if you were religiously inclined, which neither one of us were growing up, although I do consider it something cosmic which I suppose is spiritual and divine in a way, although it's a very different kind of religious than the one you and I rejected in Sunday School.

It's a bit ironic considering that Newton eventually came to believe that math itself concealed a divine presence.

I have more of an understanding now—five decades later—of what Jack was getting at, which doesn't mean I have come to believe it with the same fervor that he did. He was one hundred percent certain there was a spiritual and matter-less basis to our existence and a form of consciousness beyond the reach of our senses that was independent of our bodies and our breath. A consciousness that was as tiny as a single atom and as large as the entire universe; a consciousness that was both in the moment and timeless.

I can't deny that I have come closer to Jack's way of thinking over the years, though not close enough to find the same level of comfort he did as he lay there breathing his last.

In one of Jack's later letters, one I have not been able to find, he quoted a line from *The Prophet* by Kahlil Gibran. It was one of his all-time favorites. I bought a copy of the book not long ago and read through it until I found the line that had so impressed him.

"And what is it to cease breathing, but to free the breath from its restless tides, that it may rise and expand and seek God unencumbered."

Jack loved that passage, although he said he would substitute "the cosmos" in place of "God."

I could not picture an old man with a white beard sitting on a cloud any more than he could, but I can't deny there is a lot to the universe—to our existence—that we don't know. Our spiritual sight is limited much the way our actual sight is by the horizon.

No one would ever deny that there isn't a world beyond the horizon, so why shouldn't there be an existence beyond our last breath.

Simply because we cannot see or feel what comes after does not mean there isn't something beyond that spiritual horizon, including an unfathomable state of consciousness that accompanies us as our atoms continue their travels around the eternal circle of existence. Billions of people on our planet fervently believe it.

I ask these questions late at night now without scoffing or pretending I know the answer and I find comfort in admitting my ignorance, especially when I combine it with Jack's certainty.

As Jack once reminded me in one of his letters, "We can't always see things the way they are, we can only see them the way we are."

Admitting what we don't know, Jack wrote, is how we begin to learn and love.

Perhaps that helps explain why I never found true love and came to insist to anyone who asked that "not every life is about love". People who become lawyers—the 24/7 big business types like me—succeed because they are good at pretending that they know the answers to everything. Our clients expect that when it comes to the law and the courts.

Do that long enough and you begin to believe it yourself.

While it might be helpful when it comes to advising big businesses and preserving law and order, it isn't very helpful when it comes to finding love.

I think you need to suspend judgment and welcome doubt to be open to love.

The very moment Kai sat down beside me, remember, it was shortly before Richie Havens started playing, I knew I was meant to be with her, and she was meant to be with me. I know you couldn't see it, neither could her brother, but there was a light we both saw and a warmth we both felt. We were cosmically connected and meant to journey together in this life, just as we had many times before and will again in the lives ahead.

Similar in a way to how you and I must have felt when we first met as preschoolers. I wish I could remember it, but I'm sure that connection was instant and just as natural. Our shared journey didn't begin that first day at Preschool Playhouse, it goes back eons, and it doesn't end simply because we are no longer side by side in space or time.

The concept of infinity is a basic tenant of math. Pi goes on forever. Circles never end. George Cantor, a great mathematician, said that some infinities are larger than others. Our infinity, our journey, yours, and mine, mine, and Kai's, are the largest of all infinities. Time and space are never obstacles to interconnected souls.

Our journey is and always will be endless.

I dismissed Jack's rhetoric back then as hippie talk. It sounded to me like he had found a new religion, the Far Eastern reincarnation kind that I didn't consider all that different from the religions we had at home, albeit with a different iteration of heaven and hell that was less terrifying and easier to swallow.

How could an eternal soul be condemned to purgatory forever for behaving badly during its short time on Earth? I posed that question once to a minister at someone's wedding reception during law school. He had a ready answer, no doubt because he had been asked the same question a thousand times before.

"No finite transgression requires infinite punishment," he said. "That's up to the sinner. A soul can always enjoy the light of God's afterlife once it turns away from its mortal sins on Earth and seeks God's forgiveness."

"Does that mean a simple sorry at Saint Peter's Gate is the get out of hell free card?"

I was dissatisfied with his answer and being young felt I was entitled to joke about it, which I regret looking back on it. Even if it was obvious that I was being facetious, his belief was genuine and based on two thousand years of thought and study—like the law in a way—and it deserved more respect.

Being older and wiser, he did not react angrily or turn away and dismiss me. Instead, he looked down at me—he was well over six feet—with a slight shake of the head confirming that he had heard the same wise-ass remark a hundred times before.

"It's not quite that simple, son. Asking forgiveness must be genuine, the turn toward God and love must be total and without reservation, and a reasonable period needs to pass before forgiveness can be earned and given. In Judaism, it's twelve months after death. We believe the duration is not fixed but reflects the seriousness of the sin. Some time spent in hell can burn out the evil in any soul."

Before I could ask why God would create a soul with evil inside it, he raised his empty glass and walked off to the bar.

There is a cosmic element to the universe which isn't visible, or matter based. It can be sensed and heard by someone like Kai who is open to it. We all need to be more attuned to the cosmic vibrations around us. Kai says she can feel it from time to time, even hear it, and when she does it's as clear as if she were listening to the morning birds calling out the sunrise. She thinks living close to nature and being in the moment brings us closer to it.

I'm trying my best to hear it as well.

Jack's words reminded me a bit of Timothy Leary's mantra. The turn on part came first because it was what you needed to do to be able to tune into the cosmos which in turn would convince you to drop out. I figured Jack's new religion had to be based on psychedelic drugs.

A couple more here and now notes, Kai sells a lot of clothes at the store. She is an artist when it comes to embroidering flowers on jeans. She calls them her flower children. You should see my jeans; they look like a garden. And I'm not on the road crew anymore. The government bureaucracy inevitably filters down to the ground level and I couldn't take it. Too many rules that made no sense and too much paperwork. I'm working for a construction company now that builds houses and learning carpentry.
Can you believe it?

No, I could not. Jack worked two summers at the town library shelving books and with me the summer after graduation at the drive-in theater snack bar making popcorn and filling cups with soda. He never did anything very physical. The only things he built growing up were electric circuits and model planes that required glue and fine motor skills, he never worked with real tools like a hammer and a saw.

I started out on the framing crew, but it turns out I'm good with my hands when it comes to the finer work. I suppose it's not all that different from what my father did with his bird carving, and I used to do with my models. I'm working more now on the window installations and trims. There's a certain math required to put it all together and it's a good feeling when everything fits and doesn't need a ton of wood putty.
Kai and I are planning a trip together, not the kind you might be thinking of to the city or the beach. It's more distant than that, a trip through space and time with

the help of some LSD she took in trade for a pair of embroidered jeans. She said she did it once before in Buffalo and saw the world from the perspective of a bird. Kai thinks it will help us better understand the cosmic nature of our existence.

They don't really bother you up here when it comes to things like that if you're quiet about it and not dealing. The local police get high like most everyone else.

We've hidden a few draft dodgers from time to time making their way up to Canada. We're like a rest stop on the new underground railroad. I also cut up my draft card and mailed it back to our draft board. I saw you got a high number so there's no way they'll get to you. My number is not very good, and I expect they will try to draft me before too long.

Did you know you are required by law to always carry your draft card with you? And it's against the law to deface it because it's considered government property. Can you imagine a cop stopping you and asking to see your draft card. What is he going to do if you don't have it, or if you've scribbled all over it? Do you get a ticket or thrown in jail?

You'd probably get the ticket as a professional courtesy, and I'd get the jail cell.

In my case, the authorities won't have to ask to see mine since I've already returned it to them in small pieces. They can't move me up on the draft lottery list without changing my birthday, so I suppose they'll have no other choice but to arrest me for destruction of government property.

Believe it or not, it wouldn't be the first time. They've done it before.

There was a case that went all the way to the Supreme Court which confirmed that defacing a draft card was a serious crime, evidence beyond reasonable doubt that the government thinks it owns you lock, stock, and barrel. No big surprise that one branch of the government is as corrupt as the other, but I still find it shocking. Imagine going to jail and losing your right to vote for ripping up their little id card.

These are the kinds of laws you lawyers love to write. Laws that require abject obedience and make absolutely no sense. The government tolerates no dissent, not when it comes to their bureaucracy, their machinery of war, and the elections they need to stay in power.

Let them come for me, I'd sooner go to jail for destroying my draft card and refusing induction than serving two years as a cog in Washington's killing machine.

There was a bonfire winter term where students were encouraged to burn their draft cards. A lot of them did and none of them got arrested probably because there were too many and the local police, friendly with the college administrators, agreed to stand off to the side and do nothing.

I didn't burn mine, not because I didn't support the protest—I did and wouldn't have missed it because it turned out to be a great fire and everyone was there—but because I wanted to keep my draft card as a souvenir of my journey from eighteen to twenty-two. I wanted to be able to show it to my grandchildren one day when they doubted that I was ever young enough to go to war, at least that's what I told myself.

I looked for it a few years back, even though I don't have any grandchildren to show it to, but I couldn't find it. Perhaps it incriminated itself by disintegrating into dust. Of course, once the draft ended so did the obligation to carry your draft card.

Haven't done much lately to disrupt the military-industrial complex, but we did sabotage the electric lines into a local Dow Chemical plant responsible for making an ingredient for the Agent Orange the government uses to destroy the jungle and poison the land. It took them a few days to get it up and running again. We thought about doing it a second time, but it's too risky now because they put cameras up everywhere, even in the trees.

We'll come up with something else to do to throw another monkey wrench into their war machine. One day they will get the message. People don't want war. There are better ways to work out our differences than killing each other.

Hope you are ready for law school. If you ask me, the world needs less lawyers and more philosophers, teachers, and bakers. Think about it, you could move up here and teach high school, maybe even elementary school. There are more and more little kids running around, and some of us are talking about starting our own school that focuses more on the arts and deep thinking and less on football and rote memorization.

The public schools are all tied up by state rules and regulations. They're wedded to the state's curriculum guidelines in elementary school and are required to teach to the regent's exam in high school. The state bureaucrats have yet to realize that children learn differently, and no one size fits all, or perhaps they do but can't be bothered. They don't want their citizens to be independent thinking individuals, so why would they be interested in raising children with creative, questioning minds.

I think teaching young kids would be a bigger challenge than teaching high school or college and much more rewarding than arguing in court on behalf of large corporations, at least if you use a measure other than income.

Yours in peace and harmony,
Bohdi

If anyone had told me at our high school graduation that Jack would drop out of college before starting and wind up living in a commune in the Catskills, madly in love with a flower girl two years older than him, and railing against institutions that have served us well for generations, I would have called them delusional.

I could have imagined Jack teaching advanced calculus at a well-known university, writing complex computer programs, even building complicated clocks that sold for obscene prices, but never in a million years could I have imagined him changing his name to Bodhi, soaking crystals in salt water to help release their healing powers, and swearing off hamburgers and hot dogs.

I still believed Jack would rejoin society before too long. Maybe he would sleep with a one of his housemates, switching partners being part of the hippie creed as I understood it—free love, love the one you're with, that sort of thing—and realize that the first one did not have to be the last one or even the best one.

There were plenty of other opportunities waiting for him. At our age, the world was a sea of love. The hippies did not hold the monopoly on that. Surely, the siren calls of math and computers in his blood since birth and nurtured by his father would eventually drown out the Hari Krishna chants echoing in his head.

I'm glad I didn't hold my breath.

I thought a lot about Jack during college. I wanted to figure out a way to reach out and convince him to escape the new invisible bonds holding him down, but I didn't have an address to write him, and I was too busy with my own college experience and girlfriends to consider traveling to Woodstock to look for him.

Perhaps I was not as good a friend as I thought or perhaps not interfering with Jack's choice meant I was.

Seeing what Woodstock and one eager girl had done to Jack made me reluctant to make any serious commitments of my own during college. There were enough pretty coeds to keep me busy without settling down long term with any one of them. I was especially careful to stay away from those who appeared too artsy, too rebellious, or too eager to make a long-term commitment.

Unfortunately, that caution came to define my life.

I remember another incident when Jacko and I were in fifth grade. Our sisters were driving us both crazy and neither one of us wanted to spend a lot of time after school hanging out at home. We were only ten, but this was 1961, a time when children were allowed to wander the neighborhood if they were in shouting distance at dinnertime.

Not too far from Jacko's house was a large patch of woods that in a couple of years would be replaced by a dozen streets filled with split levels, high ranches, and colonials. There was a narrow path into the woods that Jacko was sure had been worn down hundreds of years earlier by the native Indians who once lived there. Not too far in was a swampy area filled with frogs that we called Hopping Pond.

We'd often go there to catch frogs and put them in a big metal bucket we had found at a construction site. Taken would be a more accurate word than found, but a lot of kids did things like that back down. The construction sites were like candy stores. We took nails, two by fours, anything we could use to make forts in the woods.

Sometimes Jacko and I would pick the two biggest frogs we caught and race them. They always headed back to the pond, the winner usually being the one who took the most direct route. Sometimes we'd put two frogs alone in the bucket and watch them try to claw their way up the metal sides. One would always climb on top of the other, who appeared willing to give himself up for the sake of his fellow frog's freedom.

For some reason that always astounded me.

The top frog might make some progress but usually it would lose its grip and slip down the metal side. That didn't stop them from trying again and again, and if one of the frogs did get close to the rim, I would push it back down despite Jacko's objection. Cruel, I know, but we were only ten, and we did set the frogs free when it was time to go home.

Jacko was my partner in the frog Olympics, as we called them, until we stopped going to the pond. It happened one spring day in fifth grade when we came across the biggest frog we had ever seen, bigger than any I ever imagined living in our little pond.

Jacko called it the "Frog King." I thought it had to be a freak of nature, a one in a million kind of frog, the last descendant of some ancient frog dinosaur. It had to be half the size of a cat, and as it sat there, we could see its muscles rippling through its legs.

It was too big to pick up, not that we couldn't have, but we were afraid of what it might do to us. We didn't want to let it get away—at least I didn't—because I knew no one would believe us. We had to catch it and I came up with a plan. We would sneak close enough to put the pail over it and then slip a piece of plywood we had taken from another construction site underneath the opening to trap it as we flipped the pail back over.

"It'll be able to hop out in a second," Jacko said after I explained my plan. "The pail won't hold him. He could practically step out of it."

"Not if we keep the cover on."

To my amazement, it worked. Maybe the frog was big, but that didn't mean it was smart or quick because we caught it without any resistance, as if it had been napping with its eyes open. We peaked under the plywood after we flipped the pail back over and it just sat there looking up at us, as if it was happy in its new home and had no intention of trying to escape.

Jacko said the frog was probably as scared as we were.

"Maybe it's just curious," I countered.

"It doesn't look curious to me."

I shrugged. Only a frog could read another frog's expression, I didn't see how Jacko could.

"It's probably bored," I said, trying to imagine how I would feel if I were a frog in a pail.

My plan didn't include what to do next, and we spent the next hour staring down at the frog while we discussed the options.

I wanted to take the Frog King home and bring it to school. Charge everyone ten cents for a look. Jacko wanted to tip over the pail and see how far it could hop. He bet the King could jump two to three feet at a time. I thought Jacko was nuts, although I was curious as well to see if he could.

"No one will ever believe us if we let it go," I said, shaking off his suggestion. "They'll laugh when we tell them."

"So, we won't tell anyone. It'll be our secret."

I appealed to Jacko's love of science.

"What if it's the last of its kind, a missing link, some new species, and we become famous."

Jack looked at me like I was crazy. "It's a big frog, some people grow seven feet tall."

He had a point, but I remained adamant.

"I say we bring the King home and take it to school. Let's see what the teacher thinks."

"How do you propose feeding it over the weekend?" Jacko asked. "It's not going to eat my mother's coq au vin or your mother's meatloaf."

"We'll find some worms."

"How do we get the King to school? Does it hop along on a leash?" Jacko was more practical than I was and had a lot more common sense. "The bus driver is not going to let us take it on the bus and we're not going to be able to charge anyone anything to see it. The principal will take it away and set it loose behind the school."

We both knew what that could mean. A call to our parents—after all, we'd have to do all this behind their backs—and the likelihood that some of the other kids, the older and meaner kids, might find the King and torture it, maybe chase it out into the road where it would get squashed by a passing car.

We really had no choice, and I eventually agreed with Jacko's suggestion that we dump the King from the pail and see how far it could hop. We would follow it back to the pond, see where it jumped in, and look for it the next time we came back.

"Wouldn't it be cool," I said, "if the King got to know us and came out to greet us when we showed up."

"Or maybe it's a magic frog and it'll be so grateful," Jacko said once he stopped shaking his head from side to side, "it'll grant us three wishes."

That started a story brewing in Jacko's head because we spent the next ten minutes arguing over what those three wishes should be. I don't remember what they all were, but mine had to do with us becoming rich and famous and having special powers like Superman and the Flash. Jacko's wishes had to do with meeting someone from another planet, as well as ending disease and hunger.

The first part of the plan worked well. We dumped the King out of the pail, but instead of hoping back to the pond as we expected, it just sat there. It didn't hop away even when we waved our arms, yelled at it, and stomped our feet. The King remained unmoved by our antics, staring at us with one eye like he was expecting us to do the running.

"Maybe it's too old to hop," Jacko said.

"What should we do?"

"Leave the King alone, just like we found him."

Jacko looked up at the sun which was beginning to sink below the trees. "We have to go back," he added, "it's getting late."

I started walking away, but then I stopped and turned around. I had an idea, a good one, at least I thought so at the time.

"The King will jump if we really, really scare it."

"How do we do that?" Jacko asked. "Do you have some firecrackers and a match in your pocket?"

Jacko was still standing next to the King, looking down at it and rubbing his chin like he was in class trying to solve a math problem.

"Throw a rock," I said.

"At the frog?"

"No, not at it, behind it, but close enough that the King can feel it coming. It'll hop like hell after that."

Jacko covered his mouth with his hand while he thought it over. He couldn't deny it made some sense.

"It's worth a try," I added. "At least we'll find out how far he can hop."

"Okay," Jacko said after giving it some more thought, "but be careful."

"You're closer."

Jacko stared back at me without blinking, just like the frog.

"Come on, I'm betting you're right and the King can jump three feet. Four jumps and it's in the pond."

When Jacko didn't respond, I egged him on.

"What are you afraid of? It's gonna head back to the pond. It's like one of those scientific experiments you're always talking about."

Jacko sighed, then looked around for a stone. He picked one up, but I said it was way too small. He picked up another and I told him it had to be bigger, big enough for the King to see it coming out of the corner of his eye and feel the ground shake when it landed.

"A big rock," I said, "is what you need to scare a big frog."

I suggested Jacko pick up the large rock by the tree, the one we sometimes sat on, and drop it behind the King.

"But make it close or it won't work."

Jacko looked uncertain.

"What's your problem, is it too heavy for you? Do you need help or are you just chicken?"

No kid likes being called a chicken at ten years old, and Jacko bent down to pick up the rock. It was big and he struggled to carry it over to the King. He stood behind him, the ground wet and uneven, and lost his balance as he let go. Instead of falling behind the frog, the rock fell partially on it.

Its body was partly squished, but its head and front legs were untouched. The King blinked a couple of times without taking his eye off us. That look I recognized. It was the angry talking eye I got from my mother sometimes when I was mean to my sister. Then the King started hopping, crushed body and all, not toward the pond but toward us and we both ran out of the woods. We didn't stop until we got back to Jacko's house.

"I killed it," Jacko whispered, whimpered really, as he wiped away tears from both of his cheeks.

"It was an accident."

Jacko sniffled in response.

"It was only a frog," I added, a little louder this time.

We'd seen dead frogs before, mangled squirrels, and field mice, but this was the first time we'd killed anything other than a mosquito or a fly. Some of the boys we knew would burn worms and other bugs, even shoot birds with BB guns, but not Jacko and me.

He always said that animals had as much a right to the woods as we did, and I always agreed with him because Jacko said it so seriously and it seemed so important to him. Besides, I didn't see the point of killing something that wasn't bothering me the way the mosquitos and flies did.

I felt badly about what had happened to the King, but not nearly as badly as Jacko since he was the one who dropped the rock on him.

"It's like a squirrel getting hit by a car," I said to make him feel better.

"That's an accident. I dropped the rock on purpose."

"You didn't, you meant it to fall behind him, not on him. That's the accident. It's no different than running over a squirrel."

"It's very different. It didn't dart in front of the car. I was trying to scare him, trying to drop it as close as I could. It was a rotten thing to do."

"It was my idea."

"I went along with it."

"You still didn't mean it to happen."

Jacko sighed in response.

I knew I wasn't going to change Jacko's mind, so I shrugged and headed home.

Jacko talked about it constantly over the next month and refused to go back to Hopping Pond ever again. I did go back a couple of months later to see what I could find. The pail and the plywood were still there, but there was no evidence of the King. When I told Jacko, he said the King had probably been eaten by another animal "higher up on the food chain."

He closed his eyes after saying that as if he were replaying the afternoon again in his head.

I suppose I should have taken Jacko's over the top reaction as a sign he was more sensitive to things like that—to life and death—because while I was able to put it out of my mind and forget about it, Jacko couldn't. He continued bringing it up from time to time throughout junior high and high school, and always brought it up on the anniversary of the King's death. He remembered that date like it was his own birthday.

Jacko talked about the King more often than he talked about his Uncle Francis. Of course, he had nothing to do with his uncle's death. It could be that the King's death started Jacko on his quest to understand the meaning of life and death and one of the reasons he joined the hippies because they made it easier for him to believe that nothing ever truly died.

There was another incident that comes to mind that took place after we turned thirteen. The son of one of his father's second cousins had enlisted in the army and been sent to Vietnam. I can't remember his name, but I do recall meeting him once in 1960 or 1961. The only reason I remember is because he had this cool sky-blue Chevy convertible with big tail fins, and he let us sit in it with the top down and pretend to drive.

He had been in Vietnam for about four months, but he wasn't fighting. Jacko said he was in a supply unit behind the lines that delivered food to the guys doing the fighting. He was with a group of six soldiers supplying a forward base, still miles behind the front line, when they were ambushed. They were all killed, and the food stolen.

While Jacko said he barely knew him, he did say he often heard his parents talking about him. Apparently, he was drifting through life without direction or purpose. He didn't want to go to college because none of the guys he hung out with were going. He worked at a lot of different jobs that never lasted long and was always getting into trouble. His father was the one who convinced him to join the army to "find himself." It seemed to be working according to the letters he was sending back home, at least until the Vietcong caught up with him.

After he was killed, Jacko started reading every article he could find about the Vietnam War. He was particularly interested in the history of the fighting there and what our goals were. About a month later, he announced that he was against the war. He had some pretty good reasons, but I wasn't going to let him convince me to go against America, especially considering how gung-ho my father was about stopping the Communists.

Jacko also announced that he was now a pacifist and would rather go to jail than fight in Vietnam or anywhere else.

"I'm not going to kill anyone," he said.

"You won't fight for America's freedom if the country needs you?"

What kid could say no to that?

"I'll work in a field hospital, but I won't fight."

"What about if it were World War II and we were fighting the Nazis?"

In my mind everyone wanted to kill Nazis.

"Wars always need medics. I'll help the injured."

I told Jacko he was being un-American. We had the biggest fight we'd ever had and didn't speak for a week. I can't deny that he was way ahead of me morally, ethically, and politically. Indeed, one of my favorite TV shows at that time was called *Combat* and it always made the fighting during World War II seem daring and romantic. None of the stars ever got seriously hurt and every show had a happy ending. Women and children were rescued, the evil enemy vanquished, and the world made a safer and better place.

Jacko thought that fighting anywhere whether it was behind the school or on the battlefield was a failure of intelligence and reason.

"Fighting is contrary to human nature," he said to which I responded, "you're nuts."

I told him it was the stupidest thing he'd ever said. There was fighting in practically every movie I'd ever seen. Even the Bible was filled with fights, battles, and killing. It went back to the caveman. It was as much a part of human nature as hunting, fishing, and kissing.

A year later, just as I was about to graduate from college, I received another letter from Jack. Inside he wrote one word, congratulations. Below that he drew a smiley face followed by his return address.

I wrote a letter back later that night.

Hi Jack,

I was hoping for a handmade leather briefcase, or jeans embroidered with Kai's flowers as a graduation present, but I guess I'll have to be satisfied with your mailing address. I assume that means you are ready to hear from me because you're thinking about rejoining the real world.

I hope so.

We were best friends for sixteen years and I thought we knew each other about as well as we knew ourselves, but after Woodstock sent you flying off into outer space, I began to think maybe I didn't know you at all. Four years of one-way letters certainly didn't bode well for that lifelong friendship we always talked about.

I couldn't hide my bitterness and I didn't want to. But it wasn't as if it had been four years of total silence. I had taken his yearly letters as evidence of Jack's interest in continuing our friendship by refusing to cut off one part of his past, the part that tethered him to me and my reality. It confirmed what I still believed that one day Jack would come to his senses and embrace us and our dreams again.

I viewed his invitation to write back as the first step on his journey home.

In truth, I needed Jack as much as I thought he needed me because while I had made many acquaintances during my four years of college, I had found no friend quite like him. Indeed, none of my college relationships would survive law school.

Still, I accept your olive branch, so let me start by bringing you up to date.

Yes, I did well in college. Summa Cum Laude. You know me, I'm great at remembering facts, meaningless or otherwise, and calm as a Buddhist monk when it comes to tests.

I figured that simile might put a smile on Jack's face.

I found out I wasn't bad at writing either. While the first paper I did as a freshman was returned with a C plus because it had forty-four comma errors, once I corrected them the professor changed the grade to an A minus. I studied up on commas and didn't make that mistake again. The simple rule is when in doubt leave them out.

Being able to write well will come in handy as a lawyer. That's what the professors kept telling us, so yes, it means I am going to law school. I'm staying in New York City and continuing at Columbia. It's as easy as crossing the street. I'm not sure what kind of law I'm going to practice, but it will have to do with business, not the environment or conscientious objectors, sorry old buddy.

You know, I was never very political and always way more interested in doing well than doing good. The way I look at it, if you do well, you do good by contributing to society as a successful, tax paying citizen and by giving to charity. Moving business forward, generating jobs, and upholding the rule of law are essential when it comes to preserving our country and the world.

That's my way of doing good. You have your way. The means may be different, but the ends are the same.

It's funny when I think about it. We both grew up in the same suburb, a couple of streets apart, but while you moved up to the mountains, I moved down to the city. You live in a house on a country road where you probably have one neighbor who you know well whose house can't even be seen from yours, and I'm moving into a large building on the Upper West Side with 104 apartments. Maybe I'll know a couple of my neighbors by name, a few more by sight, but the vast number will be complete strangers.

You probably know the squirrels and their families better.

I like the anonymity of city living. It's a different kind of alone from yours in the forest, but it gives me the time and space I need to think and go about my business. I may always be in a hurry, but that's the nature of life in the Big Apple. Stopping to say hello every few minutes to exchange small talk or to gaze up at the shape of the cloud overhead is not high on my list of ways to spend my time.

In my opinion, too many of those superficial relationships—remember I will have 103 neighbors in my building—would hold me back a lot more than your dreaded past.

With that, back to the news.

Freshman year was the hardest for me. A lot of the kids were rich and came with their own checkbooks and trust funds. I had to work part time in the dining hall. Of course, I missed being able to share that experience with my best friend or even talk to him about it. For most of my life, you were the one I could talk to about everything, especially the things I didn't want to talk about with my parents, which you might recall was quite a lot.

You were the mirror that helped me see myself better, and I assumed I was yours. Don't get excited, I didn't come up with that analogy on my own, it's from the intro to psychology course I took. It was in the chapter on friendship.

I suppose you didn't feel the absence the same way I did since you had Astra . . . sorry Kai . . . to share things with. I had my freshmen year roommate, Chuck, a tackle on the football team who drank two beers every night to help fall asleep and turned on the light in the middle of the night when the beers wore off to read Sports Illustrated and look at the pictures in Playboy. The freshmen team didn't win a single game, nor did varsity the year after, and he was gone by junior year.

Fortunately, I was lucky enough to get a single room for my sophomore and junior year before moving into a studio apartment in a small building the college owned off campus for senior year.

I majored in government, minored in economics, and yes, I took some other courses. It's required for a liberal arts degree. You need a certain number of credits in the sciences, the humanities, the social sciences, and two semesters of a foreign language. I also had to take two gym courses freshman year and swim the length of the pool in under a minute to graduate.

I took a second course after the intro to psych called abnormal psychology. It sounded interesting and it was. I thought it would help when it came to dealing with troublesome clients, obnoxious adversaries, and old friends like you . . . just kidding.

I took a Spanish course which allowed me to study abroad in Salamanca, Spain during Spring term sophomore year. That was cool. Wine at four cents a glass which included a small plate of tapas (snacks). I even took an astronomy course to satisfy the science requirement. It was a gut, but I did learn how to identify most of the constellations.

My favorite non-prelaw courses were in English Lit. That's right, I found out that I do like reading novels and discussing them in class. I took two courses, the first was on 20th Century English writers and the second on Greek and Russian writers. Nikos Kazantzakis was my favorite. Have you read anything by him? His autobiography, Report to Greco, blew me away.

We also read Dostoyevsky's Notes from Underground. You should read it if you haven't already, although I have this vague recollection of you reading it over the summer after our sophomore year. Perhaps you should consider re-reading it again now that you have become a card-carrying hippie with a radically different view of life.

Dostoyevsky did not believe in utopia the way the hippies do. He believed that the pain and suffering utopians wanted to eliminate were what people needed to be happy. He argued that removing pain and suffering from society destroys our compassion, diminishes our intelligence, and reduces our freedom.

He was sort of an anti-hippie.

I didn't have a serious girlfriend in college. I had semester girls which is what I called them. One girlfriend per semester to put it in a more mathematical perspective. The last one, Briana, was the exception, she lasted almost the entire senior year. She's going to med school in St. Louis. We both knew we couldn't survive that, but it's okay, I took college as an opportunity to get more experience. I wasn't looking to settle down. Not like you . . . or perhaps because of you.

One of us had to fool around in college.

Telling you about the education and social part is easy. The other part not so much. I never did get into the antiwar protests, although they were everywhere on campus. Without you in my life, I've become even more apolitical. I did a lot of pot, some uppers when I needed to pull an all-nighter, some hashish, opiated once which made me think I was sitting on the beach watching the waves wash over me, instead of in the dorm listening to the Moody Blues, but that was it, nothing psychedelic like you guys.

Lawyers—like the law—need to be black and white with occasional shades of grey. Too many bright colors and fantasies would be hard to fit into my soon-to-be-lawyer's world view. Hope you laughed at that.

For me, college was either studying or partying, not a bad way to get a higher education, although I did spend some late nights a little stoned, wondering what the hell happened to you. We never did get a chance to talk much about Woodstock since you took off so soon afterward.

We had pizza a couple of days later, I'm sure you remember that. All I got out of you was that you were madly in love, moving up there to be with Astra, and dropping out of college before even starting. It turned out to be a lot more than that since you dropped out of your whole life as well, including your family (yes, I have bumped into your mother twice over the past four years and gotten an earful) and me, although I appear to have been the lucky lottery winner when it comes to letters.

Do you think the sex and pot at Woodstock was responsible for it or was it all Astra/Kai? I know what you'll say, but it's a fair question. If she can predict the future and talk to animals, maybe she is some kind of witch. I'm joking, but she must be a very special person with unusual talents to have changed your trajectory the way she did, I'll give her that.

I wonder sometimes what I missed when we were growing up because I never saw this coming. You were always quieter than me, I did a lot of the talking, and I feel a little guilty now because maybe I should have forced you to talk more, asked you more questions, and listened more carefully.

One thing I've learned from all this is that you can feel guilty about the strangest things.

Oh well, I suppose it's not a simple matter of a cause and effect, it rarely is. There had to have been a combination of factors, some not so obvious. I wish I knew what they were.

Do you have any regrets? Even the slightest?

Who doesn't have a regret or two whatever road they take? I never left an oral argument in court not wishing I had said something that I didn't or could unsay something that I did. I'm sure Jack had a few regrets, even if his letters never hinted at any, and his eyes were clear and content as he lay there dying, different from the way I imagine mine are going to appear, assuming there is someone there with me who cares enough to look into them.

I have more than my share of regrets. The biggest one being that I never found the kind of love Jack did or anything close to it. Not a lifetime companion like Kai, someone who would come to know everything there was to know about me and still be willing to stick around. Someone who wouldn't run away no matter how disappointing my words and actions.

For that reason alone, I wish Jack had outlived me. I would love to have him around when my time comes.

College was a blast and Kai could have shared it with you, even if she took a job working in town while you earned your degree. What happened to math and all those new equations you hoped to discover that would help us better understand how the world worked?

What is it you used to say . . . mathematics will never be complete because there's always more math to discover.

Anyway, I know love can move mountains and make grown men—and women—live their lives differently, but rarely is it as early and differently as yours. From what I've read—both in my psychology and English lit classes—finding a "lifetime" love is rare, almost impossible, at eighteen.

The initial falling in love begins at a young age, I get that. It starts with our parents and continues from there. It's how we learn and develop social and emotional skills, among other things. As you can see, I paid attention in the intro to psych class; there was a whole chapter on love.

It's easy to find young love as a teenager because everyone is looking for it. The only certainty about love at eighteen and twenty-one for that matter is that it will end, and another will follow. I've read more about love over the last four years than I ever did in high school. Learned more about it as well.

Love is everywhere, in everything we see and do. You can love an idea, a sunset, even a period of history, just as you can a person. Why should love be limited to a single person or thing? And it doesn't have to be earth-shattering or radically change one's life to be meaningful and lasting. People don't usually abandon their lives for love. They adapt. Life is full of different doors. Why only open one?

Anyway, that's my view as a college grad who has taken two psych courses, read a bunch of novels, and had a half dozen girlfriends. I know yours is different.

Rereading it now, I realize how much I sounded like a pompous college graduate who thought his degree provided him with all the worldly wisdom he needed. What did I really know about love or life back then? I'd found a certain type of love at school—a kind of free love without any real attachments or consequences. It was nothing like the kind of love the great novelists wrote about.

Jack a/k/a Bodhi had come much closer to that at eighteen than I ever would.

I always figured I'd find it one day, a love that would be perfect for me, one that didn't require me to surrender my dreams or change my lifestyle. A love that would both burn and last, although I can tell you from experience that kind of love is hard to find. Most love either burns or lasts, it rarely does both. Unfortunately, being the type of lawyer that I was, a litigator, I was addicted to the burn.

Despite that, I did believe that one day I would find someone to settle down with, someone who would appreciate the life I had chosen and the demands and responsibilities that came with it. Perhaps another lawyer who had picked a less demanding area of practice like real estate or wills and trusts. Someone who appreciated what the law meant to society and the challenging and rewarding future it offered.

It might not be the all-encompassing love I'd read about or saw in the movies growing up, but it would be love, nonetheless. I figured there had to be as many kinds of love as there were snowflakes, and mine would be comfortable and undemanding, much like the love I witnessed growing up.

Love like that is more than enough for most people.

Unfortunately, I was not lucky enough to find even that. Perhaps because I refused to make the time for it or didn't want it badly enough, at least not when I was in my late twenties and thirties and there were more opportunities to find it. The truth of the matter as I see it—and have rationalized over the years—is that not every life has to be about love. Some lives are dedicated to career and service, they are about achievement and accomplishment.

I have repeated that line to myself many nights as I lay alone in bed, more often after I reached my late sixties. I have said it out loud to acquaintances when they've asked, and to neighbors who wanted to set me up with some widow they knew or an older woman like me who had never settled down.

I tell them—reminding them of something they must have thought about at one time or another—that there is more to life than love. I always say it softly, without great emotion, but forcefully, as if I were responding to a rhetorical question or concluding a winning argument to a jury.

"Not every life is about love," I have said it countless times, referring to romantic love, "and history is filled with famous people who will back that up."

Mother Theresa is the first one I always mention.

I convinced myself it was a true and noble sentiment, although it was easier to believe while I was still actively practicing law. I was super-busy, and lawyers are easily seduced by their own words. These days I have stopped thinking of myself as a lawyer and those words sometimes get stuck in my throat.

> *I'm betting that you will find your way back here one day whether with Kai or someone else. You can have more than one love in your life. Didn't our fathers have their wives and their careers, or in your father's case his hobbies, as well as their children? There are many kinds of love, some run deeper than others, some last longer than others, some burn hotter than others, and some burn out quicker than others.*
>
> *They all count. They all matter.*
>
> *Anyway, that's my philosophy of life and love based on four years of higher education and two psychology courses. I wish I had taken a philosophy class or two so I could express it better and throw in a few impressive references.*
>
> *Computers were indeed big on campus as your father predicted. The President of our college helped*

write Basic, which is one of the more popular computer languages. We had a giant computer in the student activity center where a lot of guys took their dates to print out their names in the shape of Snoopy. I'm sure there are much better uses for the computer and I have no doubt that one day you—or someone like you—will find them.

What do you guys do when you are not working at the store and growing vegetables, I mean for fun. Do you go to the movies? Do you have a television? Do you ever dream about the future? Talk about seeing the world, getting married, having a family . . . things like that? Or do hippies refuse to make plans as well as money, preferring instead to sit around getting stoned, listening to psychedelic rock, and waiting for the inspiration to hit about what institution to bring down next and what tradition to attack.

Just kidding. Remember, I was always the one with the sense of humor.

I was kidding but at the same time I wasn't. I was still bitter at what the hippies had done by taking Jacko away from the life he was meant to live and share with me. I still couldn't believe it was a conscious, calculated decision with Jacko using his mathematical mind to weigh all the variables and unknowns, as well as the risks and rewards.

Jacko used to agonize for weeks when we were kids before deciding what to ask for Christmas. He would spend half the month of August talking about the type of bookbag he wanted for the new school year. How could he be so sure at eighteen that he knew what he was looking for in life and without discussing it with me or saying a word to his parents decide he had found it one weekend at Woodstock?

Where was the math and probability analysis when it came to Jacko's first love and his new aimless life?

I had no idea what the attraction was for the longest time other than drugs and a woman, motivation enough at eighteen, but not forever, and not for someone as focused and analytical as Jack.

I do wonder sometimes where you would be now if we hadn't made it up to Woodstock. I heard thousands of cars were turned back after the Thruway turned into a parking lot which could have been us if we hadn't gotten such an early start.

How could your whole life hinge like that on an hour or two? Would it have turned out differently if we had been turned back? I think so. You would have found someone else at college and taken a very different path. One much closer to the one we always talked about. That's probability theory talking, I'm sure you remember that.

It makes what happens sometimes, even the decisions we make, seem so random.

I know I sounded a bit maudlin, but I couldn't help it. Losing a friend like Jack at such a young age was hard to accept. I had not replaced him in college, nor would I in law school. I'd make many friends once I started practicing law, but none would come close. I'd know lots of people and attend lots of expensive, celebratory lunches and dinners over the years, but I can't tell you where most of those people are now, except for the ones who remain Christmas card friends and occasional dinner companions when they find themselves in Florida.

My first and only wife seemed like a close friend for a while, but that didn't last beyond the divorce less than two years later. It was easy for her to cut me out of her life—and for me to cut her out of mine—since we had no kids and were both successful lawyers who did not need support and the few things that we had purchased together were not worth fighting over.

I have no idea what she is doing now or whether she is even alive.

No one would ever know me the way Jack did. No one could ever be there like he was for every milestone of those important formative years. I suppose that is sad, but probably not uncommon. A single best friend over the first eighteen years of life is hard to replicate, impossible it turns out for someone like me.

> *Jack, the home builder, has a nice ring to it, although it is hard for me to believe since I never saw you holding a hammer or a saw. Building model airplanes is not nearly the same. Maybe when I buy my beachfront property you can come down and build the house for me.*
>
> *I forgot to mention that we had a Greek system in college with fraternities and sororities and anyone who wanted to join had to pledge at the end of freshman year. I pledged Phi Alpha Delta which was known on campus as the prelaw frat. A lot of prospective lawyers like me, but a lot of big partiers as well.*
>
> *I was president senior year, and we threw a big toga party in the middle of the winter. We brought in a couple of thousand pounds of sand to give it a beach feel, and months later we are still finding sand everywhere. There will probably be grains of sand popping up a hundred years from now. Silly, I know, but that was college. We didn't have school dances like we did in high school.*
>
> *Anyway, when I get my law degree, I will be happy to legally change your names if you guys haven't done it already.*
>
> *Your old friend and still a card-carrying member of the establishment,*
>
> *Ryan*

No one had called me Bry in years. I was Ryan now. I liked it much better. In a way, I felt a little like a spurned lover writing a letter hoping somehow to win her back.

Don't get me wrong, I loved Woodstock. I loved the music. I loved getting high and watching the endless ebb and flow of people. I loved staring at the crowd from up on the sound tower until it turned into a single living organism writhing to the music. I liked the one-off experiences with women whose names I couldn't recall the next day. It felt as if that weekend had been my true graduation from high school and the beginning of my higher education. However, I hated what it did to Jack and our relationship and while over the years people would get excited when they found out I was there, I was never very eager to talk about it.

Subconsciously, I think what happened to Jack pushed me in the opposite direction. I never considered turning on, tuning in, or dropping out. I avoided the coeds at school who painted their cheeks with flowers and wore embroidered jeans. I also avoided the harder drugs and after getting my college degree, I stopped smoking grass almost entirely, largely because there was a lot less frivolity and diversity in law school.

Most everyone seemed like me.

I also avoided the kind of love that Jack had found, the kind of all-encompassing love that could bend the arc of one's existence in an entirely different direction. The kind of love one poet we read about in the intro to psychology class said he would happily drown in. I did not want to drown in anyone's love, nor did I want anyone to divert me from my goals.

Jack's rejection of society and his youthful dreams made me eager to hold mine closer and tighter.

THE REAL WORLD
CHAPTER FIVE

Six months later I got a response. I figured time passed differently for Bodhi and Kai living in an upstate commune surrounded by forests and cut off from the world. Perhaps Jack no longer wore a watch or kept a calendar and measured time solely by the rising and setting of the sun and the changing of the seasons.

Maybe there was no such thing as a weekend or holiday in Jack's Catskill hippiedom, each day being the same as the next, clock time rendered irrelevant except as it applied to daylight and darkness. Perhaps the twenty-four-hour days, seven-day weeks, and thirty-something months which ticked loudly in my ear did not register above the bird songs and crickets. For Jack/Bodhi, it probably took a couple of turns of the season to remind him it was time to reply.

Don't get me wrong, six months passed quickly for me as well, time always seems to do that whether you're young or old, at least when you're not standing around staring at it, even if I did check my mailbox most days expecting Jack's response and was disappointed when I didn't find it.

I still remember some of the things we read about time in that abnormal psychology course I took junior year. One author believed that the perception of time varied from species to species. He said that tiny animals perceived time on a smaller and slower scale which explained why flies were so good at avoiding the swatter. He considered fly-time to be very different from dog-time, bear-time, and human-time.

It didn't make much sense to me when I read it, but nothing about time made much sense, not back then and not now. I have done some more reading on time lately. You can find anything these days while sipping scotch and sitting in your armchair provided you have a laptop with an internet connection.

The French philosopher Bergson had an interesting take on time. He believed that time had two faces: "objective time," the kind we measure on our watches and desk calendars, which he described as constant and relentless, and "lived time," which is amorphous, moody, and unpredictable, moving at various speeds depending on our inner experience.

That would explain why a weekend of fun flies by while a weekend of hard work slows to a crawl.

Bergson said that people do not pay attention to "lived time" until it has passed which is why it seems so quick, while people are always aware of "objective time." January 15 is always January 15 whatever the year is, and the 6:42 train is always the 6:42 train whatever day you catch it. "Objective time" is always visible whether it's coming, going, or gone which gives the illusion, at least in the moment, that it's moving slower.

For Jack, the six months that passed between my letter to him and his reply was "lived time." Since I was a time counter like all lawyers whose days are broken down into six-minute intervals for billing purposes, I lived in the world of "objective time."

Hi Ryan,

I suppose Ryan is more appropriate for a lawyer. I looked it up in the name book we have in the store. It's Gaelic and means "little king." Perfect really, isn't that how most lawyers see themselves? You seem to be happy following your well-trod and long-planned path and I suppose that's all that truly matters, although what makes you happy would not necessarily make me happy or anyone else for that matter.

Remember how much we used to love playing in the woods? Well, I still do. I consider my path the most natural one for me. Because we grew up together and had some of the same fantasies as children, even as teenagers, did not mean we were bound to arrive at the same place or follow the same path.

You need to get over it.

Dreams change, as do people. The changes can come slowly, painfully sometimes, just like social change, or they can come quickly and dramatically, yes, even over the course of a weekend.

Not everything is obvious when you're a teenager because what you feel and think isn't easy to express, let alone understand. It's not that you didn't listen as much as I didn't tell. Did you know that people lie more as teenagers than they do at any other stage of life? I read that in the library recently. They lie to friends, and they lie to themselves. They don't just lie to get out of trouble, they lie to protect the feelings of others, to protect themselves, and to preserve their privacy.

They lie to maintain their independence and autonomy.

They lie to keep their options open.

If you thought that I was a carbon copy of you based on things I said or didn't say, I apologize. Nothing could be further from the truth, but since when do two people have to be identical to be friends or lovers?

I got it, our dreams—once intwined like two vines climbing the same tree—diverged one wet, wild weekend in the Catskills, although I still didn't understand why, and I certainly didn't believe that Jack had pulled a fast one by lying all those years to me or himself. I suppose the truth is that Jack had a tremendous capacity for change, and I did not.

> *Let me turn to something more pressing.*
> *The other day it finally came. I've been expecting it for quite some time. I don't know how they managed to find me because I didn't put a return address on the envelope. Can you guess what I'm talking about . . . the notice from the draft board. I am required to report the Monday after Thanksgiving.*
> *They are thoughtful enough to give me some time to get my life in order and have one last turkey feast before they train me to kill and send me to Vietnam to shoot at strangers. I guess the draft boards have their own perverted sense of humor, or maybe I should call it a perverted sense of honor.*
> *Of course, I won't be eating turkey, you know that. Turkeys are smart, they are sensitive, affectionate, social and love to play, and I will never understand why we give thanks by murdering and eating 45 million of them.*
> *I won't be reporting for the war either.*
> *Astra says we should move to Canada because if we try to hide in Iowa or anywhere else in the country, the government will find me. I suppose that's one thing they are very good at, but I don't want to go anywhere. I'd miss the Catskills too much. There's a cosmic rhythm to life here that I find as reassuring as the seasons.*
> *I don't ever plan on leaving.*
> *Let them come for me. These mountains are wild and deep. I know them as well as we once knew the woods around Hopping Pond.*

Cosmic rhythm to life? I had no idea what Jack was talking about. I doubt many twenty-two-year-old law students would. It sounded to me like Jack had smoked a few too many bongs and taken a few too many acid trips.

I like living surrounded by trees and animals. I like building things that fit in with the environment, that become one with nature, and stand the test of time, not the shoddy, disposable houses we grew up in where the trees had to be taken down to make room for grass, as if the goal was to turn the planet into one giant putting green.

One hundred years from now, our old houses will have fallen apart, the lawns taken over by weeds, but it will be different up here. The homes we are building will last two hundred years, even longer, the way they used to build them when this country was first founded. The forest will make a little room for them, but the trees will always remain their closest neighbors.

There is a tavern outside of town built just after the Revolutionary War that's still operating.

If we do go to Canada, it would only be for a little while, the war can't last much longer, and we'd go by way of Vermont. There are easier places to cross the border there and we have the names of some people who will help. Kai and I have been assisting draftees on their journey for some time now.

We will have to use different names if we go, and I won't be able to write because it should come as no surprise that the government watches all of us and doesn't take no for an answer. They will search for me wherever I go and watch my old friends for answers.

Why not wage war against its own citizens to go along with the one it's waging in Southeast Asia?

I won't tell you the name I've been thinking about using, but I bet you can guess it. If we do go, and I very much doubt we will, I intend to leave a little reminder of how I feel about the war. That National Guard base I mentioned, the one that helps ferry supplies to the innocent boys dying on the other side of the world, doesn't fit in with the environment and needs to be removed so the forest can reclaim it.

> *Best,*
> *Bodhi*

Another threatened crime I had to ignore. It wasn't hard this time because I did not believe Jack capable of doing anything that stupid and dangerous. Hippies talked a big game. They prayed for a lot of things to happen and threatened to do them as well, but in the end they did very little and few, if any, of their prayers were answered. They claimed to be tuned into the cosmos but apparently the cosmos was not listening or in agreement.

Hippies like Jack were very different from the SDS, the Students for a Democratic Society, who looked and sounded more like a paramilitary group than a political movement. They were the ones who set the army recruiting offices on fire and died when something went wrong at their bomb making factories.

The hippies were too focused on their alternative lifestyle, their music, their dope, and their peace signs to do anything like that. They were more likely to deface a sidewalk by painting it with flowers or disturb the tourists by blasting the Jefferson Airplane from speakers hidden behind the Washington Monument than they were to write political slogans in blood on government buildings or set off incendiary bombs.

I remember sitting there trying to guess what name Jack might use if he did flee to Canada. We liked superheroes when we were younger and I wondered if he might use Bruce Wayne or Clark Kent, the alter egos for Batman and Superman, but those names would be too obvious. Then I figured he might take the name of a famous mathematician. He used to talk about them all the time, but they tended to have one-word names like Pythagoras, Euclid, Kepler, Descartes, Pascal and Newton and a name like that might also draw attention.

I cannot find a copy of the letter I wrote in response to Jack's letter, but it turned out that he did not have to choose between hiding in the woods and fleeing to Canada because his draft notice was cancelled. The war was winding down by the end of 1972. While Jack had a relatively low number, ninety-six, compared to mine, three hundred and twenty-two, the number of young bodies our draft board was ordered to provide had been reduced substantially by the fall of 1973.

> *Hi Ryan,*
>
> *Didn't have to choose between Canada or joining the bears in the woods because the vampires at the draft board cancelled my notice when the government reduced their demand for new blood and only the first seventy winners of the birthday death lottery won free vacations in Southeast Asia.*
>
> *We had already decided not to go to Canada before the draft board withdrew its death threat. We both like living in Woodstock and Kai and I figured that if they did come after me, I'd be able to elude them just as well in the mountains. There are a lot of like-minded people up here who would have helped. We would have helped anyone in my place.*
>
> *And if they caught me, so what? I'd get convicted like Mohammed Ali. I told you when we were kids how much I liked him. Not only is he smart, funny, and the best boxer in the world, he's also a man of principle. Unfortunately, I wouldn't have been able to pay for the kind of attorneys he had. Maybe by then you'd have become one of those volunteer lawyers helping the draft*

dodgers, although it's more likely you'd be one of the prosecutors.

I remember well when Ali fought Sonny Liston for the heavyweight championship. He was called Cassius Clay back then and he beat Liston twice. Both times I rooted for Liston, along with my father and most of the other kids in our lily white, suburban junior high school.

Most of the fathers thought Clay talked too much and did not show enough respect, although for whom and what was never very clear. I suppose it was more for the country, the government, and the order of things in general than it was for Sonny Liston, although he certainly had no respect for Liston calling him, among other things, "a big, ugly bear."

My father thought Clay bragged too much and set a poor example for an "impressionable kid like me" and needed to learn a lesson. Jacko's father got a kick out of him and Jacko, alone among all the other kids I knew, was rooting for Cassius Clay. I thought he was just being contrary, as Jacko often was, but he had given it a lot of thought and had his reasons.

I can't remember all of them, but I do remember he liked Clay's poetry and thought he was much more fun to listen to than Liston. He thought it would be much easier to be his friend since he was always smiling and laughing, as opposed to Liston who always had a scowl on his face, especially when he glared at the camera with those scary, killer eyes of his.

"This country needs more people like Clay who are not afraid to speak out," Jacko parroted like something he'd heard from his father or read in one of his parent's magazines.

It was 1964 and looking back on it now, I'm sure Jacko was referring to the civil rights protests taking place around the country, as much as the war in Vietnam.

I'd rather go to jail than shoot at someone on the other side of the planet who's never done anything to me, as Ali said, but it'll all be moot soon enough, to borrow one of your lawyerly expressions, since the war is going the way of Nixon. I'm proud that Kai and I did our part to help send them both off to oblivion.

Kai is working in a bakery now. She goes in at five in the morning to help make the rolls, bread, and muffins. I'm still doing construction, but not full time because I'm also building a little cabin on a piece of property we bought. It's almost ten acres, half of which is mountainous and there's a wonderful babbling brook not far from where I'm putting in the footings.

No sewer, only a septic tank, no town water, well water, no electricity from some big fat utility, just a generator, at least for the time being. I can't wait to be completely off the grid.

Kai helps as well. She's good with a hammer and you'd be surprised at how much I use my old math skills when it comes to framing and angles.

There's something else I suppose I should tell you . . . Kai is pregnant.

Did you catch your breath yet?

I'm sure you're wondering how that can be possible considering you're still worried about getting good grades and finding a date for Saturday night and haven't given a second's thought to settling down or going out into the real world to live, but as you may recall I was always one step ahead of you when we were growing up, so why should that be any different now.

Clearly, it's more than one step these days. It's more like I've lapped you a couple of times.

You're not the only one who can make jokes.

Maybe it was a joke, but I was in no mood to laugh. I couldn't imagine Jacko a father anymore than I could imagine myself as one. He was still a teenager in my mind, as was I, at least until I opened my mailbox and pulled out the bills addressed to me.

It took a little while to get used to the idea since it wasn't something we had planned for or talked about. It just happened even though we were being careful, but I suppose that's the way it's been for thousands of years. When Mother Nature is ready, there's no stopping her.

Kai didn't have to remind me that there were bigger forces at work here, cosmic forces, and that doing anything about it was out of the question. Buddhism, which we have both been studying, believes a new birth bears the karmic identity of a recently departed soul, someone we have traveled with before.

We are both very happy and excited. This will give us an opportunity to raise a child in a more natural and inclusive environment, one where all creatures have the same right to the moment and the place, and kindness is the only religion that matters.

If we were all raised that way, there would be no war and no inequality because we would be able to see ourselves in everyone else and look at things through their eyes, not just our own.

Utopian wishful thinking, I whispered as I read Jack's letter. Hippies were crazy if they thought raising a few kids differently would end the world's unfairness. It would take me a few more years to realize that no one is born filled with hate and anger—that it must be taught—and that the biggest mistake you can make is to do nothing because you can only do a little.

Big changes are almost always the result of small steps.

I realize that ending injustice and violence will take a while which is why the best time to start is now and the best place to start is here. Children are the future and the best way to bring about the change we so desperately need.

I remember thinking as I read Jack's letter that there was no way I was going to have a kid in my twenties, and when I finally did, I would not raise him like a guinea pig trained to put the world before himself. I might only be a law student, but I already knew that life was hard and taking care of yourself had to be a priority. Taking care of the world would follow naturally from that.

What's more, Jack was nuts if he believed he could isolate a child and keep him or her away from the influences of other children. He was also ignoring the dramatic changes computers would soon have on their upbringing, even more so than television. Hate was going online, and the crazies among us would soon be participating in raising our children whether we liked it or not.

I intended to stick to my plan which was to marry in my early to mid-thirties—after becoming a partner—and wait a few years after that to make sure it took before bringing a kid into the world. Of course, that meant marrying a younger woman.

I'm a bit nervous for sure. I can't help wondering how we will do this and if we're ready. I guess we'll find out soon enough. Kai says no one is ever ready at first, but we will be by the time she comes. Kai is certain it's a girl and I have no doubt she is right. She's always right about these things. She's batting a thousand when it comes to the other women that we know who have given birth.

Rainbow calls it kismet. Bear says it's a cosmic blessing. Kai is feeling nauseous but has created an herbal tea for that. When she's not baking, she's busy thinking up names. I'm truly excited at the challenge of raising a child differently from the way you and I were raised. A child who can see beyond herself and who is not as intent on conquering the world as finding her place in it.

I'll keep you posted.

Please don't mention it to your parents or mine. This goes in the pledge box.

Peace and Fatherhood,

Bodhi.

It was hard for me to picture Jack as a father, particularly since the last time I saw him he was eighteen, eating a slice of mushroom pizza, and talking about running away from home. I didn't even have a steady girlfriend. The big difference in my mind was that I had a plan and Jack seemed to be winging it from day to day. It was the difference between a hippie drifting through life and a law student striving determinedly toward a bright future.

I understood why Jack would not want the news to get out back home because even by hippie standards, it couldn't be right to deny his parents a role in their grandchild's upbringing. I do not know if he ever told them or if they ever saw her, but they would be dead soon enough, so it didn't really matter.

Unfair, I know, but as a lawyer I often remind my clients that not everything in business or the law is fair, the same as in life. Indeed, few things are.

I wrote Jack back right away. I couldn't help myself.

Hey Jacko,

Hello from the Columbia Law School Class of 1976.

This is indeed a serious place; the students are serious; the professors are serious; even the hallways feel more like a hospital than a college. There's no fooling around and very little partying because everyone wants to make law review and get a job clerking with a federal district court judge after graduation, perhaps moving up to the Circuit Court or the Supreme Court after that before landing at one of the big law firms.

It's a path that guarantees you the good life, the grand life really. You could not believe how much they pay at the national law firms. It's obscene. As one of my classmates likes to say, "it's like being given the keys to the kingdom."

I'm sure you'll start jumping up and down once you hear that I've accomplished the first step, I've made Law Review. To get invited I had to write a memorandum in twenty-four hours on a legal issue devised by the editors. Only twelve of the first-year students were picked based on some mysterious score that combined their first-year grades with the points they received on the memo. In my case, I think it was mostly my grades because I had a terrible head cold the night I wrote the memo.

I need to come up with a proposal over the summer for my law review article.

As you can see, I'm well on my way. I know that doesn't thrill you, but it does me.

My sister is in college, can you believe it? She was not particularly friendly with your sister, but they did bump into each other from time to time. She says your sister is angry as hell because you hardly ever call. You really should. I don't see how a call, or a letter now and then would be letting the dreaded past back in.

It's the right thing to do. You owe it to the non-hippies in your life.

If you can write to me, why not your parents and sister?

Can you really hate their world, my world, the world we grew up in—the real world—that much? After all, it's the world that made you who you are, and you seem quite satisfied with how you turned out, unless you believe it was despite that, because you saw the light at Woodstock like Paul's conversion on the road to Damascus.

A joke yes, but bullshit if you do.

I almost crossed out the last six lines because I was afraid it sounded too preachy and dismissive and might cause Jack to stop writing. I did not because the more I thought about it the more I realized my words had stopped having any effect on him, and a lawyer should never be afraid of zealously arguing his position.

I had a lot more to say, but I was intentionally saving the hard part for the end. Let Jack squirm a bit with curiosity while he waited to hear my reaction to him turning into his father.

Your sister is going to college as well, NYU, and I hear she wants to study biology and become a researcher or a teacher. I suppose I might bump into her if I ever get down to the village. I don't have much spare time these days to wander around the city like we did that summer after graduation. Law school is a bear, very different from the bears you're accustomed to. There are always a dozen opinions I need to digest before every class, and I like to prepare index cards for each of them in case I get called on.

Bumping into her might be rather awkward anyway. What would I say to her . . . that I haven't seen her brother since Woodstock, although he writes to me, which means I have more contact with him than your parents?

Do I tell her the big news?

Does our pledge really cover something like this? I wouldn't think so, it was a childhood promise meant to protect childish secrets. I could argue both ways like any good lawyer, but don't get excited, I won't say anything.

I will leave the great reveal up to you. I can't understand why news like that should ever be kept a secret, but I assume you'll do the right thing eventually. They deserve to know and be a part of their grandchild's life.

Your world won't collapse if they come up to visit occasionally or speak to her on the phone.

Perhaps I'll accidentally let it slip if I bump into your mother again during one of my rare visits back home. It's the least I can do considering all the times I ate over.

I don't know what Jack's parents knew if anything. It wasn't too many years later that they died in the car accident. His sister did not mention Jack's daughter when she spoke at the funeral or later at the house before Jack called. And I did not see any photographs of another little girl around the house, other than his sister.

I found it hard to believe Jack would keep it a secret, but I found most of Jack's decisions after Woodstock hard to understand.

Perhaps he was waiting for her to get a little older and more certain about their hippie lifestyle before letting his parents into her life. Unfortunately, by the time she was ready it was too late.

I could never bring myself to ask Jack about it and I lost touch with his sister long ago.

In some ways—I know you won't want to hear this— you are not all that different from the government you profess to despise. You have your own secrets and your own hard and fast rules that may work for you and Kai but not for the rest of us, and the reasons for them are just as unfathomable to outsiders like me and your parents.

I was acting like a lawyer with Jack's parents as my clients.

My advice to you, old friend, is to let go of your secrets. Secrets will weigh you down as much as the past, if not more so. No charge for that bit of therapeutic, legal advice.

Feel free to share it with Kai or anyone else.

I am happy about the good news and the little addition to your family. I may not agree with the timing, but if you're happy I'm happy. After all, as you often remind me in your letters, it is your life and how you feel about it is all that matters, a truism that applies to all of us.

I had concluded by then that there was no point in challenging Jack's decisions any more than there was arguing with him about mine. I could never consider happiness—and life—as a moment-to-moment thing the way he did; it would always be a journey for me, a journey that brought me closer and closer to my destination.

Unfortunately, I would come to regret that perspective.

Now a little bit more about me.

I am focusing on corporate law, business related matters, and am currently taking a high-level tax course. I will need it if I want to go into mergers and acquisitions. It's the hottest thing in the law these days and where all the money is. It's the quickest way to my beach house in the Hamptons.

I did meet someone during my second year of law school. Gayle was into theater in college, but she decided on law as a career. She would be the first to admit that the theater is a long, hard road with lots of dead ends. It requires good luck and good timing as much as it does talent. She likes to joke that having a small talent can be more a curse than a blessing.

When it comes to the law, success is entirely up to you. Determination and effort are what you need, along with some brains, of course, but even a small talent can take you far.

Gayle and I formed a study group of two and as you might suspect we do a lot more than study. I really like her, but it's way too soon to settle on anyone since I intend to spend two years after graduation clerking in a federal district court, which could be anywhere in the country, before becoming an associate at one of the big national firms. Both mean long hours, seven days a week in many cases, and will require my undivided attention.

If I want to become a partner, a wife this early on can only hold me back. I don't see any sense in settling down at this stage in my career. Gayle understands my thinking and she's not ready either, although she is interested in environmental law and working in a non-profit which does not have the same kind of time pressures and demands, or anywhere near the same compensation for that matter.

Gayle is more like a hippie version of a lawyer, which means we are sort of opposites. The way I see it, we don't stand much of a chance, not this early on. Time will tell.

The hippie version of a lawyer was a joke.

We practically lived together the third year of law school, but Gayle moved to Washington DC after graduation to work at an environmental non-profit for practically nothing, and I got my clerkship in the United States District Court in the Southern District of New York. I didn't have time to travel to DC and she didn't have money to travel to New York. A good excuse I realize now since we both recognized it was time to move on.

The relationship ended a few weeks before Thanksgiving.

I know she left her job in DC after a couple of years and moved to Seattle to join another nonprofit. I never heard from her after that and to this day I have made no effort to learn anything more about her. What's the point of finding out that she's been married for forty years, has two adult children, and is now a grandmother of four?

Gayle got me like no one else ever had to that point in my life and liked me despite what she saw, as good a definition of love as I can come up with these days. She is on my list of regrets, although not near the top, but that's only because it's a rather long list.

Who arrives in their eighth decade without regrets? Particularly when they arrive alone.

Some regrets feel like memories, just like some memories feel like regrets.

Some nights when I lie in bed unable to sleep, I wonder what would have happened if I had traveled down to DC to visit Gayle and cared as much about her career as I did about mine. Not knowing the truth about how her life turned out makes it easier for me to put her out of my mind on those nights when the past is making too much of a racket for me to fall asleep.

Maybe someday I'll buy some land up in the Catskills and you can build me a vacation home. Why not have one up in the forest to balance out the one down by the ocean. The lullaby of the tides and seagulls on some weekends, the buzzing insects, croaking frogs, tweeting birds, chirping crickets, and rustling leaves on others.

First, you'll have to expand your repertoire to include running water, sewer lines and electricity, and perhaps an indoor pool and sauna.

Sort of a joke, but not entirely. I would have liked to spend a little time in Jack's world.

> *Well, it's time to work on my outline for Corporations.*
>
> *Congrats again on the baby. Yes, you always finished ahead of me in cross country and in class rank, but if getting married and having a baby was a race as well, I wasn't running very hard and I am glad you won because I'm not nearly ready to cross that finish line.*
>
> *I'm betting on a boy because boys are more likely to rebel—best evidence being you my friend—and it only seems fitting that one day you get a taste of your own medicine. If it's a boy, I'm betting he grows up to become a career military man, a four-star general who gets sent around the world to put out fires and spread "American Democracy."*
>
> *Wouldn't that be ironic.*
>
> *One question, did you guys ever get married? If not, you should consider it. It will be easier in the long run when it comes to inheritance, parental rights, and things like that. We touched on it when we covered family law and trusts and estates as part of a required overview course.*
>
> *If you did, why wasn't I invited? I would have attended and lent an air of social normalcy in my three-piece suit. I'd even have brought Gayle as my date, so you could see that my eventual surrender to love is just as possible as yours.*
>
> *Let me know how the birth goes. I don't want to hear about him—or her—for the first time after he/she graduates kindergarten.*
>
> *Your cosmic friend,*
> *Ryan.*

I thought I was being funny with cosmic friend. Jack and I had very little in common at this point, so perhaps there was some invisible cosmic force keeping us connected, something infinitely stretchable and impossible to break. Just the thought of it made me chuckle back then since I had no doubt it was the past that held us together, our shared childhood as opposed to the universe, a force that was more nostalgic than cosmic.

I did hope that Jack and Kai had gotten married. Maybe Jack didn't care about the bastard thing, but I had learned enough in law school to know there could be problems for a child born out of wedlock, as well as for the father, if the couple breaks up and winds up in court fighting over custody and visitation.

I am sure Jack didn't think breaking up was possible, but as a former mathematician he could not deny it was a statistical possibility. It was an even bet considering that almost fifty percent of baby boomer marriages back then ended in divorce.

It was a long time before I received Jack's next letter. It was the middle of my last semester at law school, and I already knew by then it wasn't going to work out with Gayle. She was taking up way too much of my time and there wasn't a lot of that to spare between classes, law review, and interviewing for federal court clerkships.

Her ambitions when it came to the law were very different from mine. She believed in that line about working to live, instead of living to work. I did not see much of a difference between the two—living and working. She talked about the importance of finding the right balance in life. As far as I was concerned, it was the graduate school version of meaningful and relevant.

She sounded like a preacher sometimes. You know, the stop and smell the roses kind who is always reminding his congregation that to be happy you need to focus on what you have, not what you don't. In response, I kept reminding her that she couldn't consider the law as just a job if she wanted to be a big success. It had to be a burning passion and at times an obsession.

I began seeing Paula, an MBA student, on the side. I thought a JD and an MBA might be a better combination, but Paula was as driven as me, and just as inflexible so it did not last very long.

> *Hey Ryan,*
>
> *No, we never did get married, and we don't plan to. Why would we need a piece of paper confirming our union according to some meaningless laws passed by a roomful of lawyers feeding at the public trough? Kai didn't even give birth in a hospital. It was at home, although the bureaucrats managed to get their pound of flesh before agreeing to issue the birth certificate. They love to give you a hard time when you refuse to genuflect to their rules and regulations and do things the way they want you to.*
>
> *It was indeed a girl, as Kai said, and we didn't pass out cigars, just joints and cookies. We had a midwife, and it went smoothly. No drugs, all natural. Kai was great. According to the midwife, she has the perfect pelvis. I could have told her that since I know it so well.*
>
> *Having a baby really is—or should be—the fullest and most poetic expression of two people's love and cosmic connection. Kai and I have never been happier. It confirms that our union—or reunion—in Woodstock, and I mean that in a larger-than-life sense, and our pledge to continue our journey together was written long ago in the stars.*
>
> *Naming her was the hardest part. We thought about Cloud, the part of nature that offers you a silver lining in dark times, as well as lifegiving rain. Then we toyed with Cypress after the beautiful tree. Thought about Dawn for the obvious reason and Heather which is the prettiest purple flower. We considered Willow, Leaf, Meadow, Moon, Petal, Rain. Sky, Summer, and even Storm.*

We were leaning toward Willow when the name came to Kai in a dream. In her dream, all the trees surrounding our house started singing about the new addition to the forest. She couldn't understand any of the words, but as strange as they sounded the trees sang them together in perfect harmony.

That was the first word on Kai's lips when she woke me up and told me her dream . . . harmony. We both love saying it and it seems as if Harmony smiles every time we do. Kai says Harmony will never wear store bought clothes or eat processed food. We will feed her as best we can on what grows locally until she's ready to make her own decisions.

We both agree that we won't weigh her down with all the demands and expectations we had growing up. We will let Harmony find her own way and when she feels the need to move on one day, as she surely will, we won't try to stop her or point her in any one direction.

How she relates to us, and the world will be up to her, and she'll have our full support whatever she decides to do. Moving out and moving on is the way of nature. Observing the animals in the forest makes that clear.

Easier said than done, I remember thinking. A lot happens between birth and eighteen. Parenthood comes with its own aspirations and dreams; I certainly saw that with my parents.

When Harmony's time comes to rebel, influenced by her friends, the internet, or a tweak in her DNA, it could mean going to college, getting an MBA, dressing in a suit for business every morning, and reporting for work as a small cog in a large corporation, or worse yet as a government bureaucrat.

The three of us are sharing a room at the back of a small house we are renting with Rainbow and Bear and their little boy, Orion, the brightest constellation in the sky, while we work to finish our cabin, so we can grow food in our own garden and become more self-sufficient.

I've come up with a better way to raise the money we need to finish it, which I'm sure will raise the hairs on the back of your legalistic neck. Kai had to cut back on her baking and embroidery for a while to attend to Harmony, although all the mothers in our little community are helping. It's very different from the way it was when we were growing up.

My construction work is not bringing in enough, so I started growing pot on a piece of our land that's out of sight in a little clearing near the top of the mountain. You can relax because I'm not walking around town selling it. I'm wholesaling it to a guy who sells it to the students at some of the nearby colleges. The administrations all have deals with the local police to leave the students alone. Really, I could probably set up a stand on the college common and sell it myself.

Think about it, why should marijuana be illegal? It's no different than beer, wine, and liquor, and despite what the government wants you to believe, it doesn't lead to heroin or crime. That's just a scare tactic they use to keep people in line because the government doesn't want anything around it can't control or doesn't understand, particularly something that the bureaucrats didn't enjoy when they were young.

It's the government's irrational rules and excessive regulations on top of society's unreasonable demands and expectations that push people to crime and heroin, not pot. One day when the Woodstock generation takes over it will be legal and there will be a cannabis aisle in every grocery store.

I intend to keep the business small, just enough to make what we need for the cabin, and for our own personal use. I promise you I will keep it under the radar, and you won't have to read about my arrest in the newspaper.

Jack sold his pot to a distributor who sold it at local colleges until something happened that forced him to shut down the business. Jack continued to grow small amounts after that, not for sale but for his personal use and for friends, which ironically did result in his arrest.

He never stopped smoking grass, not until he was on his deathbed. Harmony was not a smoker, and as she got older her parents had to smoke outside or when she was not around, not because she was against marijuana but because she had allergies, and the secondhand smoke made her cough.

Never did get around to finishing either one of my books, the one about crystals or the one about letting go. Maybe another time. Right now, I'm having too much fun planting, harvesting, and building. No phone, no computer, no television . . . although we do have a radio and a stereo. Music is essential to understanding and appreciating the cosmos and is very mathematical as well. It's one of the fullest and most sublime expressions of math that I know and mathematics, as I read recently, is considered the longest continuous human thought.

Some say that God gave us math to help us understand his nature. I say that math is a mystery which helps connect us to the cosmos.

We never did change our names legally, but it doesn't matter. Our names are whatever we want them to be. The government is not in charge of what we call ourselves, any more than it is over what we think and do.

We don't pay income taxes. Kai works off the books, as do I. When the government starts spending our tax dollars on the people who need them, instead of giving breaks to big corporations and funding newer and bigger weapons of war, I'll consider paying what little I would owe.

The funny thing is that this used to concern me more than anything else because I was sure the government would catch up with Jack eventually for tax evasion like they did with Al Capone. The government's number one priority is always money because money is power. It might not hunt you relentlessly if you don't offer your body in response to the draft, but it will if you refuse to pay their tithe.

It's funny how much I sound like Jack these days.

They never bothered Jack and Kai and according to him he never paid a dime of income taxes. Perhaps because he never earned much that was reported, never kept money in a bank, and didn't use credit cards.

The local authorities knew Jack existed because he came into the County Clerk's office twice a year to pay his property taxes in cash. Jack told me he wasn't thrilled about paying that either, but he knew most of it went to the local fire fighters, schools, and roads. He also knew that they would auction off his property in a minute if he didn't because they had to obey the laws laid down in Albany.

I've been studying Buddhism with Kai, and some others including Bear and Rainbow. The Buddha teaches that life is a circle with no beginning and no end. The Bhavachakra is the Wheel of Life, also called the Wheel of Becoming, and it turns endlessly from life to death to rebirth.

There is a way to get off the carousel, but it isn't easy. To achieve that liberating existence, you need to find the meaning to your life and play a role in your own story, a story that must be bigger than yourself and embrace growth and change.

You can only reach that high plane of existence when you find the wisdom and balance that allows for change and releases all the desires that inhibit growth. When you can let go of desire and welcome change, you get to spend eternity as one with the cosmos, alongside the other liberated souls.

It was all nonsense to me. Even crazier than the gibberish they used to tell us in Sunday School about hell and heaven and how what we ate on Fridays could determine how we got to spend eternity.

What did playing a role in your own story even mean? To me it meant having a goal and working to achieve it, which is what I was doing. Why would it matter if that goal was becoming a lawyer. instead of a teacher or a photographer? And how could anyone—any normal human being—let go of desire? Isn't desire built into our DNA? Don't we need it to move forward? Doesn't it go hand in hand with ambition, accomplishment, and love?

At a minimum, we needed desire to propagate the species.

I would call it an essential element of the human condition, as basic to life as eating, drinking, and breathing. Perhaps Jack only meant letting go of certain desires, those desires that the hippies and Buddhists didn't care for, like the desire for financial success or the desire to become a leader responsible for enforcing the laws.

It sounded as nutty to me as when Jack first told me about his plan to drop out of college and return to Woodstock. By now, I had come to understand his desire to live life differently— assuming I was allowed to use the word desire when talking about Jack—focusing more on his breathing, the trees, and the sky than his cash flow, but my opinion had not changed. I still believed that people who dropped out of society like Jack did it more out of fear and lack of confidence than conviction.

Even after all these years, I remain suspicious of all religions, be they Western or Eastern, that claim to know the best way to live and the only way to reach God or nirvana.

There are three basic truths in Buddhism: first, nothing and no one is ever lost in the universe, second, everything changes because change is constant, and third, there is a cause and effect to all things that happen which is called Karma.

Only when you have learned to release your attachment to desire and self can you reach Nirvana, the state of liberation and freedom from suffering. A state that frees you from the wheel of life and allows you to exist as part of the cosmos.

Does any of this make sense to you?

I doubt it.

That's okay, it doesn't make sense to most people brought up on the traditions of Western religion. You know, go to church, think good thoughts, obey the rules, and earn the points you need to pass through those pearly gates. Don't and the alternative is endless fire.

I don't see how that makes more sense.

Anyway, it's called belief because it's something you come to feel and accept without the kind of specifications and warranties you expect when buying a new car. There are no guarantees or smoking guns like the kind your juries need to reach a verdict. Belief is the opposite of mathematical certainly, which doesn't make it any less true. It's based on what you attorneys call circumstantial evidence.   I doubt a trained lawyer could ever

> *comfortably hold tight to evidence like that as the basis for a belief and way of life.*
>
> *You're accustomed to finding a reasonable doubt in everything that isn't black and white.*
>
> *Too bad, because it must be tough passing through life doubting everyone and everything that you can't see.*
>
> *Best,*
>
> *Bodhi*

Not exactly, Jack, I remember thinking at the time. Circumstantial evidence was acceptable under the law. Indeed, it provided the basis for many jury verdicts. It was the predicate from which experience and reason helped the jury arrive at a logical conclusion. For example, if you see someone walk into a windowless room with a wet umbrella, you have a reasonable basis to believe it's raining outside, even though you can't see it, feel it, or hear it.

That's circumstantial evidence.

Where is the circumstantial evidence that life is an endless circle? Where is the wet umbrella that makes it clear it is raining on the other side of the divide? I would have liked to have that conversation with Jack back then in person, not through correspondence, but he had made it clear early on that proximity was not necessary for our cosmic relationship to continue.

The years have caused me to reconsider some of the things Jack said in his letters. He had no doubts at the end as he lay there waiting to be freed from his last breath. He had been listening to those cosmic whispers for fifty years and he could hear them loud and clear. He called them "calming and inspiring", and they gave him a warm feeling . . . "like Kai's love."

These days, I can accept that there is a spiritual aspect to life—to all existence really—that can be felt at times even if it can't be seen or heard, at least not by me, and remains unknowable like a lot of things in life. Accepting something is unknowable means acknowledging that what over a billion people fervently believe could be true.

The sincerity and passion of Jack's belief is hard for me to deny.

I think it was easier for Jack to believe in life in terms of an endless circle because he was a mathematician at heart. Algebra, geometry, trigonometry, and calculus—like pi—never end. If there are a multitude of infinities, why not a multitude of lives. Jack's infinite circles are certainly much closer to the cosmos than the linearity of the laws and rules I based my life on as a lawyer.

In my old age, I've come to believe as well that math is more essential to life than corporate and business law, and closer to God.

> *Hi Jack aka Bodhi,*
>
> *Growing and selling pot is a recipe for disaster. You will get caught, one of your buyers will squeal to avoid going to jail, giving you up in a minute for leniency, especially since you are a small, easily replaceable supplier and not the kind to retaliate with brute force. That's the way the system works, and the judges love to send the growers, the source of the drugs, away for a long time.*
>
> *You will get two to five at a minimum and miss Harmony's early years.*
>
> *I am not trying to scare you; I am just letting you know how it works in the real world, the world where the rest of us live. If you need some money to finish the cabin, I will be happy to help. You would not believe what they have been paying me and how much I already have sitting in the bank.*
>
> *You can pay me back whenever you get the money or not, I don't care. Consider it my baby gift to Harmony.*

In truth, I was trying to scare Jack. We might not be as close as we once were, but I still considered him my best friend. The passing of time and the lack of proximity has a much heavier hand when it comes to love than friendship. Friendship can survive long distances and long separations. Love is greedier when it comes to obstacles like that, at least in my experience.

I could not bear the thought of Jack sleeping in a jail cell with some heavy-duty felon.

Not surprisingly, Jack never took me up on my offer. I am sure he considered the ridiculous amounts of money I made as a law student during my summers at a large firm working on behalf of corporations to be the spoils of war, in this case the war against the working class. I would have been happy to give him five thousand dollars. It didn't mean much to me at that point in my life and I knew it would mean even less down the road.

I did not have anyone else to share it with; my parents were doing fine, as was my sister, and I knew that once I finished my clerkship and started working as an associate, I would be making more than enough to buy a nice apartment on the Upper West or East Side, and eventually the beach house.

I was right because in the end I made enough to buy a dozen beach houses, even though I never bought any. I could say that I didn't have the time to look for the one I envisioned or the time to enjoy it if I found it, but I would be lying. It was more than that. Practicing law the way I did, working twenty-four/seven, somehow extinguished that desire, along with a lot of the other ones I had when I was younger.

I have my clerkship lined up in the Southern District of New York, a Federal Court, not a state court, and highly prestigious. After that I will be able to pick the firm where I want to work which is when the big bucks will start rolling in. I am serious about the money for the house—giving it to you or lending it to you is not a problem—and I would be happy to do it if it means keeping you out of jail.

I can't wait for law school to end. It's nothing like college and not nearly as much fun. The reading is interesting but there is so much of it and the classes are long and boring probably because all the people in it are just like me.

Funny, but not a joke.

I realize it's the price you pay for success, but I can't wait to get out into the legal and business world to kick some ass and make my fortune. My dream is finally coming true. You got the girl, but that was only part of your dream. The one you talked most often about back then, the one you thought most likely to come true, was becoming a hero in the theoretical math world by creating a new computer language that would blow everyone away and then following that up by building the world's first android robot, do you remember, like Robby in that old movie we both liked, Forbidden Planet.

Funny how things work out sometimes . . . or don't.

I never really worried about the girl and the family. I always thought that would be the easy part once I rose to the top of the legal world. I'd be able to pick one out when I was ready, as if a wife was something you could order from a hi-end catalogue. It seemed logical—and more convenient—to put off that dream while I chased after the more competitive ones.

What I did not realize was that some dreams become impractical—almost impossible—if you put them off for too long.

Looking back on it now, I realize that finding the right companion, a love for life, was the most difficult dream of all because it didn't depend solely on me and my abilities; it required two people. It's not easy to find the right someone who is willing to surrender a part of herself to you and inspires you to give up a part of yourself as well, especially if means letting go of one or two of your long-cherished dreams.

It can be especially difficult for someone as driven as me, especially when his dreams are in sight.

> *I suppose that means there will be no Nirvana for me when it's all over and another round down here on Earth, but it is what it is. You will recall how fond my mother was of saying that. But I don't mind going around in circles. Isn't that what we did when we ran cross-country? Besides, that Buddha stuff is as hard for me to swallow as the stuff they used to feed us in Sunday School.*
>
> *If you ask me, I think the Western religions have better holidays which is enough of a reason to stick with them. I like the fat old man in red with his white beard and sack of toys, and the big bunny with the chocolate eggs. It's hard to imagine anything else measuring up to Christmas and Easter.*
>
> *Maybe the problem is I'm not plugged into the Cosmos like you and can't see or feel anything behind the curtains. Maybe I need a few drugs to help part them a bit because alcohol isn't doing it for me.*
>
> *Another joke.*
>
> *I should mention that I had my note published in the Law Review on Due Process in the Recoupment of Entitlements. Esoteric, I know, but a hot topic when it comes to overpayments which are common under most Federal programs.*
>
> *I spent last summer working at a big white-shoe firm and earned more than twenty times what I made in all my prior summers combined. I'm going to use some of that on new clothes and an apartment, boring I know, but*

necessary in the big city. I could use some of it for your cabin if you would like, just say the word.

The clerkship starts soon. I'm excited about that. I'll be sitting in on trials and helping the judge write jury instructions, as well as drafting decisions on motions. Seeing how judges work from the inside is the best practical training for a new lawyer going into litigation.

My girlfriend situation is in flux. Gayle is moving to DC to work at a non-profit for next to nothing. It's way too far and it isn't really working at this point anyway. We are too different, heading in opposite directions . . . sort of like you and me but without the bond that goes back to toddlerhood. It'll be mutual.

I've started dating some other girls who seem more impressed by my law degree than anything else, but that's the way things are in the Big Apple. Your prospects are everything when it comes to first impressions.

None of them will last very long, I can tell that. The connection is largely based on nice restaurants and Broadway shows, nothing cosmic about that, nothing connecting us to prior lives or the universe, if that's the way it's supposed to be. The question I have for you is how will I know when a woman is cosmically connected? Is there an easy way to recognize it? What I need are those magic x-ray glasses they used advertise on the back page of my Superman comic books.

I feel too old for another muddy outdoor rock concert. I wonder if I can find someone at one of the outdoor concerts in Central Park with their large blankets, gourmet picnic baskets, and expensive wine? Not likely, since the girls who attend those concerts tend to stick to the group they come with. Besides, I doubt a door to the cosmos would open wide enough at one of those gatherings for me to walk through, not the way it did for you at Woodstock.

Hope you chuckled at that. Still trying to make you laugh, except now I can't tell if I'm succeeding.

I've been thinking of taking a ride up to Woodstock to visit.

What do you think? I won't come up there unless you want me to, and I won't try unless I know where to *find you.*

Jack's return address had been the same since he first gave it to me, a P.O. Box at the Woodstock post office.

If not, at least send me a photo of Harmony. I'm hoping she looks more like Kai than you. It wouldn't be fair to saddle a girl with a mug like yours, although your sister turned out alright. I heard she's getting married to someone she met in college in case you haven't heard and is planning to take a teaching job.

Let me know about coming for a visit. I know I'm a face from the past, but I can't imagine seeing mine will set you back, not very much anyway. It seems to me, you're like a helium balloon without a string that has drifted way out into space, far beyond my reach, and there is nothing I could do to pull you back to earth.

A funny analogy, right?

Anyway, call if you're up for a visit, assuming you can find a pay phone and have enough change or else drop me a postcard with your address.

Best,

Ryan

It was a long time before I heard back, almost two years. I had already finished my Federal Court clerkship and started as an associate at the largest law firm in the country. My starting salary was higher than what my father was making after working at the same corporation for over thirty years.

UPWARDLY MOBILE
CHAPTER SIX

Hi Ry,

If I can't call you Bry anymore, I can at least shorten Ryan to Ry. Sounds almost the same, don't you think?

Sorry, I didn't write back sooner but I had a problem with the marijuana business. It wasn't the police. The entire crop disappeared one day just like that. No, it wasn't eaten by the bears, although they have sampled it before. They don't like pot because it makes them dizzy and hungrier, which defeats the purpose of eating it. My entire crop was taken by poachers, and I know who they were.

One of my customers who sold on a couple of college campuses got roughed up a bit by one of the major players who wanted to eliminate the competition and he gave me up. I always hated it when you're right when we were growing up, fortunately that was not very often.

My turn to joke.

Anyway, they harvested all my plants, their shot across the bow, and it came with a message warning me to stay away from the colleges or the next time it would be worse. I have no intention of buying a gun and fighting it out like the wild west. These aren't the woods where we grew up playing cops and robbers and I'm not eight anymore. I couldn't very well call the police to complain that someone had trespassed on my property and stolen my marijuana.

Kai and I decided to leave the pot growing business to the professionals. I'll just cultivate some plants for our personal use and for friends. I've gotten pretty good at growing it, so we'll have to come up with another way to make the additional money we need to finish the cabin.

Thanks for the offer, but I can't accept any of your money, just like I won't borrow from a bank. It's all dirty money as far as I'm concerned. You might think yours isn't as dirty, but it is because it's been earned in furtherance of society's efforts to perpetuate an oppressive system that keeps poor people poor and rich people rich.

Maybe I'll go back to writing one of those books or making my own line of pipes carved from trees. I've gotten pretty good as a carpenter. I made a pipe for us out of maple with a metal tube inside for inhaling and it draws well. I would need to make the bowl deeper and the pipe more artistic to sell it. The store gets a lot of tourists up from the city who like buying local crafts.

As nice as it would be to see you one of these days, and for you to meet Harmony, it's too soon. I still like keeping the past at a distance . . . in an envelope the way we do now. I don't have to think about it for too long or see it standing there in front of me. Nothing personal.

Letters with you are different, they feel more like a Star Trek time warp, as if I'm communicating back in time to the 18-year-old Bry. It wouldn't feel nearly the same after seeing Ry, the adult lawyer in his three-piece suit and polished shoes staring at me like some hillbilly cousin.

Of course, if you decide to move up here and become a country lawyer fighting against the "Man" that would change things, although I suspect there's little chance of that.

Another joke, you're not the only one who can be funny.

Really, there is nothing here to see. My hair is long, I have a full beard and moustache, a real one this time, not the kind we tried growing the summer after graduation. I wear overalls, smoke weed, and have put on a few pounds. It's mostly muscle since I do a lot of physical labor, unlike yours which I'm sure have atrophied from sitting behind a desk, eating rich food, and drinking expensive wine.

I prefer to see you as 18 in my mind's eye. It's the way I see myself until I catch my reflection in the mirror.

I'm glad my sister is doing well. We don't correspond. I don't correspond with anyone except for you.

Harmony does look like Kai. I'm happy about that too.

I hope you are also doing well, although we have very different ideas of what well is. The way I look at it, all lives are weighed in the end—all religions teach that including Buddhism—and many are found wanting to quote one of the lines they used on us in Sunday School. Remember?

Buddhism teaches that how you lived and who you were is considered in determining where you go next.

You don't get punished; you move on.

If you lived a life governed by fear, desire, and doubt, it's not hell that awaits you, but another turn of the wheel, and another after that until you find the faith and love you need to let go of that fear, desire, and doubt and figure out what your story is and what your life is truly meant to be.

That's the kind of well I am referring to.

In terms of your magic x-ray glasses, you already have them. Living with an open heart and an open mind is what will help you find your soulmate, the one you have journeyed with for countless lifetimes before and who will help you draw nearer to Nirvana.

Finding your true love is the foundation of a well-lived life. But you need to be open to it, you can't let ambition and expectations get in the way. They will blind you if you do.

It was clear that I was not going to get close to a well-lived life using Jack's metrics.

What I really wanted to know was who did the measuring? Who would determine that my life was wanting? Was there a judge or a panel of enlightened souls sitting in some cosmic court that examined the evidence to see if I was qualified for nirvana or had to return for yet another turn of the wheel?

It couldn't be some old man in a long beard sitting on a cloud, I knew Jack did not believe in that, and I'm sure the Buddha had more important things to do.

Could the judgment be based on some mechanical scale of justice that weighed each life and operated automatically according to some cosmic law? Or perhaps it was based on a vote by the liberated souls already living together as one with the cosmos.

In the end, it always comes down to a judgment, whether it's by God, the community of perfect souls, or some other cosmic litmus test. Someone or something must weigh the evidence and reach a verdict much like a jury. I wondered if I would get the opportunity to plead my case or if there would be a perfect soul assigned to represent me like in that movie with Albert Brooks and Meryl Streep.

Not surprisingly, my world—the legal world—tended to be judgmental as well, although the judges were well known and the reasons for the judgments usually clear and easy to understand. When it came to the cases I argued in court, the outcomes were always based on the evidence and the law, not on any abstract fears, desires, and doubts.

I might disagree with the outcome, but I usually understood the court's reasoning.

I think that's what I liked best about the law; the statutes and case law were there in black and white to be read and considered. With every client and in every matter, I always knew exactly what I was getting into, what was expected, and how likely the desired outcome was.

Jack's world did not offer nearly the same predictability.

Just because the war is over doesn't mean everything is right again with our government or our intrusive and biased legal system. Making tons of money is not a good enough reason to turn a blind eye to it. There is much that needs to be changed to eliminate the biases in a system that favors the rich and well-connected and allows profit to put its finger on the scale. Our society is unable to change from the inside out since lawyers run the government and the courts and they . . . like you . . . have sworn an oath to uphold the status quo.

Change must come from the outside in.

Jimmy Carter is an outsider, unlike Nixon and Ford, but let's see what Congress lets him do, nothing I expect, and how long he lasts. After all, he's a scientist, not a lawyer or a professional politician. I'm betting he'll try to shake things up, won't get very far, and will be kicked out of office after four years, replaced by another Nixon with a better smile and a smoother line.

Carter is too kind and committed to equality to turn into one of them and unlikely to get a second term. There are a lot of ugly politicians out there eager to replace him. You want to hear my wild prediction? It'll be that actor, Ron Reagan, who no doubt envisions more wars as a means of making his rich friends richer and will do his best to end the separation of church and state. Another politician who believes it's his way or the highway and that the best way to save the poor is by helping the rich.

Why become president if you can't help your friends and impose your beliefs on everyone else.

I know you're not a monk or an ascetic, I grew up listening to your dreams and even shared them for a while, but I would still recommend that you put down your statutes and regulations for a few nights and read about the life of St. Francis of Assisi. He had the good life; he came from a rich family and had all the money and creature comforts he could ever desire. Yet he abandoned it all for a life devoted to helping the poor, as well as animals and the environment.

We could certainly use another Francis of Assisi these days, instead of another millionaire consuming enough resources to support an entire village. Or perhaps you could become another Gandhi, a lawyer dedicated to fighting for equality. Inequality hasn't disappeared because you don't see it at the office or experience it when you go out to eat.

There is still a lot we need to do to live up to the Declaration of Independence and the Constitution.

They still teach those in law school, don't they?

If you want to know more about Kai and me, and our lifestyle, you could study the life of Thoreau. He was a transcendentalist. I'm sure you think that's a medium who communicates with dead spirits. It's not. A transcendentalist believes in a spiritual state that transcends the physical and empirical world. He or she achieves insights through personal intuition by opening up to the cosmos, as opposed to relying on traditional religious doctrine. Being close to nature is essential because nature is the outward manifestation of the cosmic spirit and helps open our hearts and minds to the invisible forces of the universe.

You can't find that kind of nature in a fancy restaurant or on the fortieth floor of a skyscraper. It can't be found at Brooks Brothers or in the glove compartment of a Mercedes Benz. It's not on a cement sidewalk or in the air being polluted by the black soot pouring from your clients' smokestacks.

Simple living among the trees and the animals is what Thoreau considered a life well-lived. Equally important to him was resisting unjust laws. Civil disobedience in Thoreau's time meant being an abolitionist. In our time, it means ending war and inequality, fighting for civil rights and human rights, which include the right to an education, food, and health care. It means addressing the pollution the fat cats encourage because it means more profits.

It means abandoning greed, waste, and the illusion that you are helping others by helping yourself. Accumulating riches is not one of life's essential truths. Nor is excess consumption, looking at the world through rose-colored glasses, or closing your eyes to things you don't want to see.

While you cannot come up for a visit like you were taking a tour of a monastery, so you can tell your colleagues at work how quaint and spiritual we are, you are more than welcome to move up here and join us.

I hope that better explains why there is no point in visiting.

Here's hoping that the world awakens soon to what it is doing to our planet. Earth Day, if you recall, was supposed to be more than a one-day observance, it was a warning about the terrible things to come if we didn't act quickly and dramatically and keep the Earth in our hearts every day of the year.

We must all stand up to tyranny, even if it's the tyranny of our own expectations, desires, and dreams.

Bodhi

I shook the envelope to see if a photo of Harmony would fall out, but nothing did. I was more disappointed about that than I was about the tone of Jack's letter. He didn't want to see me, not in my present incarnation. He considered me the enemy, a card-carrying member of the establishment, which I was and happy to be so.

I mirrored Jack's disdain back then since I considered him the wayward brother who had lost his way. The brother who was wasting his talents and his life chasing butterflies. The one who would realize it one day which is when our paths—at least what was left of them—would cross again.

His letter left me with a lot to unpack and I needed time to think about it before responding.

First, there was no chance I was going to join Jack up there in his effort to hold onto Woodstock forever. I was not interested in getting stoned every night and living off the grid in the Catskills, narrowing my life to a little patch of forest and a small town. I had no intention of marrying one of Kai's hippie friends and naming my kids after flowers and constellations.

My feet were firmly on the road to success, which was my transcendental enlightenment. I had nothing against St. Francis or Thoreau, but there had to be a reason they had been relegated to the dust bin of history, their names barely mentioned in any of our history textbooks. Time had judged them irrelevant.

I knew there were still Franciscan monks around, but I certainly didn't see any of them walking up and down the city streets trying to convince people to renounce their wealth and comfort so they could travel the back roads of America building churches like they did during the Middle Ages.

The people who ran the churches and monasteries treated them more like businesses. They gave tours and sold liqueurs. They were just as avaricious in my mind as any lawyer or stockbroker, and much less moral in some cases when it came to children. Mother Theresa was the exception, an exceedingly rare one, and I certainly was not interested in emulating her way of life.

Thoreau may have advocated living a simple life in the woods, but I figured I could do that anytime I needed a break by taking a two-week vacation or spending a long weekend at the beach. A week or two of fasting and purging myself of the city's excesses was all I would need.

Jack and his hippie friends were fewer and far between by the late seventies and early eighties and there had to be a reason for that. Times change, movements grow stale, and ideas turn to dust. Their hippie time had passed and mine was here. There was an economic boom on the horizon that would elevate and reward big businesses, their investors, and their law firms.

I must admit that I was insulted and hurt by Jack's last letter, and his refusal to let me come for a short visit. What did he think I was going to do? Stand on a soapbox and proselytize about the good life in the city? Plant a seed in Harmony's heart that would encourage her to run away to the big city the day she turned eighteen?

All I planned to do was bring her a present—I was thinking a bicycle—and have some tea and cookies with Kai and Jack. He and I could have gone for a walk afterwards up to his old pot farm and perhaps even shared a joint.

How painful a reminder of the past would that have been?

I was curious as hell to see what Jack looked like and how he sounded in person. I didn't feel any attraction to his lifestyle or his rhetoric, but I wanted to get close enough to see it for myself and get a better idea of what it was that had diverted him from the math and computer career laid out for him.

I thought about driving up to Woodstock anyway and surprising him. How many bakeries could there be around Woodstock? That would be the first place I'd look to find Kai. I was sure I'd recognize her. I had a P.O. address at the post office, I could go there and ask whoever was at the window where Jack lived. Or I could find their store, the Community Center, and ask Rainbow or Bear. Maybe even walk in and find Jack or Kai behind the counter.

I thought about doing that, I really did, but I never got around to it. My life was too busy and if Jack wanted to reject me because I was not Thoreau or St. Francis than I could reject him for not being Bill Gates or Warren Buffet.

I decided not to write back, not as quickly as I had before. Instead, I put Jack's letter in my desk drawer to wait until the mood hit me. Give him a taste of his own medicine. I was growing accustomed to holding tight to my anger because it fueled me in my legal battles, and the mood didn't hit me over the next two years. I was moving quickly up the associate ladder, the firm having made it clear I was partnership material, not surprising since I was making it a fortune by billing almost sixty hours a week.

I bought my first apartment on the Upper West Side with a view of the Hudson River, and not long after that I fell in love with one of my downstairs neighbors, Michelle, a graphic artist who specialized in designing fabrics, a career I didn't even know existed until we met.

Michelle and I kept bumping into each other on the elevator. Jack might have considered that a kind of cosmic intervention, but there was a simpler explanation, we were on the same elevator bank and had similar schedules. I left early and came home late, as did she. It was hard for me to believe designing fabrics could take that much time and effort, but she said it did because they were always on tight production deadlines that required last-minute modifications. She also stayed late because she loved creating new designs and found her office to be more conducive to the creative process than her apartment.

It was not love at first sight. Michelle had recently moved to the city from a small town in Iowa and was more tentative and reserved than I was accustomed to, but after a month of elevator conversations, a couple of cappuccinos at Starbucks, and a few late-night dinners we hooked up.

If I were to be truthful looking back on it now, I would have to admit we were "not a match made in heaven," as I had overhead my secretary say many times when talking about her sister's husband, which I suppose is another way of saying there was not a strong cosmic connection.

The attraction wasn't instant like with Jack and Astra. The intimacy wasn't nearly as quick. We didn't have a lot in common other than the fact that our birthdays were two days apart, we were both devoted to our careers, we were both alone, and our apartments were on the same elevator bank.

I wasn't all that wild about the fabrics she designed. I found them interesting, but they tended to be a bit too psychedelic for me with lots of bright colors and swirls, and I wasn't bashful about giving her my honest opinion, the same as I did with my clients. I suggested she try designing a few classic fabrics from time to time like the kind you might see in the store windows on Madison Avenue, but she said they didn't move her the same way.

I did like the way Michie, which is what everyone called her back in Iowa, talked about designing. Her eyes sparkled and her voice filled with passion, much like the way my voice did when I talked about whatever merger and acquisition was on my plate.

My cases might not be works of art, but I considered what I did—helping to build larger and more cost-effective businesses—to be every bit as creative and meaningful because of the difference it made to our country, our economy, and in many people's lives.

While I was getting very rich doing it, Michie was not. In fact, they paid her very little, far below what an artistic talent like hers deserved. She said she didn't mind because she worked for the fun of it, although I didn't believe anyone back then who told me they didn't care about money and worked for love. Fortunately, Michie did not have to worry about the high cost of living in Manhattan because her parents were rich and generous, which explained why she could afford to live in an apartment in my building.

She knew money mattered to me, I didn't hide that, and how laser focused I was on becoming a partner because that was when the big bucks—she liked to call them the obscene bucks—would start pouring in. I told her all about Jack and even showed her his last letter, the one I had not yet responded to.

We went out for almost two years, spending most of our nights together when I wasn't traveling, more in her apartment than mine since she found my apartment too generic and bland for her taste. She needed color.

"It looks more like a hotel room than an apartment," she once said when I declined her offer to add "some color and homey touches."

I told her it didn't bother me if it looked like a hotel room when what I really meant was that I was accustomed to it. I was traveling constantly for work and took comfort in knowing the hotel rooms would feel a little like my apartment. I suppose the only color I cared about was green.

We never moved in together, although we did discuss it. Our schedules were too hectic, at least mine was, and we were too different. I was very neat and organized, there had to be a place for everything and everything had to be in its place. Michie was the opposite. Her works in progress were scattered about her apartment and she could never find anything after she put it down, even her sketchpad.

She tossed her mail on the hall table and left it unopened for days, sometimes weeks. Her bills were piled high on the kitchen counter because she waited until the end of the month to pay them, while I opened my mail the moment that I got home, whatever the hour, and immediately paid any bills.

I couldn't live in a messy apartment, even if it wasn't my mess.

I think we both realized we needed our own space, and it would take too much compromise to share an apartment. Even though we were the same age, I felt older. I was already pretty set in my ways—lawyering is a job that requires routine and consistency—and although she denied it, she had no fixed perspective on the way she wanted to live and work.

We were both moving into our late twenties by then, so I thought that was a bit odd.

Still, I think I did love Michie, at least according to some of the definitions of love I've read over the years. I felt calmer when I was around her and looked forward to the shelter she offered late at night from the pressures of the office and the anxieties I might have over the current takeover battle. My mind was always percolating with new strategies to meet the legal challenges, even when I wasn't consciously thinking about them.

When I was with her, I could relax and focus more on the moment, for a little while anyway, just as Jack always encouraged me to do. None of the women who came before and after her were quite as good at making me feel that way. Jack probably would have considered her my cosmic connection for that reason alone.

I started thinking seriously about taking the next step, even though it was premature in terms of the timeline I had laid out back in law school. The partnership was supposed to come first, and that was two years away. I remember looking at a few engagement rings in a jewelry store across from the office, but then one of the big acquisitions we were working on took a wrong turn and I had to spend six weeks in Salt Lake City and Dallas.

Our relationship took a dramatic turn after I got back. Michie had found a new job designing wallpaper instead of fabrics and her studio was no longer in midtown but down in the village. She and her new boss, the young owner of the company, hit it off. He had artistic aspirations for his new company that went far beyond wallpaper, and he encouraged Michie to expand hers horizons as well.

She explained it all to me one night over dinner a month into her new job. She said she needed to be with someone who would be more present in her life and who shared the same interests. I worked too hard, my hours were too long, and I traveled way too much.

"Even when you're around," she said, "your mind is often somewhere else."

I hadn't seen it coming, not the way I anticipated and prepared for what was likely to come next when I was dealing with my adversaries in court, and I was at a loss for words. I was out of my element. Words of love are not commonly used by lawyers in legal briefs or during oral arguments.

"I need someone who will be around more," Michie said, "and can make more time for me . . . for us . . . someone . . . ."

"Less ambitious," I shot back before she could finish her thought.

"More flexible, less scheduled," she responded, which I found bizarre since everyone in Manhattan was scheduled to a significant extent, particularly the successful people.

She admitted we were both driven by our work, but the work was so different, as were the demands, and there was no "easy way to reconcile them," she added, using a legalistic phrase I had relied on many times in court and over the course of our relationship.

Michie added that my job felt like a "jealous lover" who would never let go.

"We are driven by different things," she whispered.

"You mean money?" That was the main difference in my mind.

She sighed and took her time answering. Michie relied much more on her heart than her head in conversations like this, while I was the opposite. I weighed my words and reviewed the precedent as if I were arguing in court.

"We all need money, but only enough to live. It's a part of life, not the be-all and end-all of our existence."

"It's a very big part," I said, correcting her.

Michie gave me a half-hearted nod. She didn't want to argue, I could see that. Her mind was made up. I had seen that same look many times on judges.

"Everyone admits there's nothing worse than being poor," I said, "yet in the same breath they condemn the pursuit of wealth."

I remembered that line from one of the old *Christmas Carol* movies. I could have used it on Jack as easily as Michie.

"Our minister used to say that it wasn't the man who had too little who was poor, but the man who craved too much."

"Money is power," was my retort, "that's an old English proverb."

It went downhill from there. I said some harsh things. I had on my lawyer's hat by then and I always made it a point to exploit my opponent's weak spots. I didn't care if I hurt her since I knew I had already lost her.

I wish I had behaved better.

Despite that, Michie said she wanted to remain friends. I knew from experience those words meant nothing, I had used them often enough, and I remember slamming the door on my way out.

I never experienced a breakup that wasn't sharp and final. That was the way I did it when I did the breaking up, which was all the time to that point in my life, and I preached the same thing when it came to mergers and acquisitions. Don't dawdle, don't linger, and don't use half measures. The takeover must be quick and complete, people will have to be let go and factories shut if economies of scale are to be implemented. I always reminded my clients that there would be no room for accommodation with the executives in the acquired company, a buzz word for friendship, after the takeover was complete.

Michie moved out of the building and down to Greenwich Village a month later. She wanted to be closer to work. I was sad to see her go, although I didn't tell her that. In truth, I didn't like being dumped and I resolved to make sure it never happened again.

The last time I saw Michie was the day before she moved out. We bumped into each other in the elevator, just like we had at the beginning. It was just the two of us and it seemed like a long ride down. We exchanged some pleasantries, as if we hardly had any history together. Then she smiled at me, the same smile she used when we first began our elevator courtship, the one I used to carry with me to the office.

As the elevator reached the ground floor, she asked me if I had written Jack back yet.

I shook my head no.

"You should," she said, "being angry hurts you more than it does him. He's the closest thing you have to a real friend and family."

Michie knew I wasn't particularly close to my parents or my sister.

"It's not anger," I said as coldly as I could, knowing how much she hated it when I used my emotionless, lawyer's voice.

"Then disappointment or frustration, call it what you want, but sit down, and write him back. I think you'll feel better once you do."

The doors opened and I waited for her to walk out first. She started to leave but then she stopped and turned around. There was no hiding from the kindness and pity in her eyes.

"Jack is right about being in the moment, focusing on it and keeping it within yourself, instead of always chasing after the next one."

With that, she turned and walked away. Those were Michie's parting words. More lifestyle advice like Jack's that didn't make much sense to me in terms of my profession or my goals. They made me just as angry as Jack's remarks did, no matter how well-intentioned or prophetic.

I never saw or spoke to Michie again, although I did hear about her six months later from an elderly woman who lived in the apartment next to hers. I bumped into her one Sunday morning on the elevator and she told me that Michelle had married her boss.

That evening, I pulled Jack's letter out of my desk drawer and wrote back to him.

> *Hi Jack,*
>
> *It has been a while. I decided to write back in response to your last letter on Bodhi time instead of mine for a change.*
>
> *A lot has happened over the last few years. I am now a senior associate working on matters that often hit the front page of the business section of the Wall Street Journal. It's interesting work, always timely and incredibly remunerative, although it's not nearly as much fun as clerking was.*
>
> *When you clerk for a federal judge, you're almost like a god. Call an attorney's office and they will pull him out of the bathroom to take the call. If he's not around, they'll track him down and you'll get a call back five minutes later. As an associate, even a senior one, I can wait days for a call back. Half the time they won't return my calls. Partners only want to speak to other partners.*

The judge I clerked for was hardnosed, short-tempered, and self-absorbed, but it was good training for dealing with judges when I'm practicing law, as well as irrational, demanding clients, and adversaries. He was smart, decisive, and overworked like all the other federal judges. His mantra—to use a word I'm sure you're familiar with—was that while he couldn't be thorough, he always had to be right.

My job was to make sure he was always right, and he didn't get reversed by the Second Circuit on my watch.

The criminal docket in Federal Court was awful. It tended to be drugs and gruesome murders of federal agents and informers. The pictures they put into evidence could radically change anyone's opinion of humanity. They did not simply kill people; they cut them into small pieces.

They do not pay law clerks very well, but as I said before, it guarantees you a job at any firm you want, along with the big bucks that come with it. I know you don't want to hear it, but you can check that box off my list of childhood dreams. I am rolling in it—my last bonus was six figures— and the offer still stands if you need some extra money for the house or anything else. Just say the word, no strings attached.

A couple of years ago, I started going out with Michelle who lived in my building one floor below me. She was a graphic artist who designed fabrics, mostly for furniture, bedding, things like that. Weird career I know, but everyone has a bed and a comfortable couch to sit on to watch TV. Well, maybe not everyone, I am sure hippies have something against creature comforts.

Her designs were a little too colorful and abstract for me, although they were very intricate, not just a jumble of shapes like your old ones. There was no denying her artistic ability, the way she used colors and swirls, although I was always surprised at some of the artwork hanging in her apartment—realistic paintings of landscapes and people that she had made in high school and college that evidenced her true artistic talent. I could never understand why she abandoned that for figurative art, but she said she had a calling, I suppose a little like you.

I thought she might be the one, but she couldn't take my schedule, especially all the traveling. I'm often away for weeks at a time now, home for a few days and then back out on the road. Anyway, she switched to wallpaper design, got a new job, and moved away.

She was a bit of a hippie in the way she dressed, you know, flowery fabrics and long flowing things, even in the way she viewed the world like it was a blank canvas waiting for her to color it in, while my suits are all dark blues and grays which is what lawyers wear, and I view the world from a legal perspective, black and white in terms of law and order. I don't see life as a blank canvass waiting for a brush, but something unstable that's always tottering on the brink of disaster and requires a lawyer's skill and effort to keep it from toppling over.

Sort of like Atlas carrying the world on his shoulders.

Life, my old friend, is not a work of art. It's not a swirl of color and abstract shapes. It's not about standing still and trying to figure out what some cosmic whisperer is trying to say. It's a full-time job just keeping the world spinning and it requires determination and perseverance. It's about working hard, establishing routines, and embracing and nurturing those little consistencies in life that the law is there to protect because in the end those consistencies are what really matter.

I remember reading in college how Oscar Wilde believed that we should all be spectators of life, particularly our own, as if we were "living inside a work of art." I didn't see how that made any sense back then or now. I believe it's incumbent upon each of us to be active participants in society and business. We have a responsibility to determine what needs to be supported and what needs to be fixed and to work hard to make things better for ourselves and in that way for everyone.

Relating to life as if it were a work of art the way Michelle did will never save the world or improve it much, despite what she—and you—may want to believe. In the end, it was clear to me that Michelle would not have been a good fit. She was too abstract if that makes sense. She had a very different kind of drive, a free-flowing creative drive, not that there's anything wrong with that, but it didn't mesh well with mine.

I need to stick to the business-types and continue the good work of upholding the law. I need to find a woman who admires commerce and ambition. Someone who plays by the rules and understands the price to be paid at times for the work I do in advancing the rule of law. There are plenty of woman around who appreciate an orderly world and the success and financial security that come with it.

I am disappointed now when I reread this letter.

What about saving the world one life at a time? Art can do that. Art touches everyone, even math does, one heart at a time; mergers and acquisitions not so much.

I really did like Michie. Maybe it was love, I can't swear to it, not after all these years. I am not sure I could have recognized it back then. Honestly, I am not sure I would know it any better now. I've read a thousand definitions of love over the years and never found any of them easy to understand.

Still, Michie was about as close as I ever came to one of the definitions that I still remember from my introduction to psychology class in college. It described love as the sudden and difficult realization that someone other than you is real and matters. Even that definition falls short because as lawyers we are trained to see all our clients as real with problems that matter, yet I can swear unequivocally that I have never loved any of them.

I think Michie and I came close, but I was too cautious which made me too judgmental. After I retired and started reading novels again, devouring them is more like it, I was struck by this line I read in a murder mystery by some obscure author:

There is a time and place to be cautious, but not when it comes to love; caution will always be fatal when it comes to love.

Later in the same book, the author wrote that *the more one judges, the less one loves.* I think that about sums up my life. I wish I had read those lines when I was much younger, although I doubt that I would have appreciated their wisdom back then. They should have taught more about love in public school from the elementary years right through high school. It would have been much more useful than geometry and physics.

I often wonder what happened to Michie. People moved in and out of my life so often back then it was too difficult to keep track. No one ever remained connected the way Jack did.

In truth, I prefer not knowing how the rest of Michele's life turned out, as with the other women I have had relationships with. What's the point?

I am sure you will be happy to know that I'm working on a big merger of two large oil companies. It is not so much a merger as a buyout. The interesting part is that if you were to call me and I were to tell you the name of the company that was about to be acquired, you could buy a few options and easily make enough to finish your house if it's not already finished, and even pay to bring up the town sewer, water, and electric lines.

I knew Jack would never call, or be interested in making money that way, but I wanted to see if I could tempt him. I'm not sure I would have given him the tip if he had called since it would be breaking the law. I like to think I wouldn't have, but because it was Jack, I might have if he'd agreed to buy no more than ten options, a number that would not have garnered any attention, and offered me the opportunity to visit him and meet Harmony.

I'm in the office six, sometimes seven days a week. I come in early, stay late and bring work home. There are always a thousand fires that need to be put out and yes, I like it. It's like Woodstock in a way . . . nonstop action and a constant high.

Everything we do is cutting edge and often appears in the business section of the national newspapers. It affects the economy which, whether you admit it or not, is the engine that drives this country forward and helps protect the freedoms that you so cherish.

Don't do anything stupid, Jack, in your fight to bring down the government and put the hippies on the throne.

You have a daughter, maybe a son by now for all I know, and they are better off with you around as opposed to making license plates for ten cents an hour.
Best,
Ry

I did not hear from Jack for a long time after that letter. It had to be two or three years. I'm sure my letter didn't endear me to him any more than his last one endeared him to me.

During that time, I read about a fire set at a chemical plant that made a weed killer protesters alleged was poisoning the pristine waters of the Catskills. No one was injured, but there was significant damage. I also read about some demonstrators who chained themselves to trees to stop loggers from cutting them down and clearing large sections of the forest to make room for more second homes and spa resorts. The Catskills was becoming popular with those people killing it in business but not making enough to afford a vacation home on the beach.

Dozens of people were arrested in the forest protest, although the papers didn't provide the names of any of them, just the name of the group, the Forest Flying Squad. There was another group, the Environmental Warriors, who lay down in front of trucks delivering PCB waste to a landfill about thirty miles from the site of the Woodstock Concert. They were arrested as well, and one man was seriously injured when one of the trucks ran over his leg.

There were growing nationwide protests in the eighties over the environment and the pollution inequalities that unjustly added health hazards to the other hardships suffered by families living in poorer neighborhoods. Nobody wants a landfill in their neighborhood, and I agreed that they should never be located near population centers. I would have liked to see more of my tax dollars going to help blighted neighborhoods, but it could not have come as a surprise to anyone that people with the most political pull were the least likely to find dumps placed near their homes.

I am sure those environmental warriors have long since grown old and retired to warmer climes, while the pollution disparities they objected to still exist. It is an unfair world, there's no doubt about it, but it seems to me the only way to make the world completely fair would be to burn it down and rebuild it from scratch, as Jack proposed in his valedictory speech, which no one wants.

A little fairer—some incremental improvement—is about all you can really hope for from generation to generation, unless you're like Jack and his merry pranksters, young, idealistic, and fervent about change of any kind.

There was never any mention of Jack or Kai in any of the articles. The leaders were named on occasion, spokespeople were quoted, but never Jack. Of course, Jack was never comfortable in the limelight, he always liked to remain in the background unless it was unavoidable. That was the way he ran cross-country, staying back in the pack until the finish line came into view when he sprinted to the lead.

I don't think I heard from Jack again until shortly before his parents had their terrible accident. By then, I had already married Gayle, a mid-level associate at a small tax firm who had spent quite a few months with me in Omaha on a pharmaceutical merger. Those takeover battles were always conducive to quick intimacy.

The relationship continued after it was over. It was convenient since we were on similar schedules, meaning we were often in the office 24/7. It satisfied both of our needs in terms of not eating late dinners by ourselves and falling alone into a cold bed at night.

It didn't feel anything like the way it did with Michie, but it was easy, and I thought it might work because we were both lawyers with similar ambitions. I think timing played a big part in my decision because I was getting older and didn't want to let another opportunity go by.

Real love, as the poets often proclaim, looks out on eternity, which might explain why our marriage didn't prove to be real or last very long. Neither one of us could see beyond the legal matters that held our attention. That's pretty much all we thought about, and it certainly was almost all we talked about.

The divorce, about two years later, was amicable since there were no offspring and no joint property of any significance. We were both earning big salaries and neither of us needed the other for financial support or any other kind of support for that matter.

I'm not sure which of the traditional definitions of love that I've read over the years would fit what we had, if any, but people marry for lots of reasons; love is not the only one.

Gayle moved to the West Coast shortly after the divorce to join a midsize LA firm where she quickly remarried and started a successful small boutique firm that specialized in capital raises for startups. I don't know whether she had any children or how long that marriage lasted. Perhaps they are still married and have a couple of young lawyers as grandchildren.

As always, I don't want to know.

Our time together doesn't stand out in my memory. I never rerun it late at night when unsaid words linger on my lips, sleep feels like a distant memory, and I am forced to stare wide-eyed up at the white ceiling where my past is often projected.

Shortly after we split, I sold my old apartment, the one we had lived in, and bought a luxury apartment across from Central Park, not the Penthouse, but one floor below. I lived there for over thirty years and didn't sell it even after I retired and moved down to Florida, not because I had any intention of returning, but because I thought it would be a nice farewell gift to Harmony when my time came. This way she would have a vacation home in the city, which I thought rather ironic.

After the divorce, I began renting a house in the Hamptons for the summer with some of the other single partners at the firm, hoping to find someone more sustainable for the long run. Marrying another lawyer was a mistake, I realized that, especially one as focused and obsessed as I was, so I was not going to do that again.

I figured someone who did not have to work as hard, perhaps a socialite or a book editor who could work from home. I also kept my eye out for a small house near the beach that I could trade in one day for a larger one on the beach or high up on a bluff with a panoramic ocean view. I continued renting for five more summers—the last two on my own—until I grew bored with the Hamptons and stopped going.

In truth, I became less and less interested in having a beach house as the merger and acquisition work dramatically increased and took me all over the country and sometimes around the globe. I suppose not having much time to spend out there contributed to that.

I met a lot of gorgeous, successful women over the next twenty years, had lots of relationships, but none that stuck. I was busy with tender offers and takeovers, camping out in hotels for months at a time while fighting protracted battles against poison pills and competing suitors. It did not change my lifestyle much since every city had beautiful women and five-star restaurants.

I do think I would have made a better husband the second time around, although it wasn't easy finding someone, preferably a younger woman, willing to accept my ridiculous work schedule and peripatetic life. It is hard to find a love that will last when you're too judgmental and most lawyers, litigators in particular, are in the judgment business. They believe that what they do is more challenging and worthwhile than anything anyone else does.

The funny thing is that in a strange way I was doing exactly what Jack had advised me to do, I was living in the moment, except my moment always happened to be the latest merger and acquisition, which I realize now is not what Jack had in mind since those moments belonged to the client and the firm, not to me. I was living in their moment, guiding them through it to make sure they reached their destination.

> *Hi Ry,*
> *Been a while even by my standards. What's it been*
> *about three years? I don't keep track of time the way you*

lawyers do.   Probably because I don't bill it by the minute.   In fact, I don't bill time at all, I get paid by the job.

That's a joke.

Ignoring clocks and calendars keeps me more in the moment.   Kai says it frees us from society's endless tic-toc.   I rarely know the date and I am lucky if I get the day right.   I can always rely on the angle of the sun to tell me when I'm supposed to be somewhere.

Time counters like you, who allow calendars and clocks to dominate your sense of place and self, turn time into your master which makes the days, months, and years rush by even faster.   Ironic, isn't it.

Moments are the place where you are.   They're all that really matter.   They deserve your full attention.   They need to be experienced, not counted.   That's what helps us rise above time.

More Buddhist philosophy, I know, a lot for you to swallow.

No more kids if you're wondering.

Too many people in the world already in case you haven't heard about the overpopulation problem and what it's doing to the Earth.   Harmony is the best thing we can contribute to the planet.   She has a good heart, and she knows what's important.   We are home schooling her at the present but will send her to public school eventually.

She needs to socialize with different kids raised by all kinds of parents.   It will make her stronger and more independent.   It will help her to see the world through the eyes of others, which is the best way to find compassion.   She wants to go and has the right to determine her own destiny.   Maybe she'll turn out to be a lawyer like you, but if she does, I can't imagine her clients being big corporations.

Jack was right about Harmony. She has a good heart which she has been kind enough to share with me. He was right about more things than I was at the end of the day, but that's hindsight and everyone knows what they say about that.

We did finish the cabin. It's small with two bedrooms, one bath and yes it does have a septic tank and a well, although it does have electricity. The utility ran lines up our mountain road without anyone asking. Apparently, it was part of a twenty-year plan they had drawn up ten years earlier. We burn wood in the winter for heat, but we never cut down trees for it. We use the trees that nature prunes.

I suppose the big news is that I spent three months in the local jail. There you go, your prediction come true . . . or was it a wish?

It wasn't much, some hikers discovered my little pot field, the one for us and our friends. Unfortunately, one of them turned out to be a New York State Trooper. They cut down all the plants and arrested me. Since I wasn't selling it—it was for personal use only—the judge said he was going easy on me.

Six months in jail, out in three with good behavior, hopefully that will help you clean up your act he bellowed from his judicial perch like some robed vulture. You're a father with obligations to your family and the community, and if I see you back here again, I won't be so lenient.

If he knew half the things I had done as part of our anti-war and anti-pollution protests, he would have thrown the book at me.

He was just another bureaucrat throwing his weight around. A pompous ass perfectly suited for the government's biased justice system. If I had any connections or money, or acted the least bit contrite, I'm sure he would have given me a slap on the wrist and wished me luck.

It shouldn't be illegal to grow marijuana for personal use any more than it is to make your own wine or beer which gave me an idea when I got out. Kai and I have been making some extra money brewing our own beer. We call it the Katerskill Falls Brew and believe it or not it's popular at a couple of the local taverns.

It's also illegal to brew and sell beer without a permit and regular inspections by some government flunkey who will visit once a year with his hand out. Despite that, no one has bothered us about it. I'm sure that's because the sheriff and the judge both like beer. The worst I would get from a home brewing infraction is a small fine. They don't put people in jail for the things they like.

It amazes me that when it comes to guns and hunting anything goes. When it comes to drinking beer, wine, and hard liquor anything goes. Drunk driving? Get a ticket, pay a fine, and receive a warning to be more careful the next time. When it comes to getting high with pot, it's lock 'em up.

Anyway, it wasn't so bad. Since it was only three months, they didn't send me to the state pen with all the murderers, thieves, and crooked politicians. They kept me local with the small-time drug dealers and shoplifters. I made some new friends and I have a lot of potential customers if I ever decide to grow again. My cellmates liked my organic philosophy of farming—no bug sprays and no chemical fertilizers, just sunshine and rain.

I'm back to carpentry as well. Bear and I have started our own company specializing in renovations. He's not as good a carpenter as I am, I think all the math helps, but he's big and strong and can do the heavy lifting. The store is doing well, but we don't make a lot from it since Kai and Rainbow don't like to mark things up too much.

We have everything we need so it doesn't matter.

Harmony is a joy that I hope you get to experience one day when you find someone willing to love you despite your first loves . . . work and money.

Ha-ha.

I've started studying math again as a hobby. I always found prime numbers interesting. In case you've forgotten what those are—which I am sure you have— they are numbers divisible only by themselves and one. Mathematicians have been searching forever for the perfect formula for finding prime numbers like Mersenne's 2n-1. Unfortunately, his formula came up with some numbers that weren't prime. There should be an infinite number of primes and the world has been looking for a foolproof way of identifying them, the math world anyway.

The Godbach conjecture is another interesting challenge. He believed that every even number greater than two had to be the sum of two primes, like 3+3=6. No one has been able to prove or disprove it, not yet. The conjecture works with large numbers, but the question is how large do you need to go to prove it? Some foundation offered a million-dollar prize to any person who could come up with the right proof, but no one was able to claim it.

Another question many mathematicians have argued about over the years is whether math was invented or discovered. If it was invented, then it would have been shaped by the tendencies of human beings toward certain ways of thinking. That's the minority view and it's certainly not mine. Most mathematicians believe math was discovered, that it exists independent of human thought and has its own timeless truth.

It could be the force that drives the Wheel of Becoming . . . the circle of life.

It's something I like to think about sometimes when everyone's asleep. No doubt it's very different from the kinds of thoughts that keep you up at night. Am I right?

He was right back then, not so much now.

I don't sleep the way I used to. Remember how we used to sleep until noon in high school? Whatever time I fall asleep these days my eyes roll up like window shades at six and there's no way I can fall back asleep. I can feel my body changing. It's thickening around the middle and there are late-night pee trips now. I suspect sleeping for ten hours at a stretch is not coming back.

I don't mind because I get to enjoy the day's bookends. The dawn in the mountains is always beautiful. Each day is like a rebirth, a new life, another taste of the season. The sunset is always astounding and the night sky without all the electric lights is filled with the "spirits of the blest" to borrow a line I still remember from a Wordsworth poem we read in school. The stars always help me let go of whatever thoughts have been weighing on me during the day.

To my ears back then it sounded like Jack might be having a few regrets, perhaps subconsciously, and was having trouble sleeping and turning back to math to calm him down. I wasn't sleeping all that well either, but I was sure it was the pressure of work, the drinking, the heavy late-night meals, and the increasing demands from the firm's big corporate clients who now considered me their go-to attorney.

My mother might have called it being overtired. She blamed everything on my being overtired when I was younger.

I don't sleep any better now that I no longer work. I go to bed early because the news is depressing and there's never anything else on television I want to watch. I read to get tired, but it takes a long time before I can fall asleep. Even after I do, I wake up every couple of hours as if my internal alarm clock is broken. I always manage to fall back asleep, at least until the sun begins to peak through the curtain, which is when I'm up for good, as if it's a wakeup call from the cosmos courtesy of Jack.

> *Harmony has asked about my parents and my sister. She wants to know what my life was like when I was her age. I told her all about them and about you. Kai and I believe in honesty. The truth is what you need to hear when you're growing up . . . once you're old enough to understand it. A child will sense it when you're keeping something from them, and secrecy will make it harder for her to find her true self.*
>
> *I've promised Harmony she can meet my parents soon. I wanted to wait until she was a bit older and better able to withstand the onslaught of their suffocating expectations and demands—and guilt— not counting the recriminations they will try to toss my way through her.*
>
> *I know you always thought my parents were perfect because I didn't have all the rules and curfews you did, and because they seemed very different from all the other parents when it came to the things they liked to do. But different doesn't always mean better. My mother was always obsessed with herself and her latest unfinished*

cookbooks, as well as what she was creating for dinner, and my father spent every free minute trying to uncover the secrets of the great magicians and searching for an unknown species of suburban bird.

They were too busy chasing their own dreams and desires to find time for much else. They were too disappointed with their own failures to pay attention to me or care about my disappointments. Demands and expectations are demands and expectations whether they are directed at yourself or your children.

Maybe there weren't all the rules and reprimands you were accustomed to, but the silences and empty spaces . . . the indifference . . . felt confining and uncomfortable in its own way. Lonely as well. Children should never feel ignored.

Still, Harmony deserves to meet them and develop a relationship if she wants.

I suppose demands and expectations come in all shapes and sizes, some loud and obvious and others more subtle, especially to outsiders. His parents' lack of interest in Jack's school activities was obvious. They never came to any of the meet the teacher nights or any of our cross-country races like my parents did, and the fact that he never showed them any of his stories, poetry or artwork should have been a clue that it was far from the perfect home I imagined.

Family dynamics are very different from the inside looking out. I am sure that's difficult for most teenagers to understand.

Unfortunately, Harmony never got to meet Jack's parents since they died in the car accident not long after his letter. Never getting them together was a loss, not only for Jack's parents, but for Harmony as well. Fortunately, she got to know his sister a bit and me a lot.

The first time I met Harmony she was twelve. Jack brought her down to the city to visit the Museum of Natural History because she'd read a lot about it and begged him to take her. She was an easy conversationalist like her mother, I remembered that about Astra from Woodstock. She had heard a lot about me, enough to make her curious, and insisted on meeting me while they were in the city. She peppered me with questions about what her father was like growing up and the kind of things we did together.

She called me Uncle Ry, without prompting I might add. It was natural affection, organic, as Jack was fond of calling things that I considered genetic.

Harmony was beautiful, bright, and easy to love.

It was the first time I had seen Jack since that day we had pizza together before he took the bus up to Woodstock and Astra, but I can't really remember what he looked like. The only memory I have is of Harmony. I remember our conversation, which was delightful, and what she was wearing, jeans with embroidered butterflies and a Woodstock T-shirt. She had long straight hair, straw colored like her mother, and the sky-blue eyes of Astra's brother. I've racked my brain, but my memory of that day begins and ends with her.

I suppose Jack stayed in the background, not wanting to turn it into a high school reunion considering the way he had rejected his past.

I would grow close to Harmony over the years, especially after she moved down to the city to attend NYU. She was gifted in art and poetry, as well as patience and compassion. Math too, but then again, she was good in all her subjects and received a full scholarship because Jack and Kai did not have any money.

We grew closer after Kai died. Harmony and I talked almost every Sunday. We talked about her kids and her life, and she always asked about mine, particularly after I retired, although there was never much to tell. I took daily walks around our manmade lake. I managed on my own for breakfast and lunch, and had my dinners delivered or picked them up. I didn't feel comfortable eating out by myself anymore.

I spent time each day managing my money and my investments. It was more a habit than anything else since it hardly mattered to me if the stock market went up or down. I was diversified and had more than I could possibly spend. I liked to play solitaire, build houses out of cards, and roam the internet when I needed to pass the time.

I also read a lot, about four books a week, sometimes more.

All I read these days is fiction. I used to read history and biographies when I had the chance during my lawyering days, which was not often, figuring they might help me in terms of adding some color to my courtroom presentations, but I prefer novels now. I've had enough of real life. I find fiction real enough and much more engaging.

Fiction is like a window that allows me to peer into someone else's life, one very different from my own. Sometimes it's like a mirror reflecting my own. I didn't make that up, I read it somewhere and it stayed with me.

I even started writing my own novel. A corporate cliffhanger where the main character, a young lawyer, tries to stop an evil energy conglomerate intent on gaining control of the planet's oil reserves. There is a love interest, of course, but unlike the corporate executives, she's an environmentalist and not a very believable character. I suppose that's because I have had very little experience with people like that.

It doesn't matter since I have no intention of trying to get it published or showing it to anyone, assuming I ever finish it. I am writing it for myself. Maybe I'll leave it to Harmony in my will. She is already getting a big chunk of my estate with the rest going to my sister and her kids. That is the least I can do considering what a rotten brother and distracted uncle I have been.

Harmony is a remarkable woman. She moved back up to Woodstock after college because she missed the trees—she called them her childhood playmates— as well as the seasons. She described the seasons in the city as "half-hearted" and complained that they quickly "grew stale."

That made me laugh.

"The seasons in the mountains are so different," she explained. "The sights, the tastes, the sounds, the smells are more vivid. They permeate everything and they linger for so long."

She found the seasons in the Catskills reassuring in their consistency, although they were never the same with each adding its own subtle differences.

I never experienced seasons in the mountains so I couldn't comment, although I did notice the seasons a lot more growing up in the suburbs than I did when I was living in the city, but I was a boy back then and the seaasons always seemed new and exciting.

"In the city," Harmony said, "it's all about the change in the temperature and your wardrobe, the shoes and shirt, the hat and jacket; the landscape doesn't change."

She was right about that; the cityscape doesn't change much except when a building is torn down, and another is put up in its place. The seasons are more a convenience or inconvenience than anything else. For urban types like me, being able to ignore that weather was one of the city's big attractions.

Harmony teaches special education and has a master's degree in art therapy. She is also an assistant English professor at the local community college where she teaches art therapy and poetry. She is married with two kids and has published two thin books of poetry.

I don't understand her poems any more than I did Jack's. I'm still too literal and legalistic for that, but she explains them to me with more patience and pleasure than Jack ever did. I'm sure a big part of that is my eagerness these days to listen and understand, which I did not have in abundance as a teenager.

If life is indeed an endless circle as Jack believed, I hope to be better at it the next time around.

Well, old buddy, let me know when you find someone and settle down. Even a rich, hard-working lawyer needs some companionship. The right woman will help you come to your senses in terms of deciding what's important in life, and I'm talking from personal experience.

One more thing before I go, Kai is a little sick. She has Parkinson's, not bad, just some tremors. The doctor says not to worry because she can live another fifty years this way. It's unusual at her age, but apparently it runs in her family. Her grandmother got it at forty-eight and she still lived another thirty-five years, although Kai is getting it at a much younger age.

Seems that there is no escaping some things from the past. You can run away from home, avoid your parent's lifestyle, and blaze your own trail, but you still carry their genetic footprints with you. There is no rejecting the DNA you are born with.

Anyway, we haven't told Harmony yet, in due time, we'll certainly tell her if she notices and asks.

Kai would get her thirty years and die at sixty-six, three years before Jack. Harmony was calm and composed both times, which doesn't mean there weren't tears. But she didn't wail and lose it like they do in the movies. She clearly believes, as did Kai and Jack, that nothing—and no one—ever ceases to be.

By the way, I do read the New York Times on occasion in the library and the other day I came across a corporate battle in the business section. Two large corporations fighting over a smaller one, circling it like

*vultures over a carcass. I forget their names, but they
were all involved in oil and gas.*

Guess whose name was mentioned?

*Your father would be happier if it was the New York
Post, but I hope you pointed it out to him.*

*Anyway,   rich,   and   now   famous,   mission
accomplished.*

How's the beach house coming?

Best,

Bohdi/Jack, anything but Jacko, ha-ha

I had fallen out of the habit by then of writing Jack right back.
I was usually involved in some urgent tender offer or acquisition
and working day and night at the office or traveling across the
country to argue in court for or against it, depending on which side
I found myself. I was after all a gun for hire and willing to work
for either side since they both paid the same obscene fees—win or
lose.

The battle Jack was referring to was one of many in the
energy sector at the time, as that industry continued to consolidate
in search of a quicker and easier way to increase reserves and
improve economies of scale.

I had more than enough by then to buy the beach house, but
no time to look. In truth, I had lost the burning desire to sit on my
back deck listening to the tide and staring out at the water. I had
more important things to do and never enough time to do them.

There was no girlfriend to write to Jack about. There were a
lot of relationships, but not any worth mentioning, none that I saw
lasting beyond the next takeover battle. When you miss all those
parties in your twenties, thirties and early forties, the single
mingles as someone in the office liked to call them, the
opportunities to find that right person, the one with the cosmic
connection, are diminished.

I was no great catch when you considered my advancing age and the weight my sedentary life had unnaturally added to what was once a thin frame. If I stood too long in front of the mirror, I looked as if I were wearing a padded body suit. Rich late-night meals and expensive wine will do that to you.

There was a constant stream of mergers and acquisitions in the late nineties and early part of the twenty-first century, at least before the 2008 crash, and I wasn't sitting around feeling sorry for myself or dwelling on what I might be missing. I liked the challenge and the excitement of leveraging the law on behalf of my clients, big businesses with big plans, as well as the megabucks they were paying for my services.

I liked working on deals that made the front page of the Wall Street Journal and sometimes the nightly television news. They were never life and death matters, and they didn't involve sexy issues of justice and equality, but they were examples of capitalism at its best, and essential to keeping America as the engine driving the world's commerce, at least that was the way I looked at it.

Even the women I dated were impressed at first. Sure, I complained about the long hours from time to time to whoever was sitting beside me enjoying the front row center Broadway seats my secretary purchased from the firm ticket broker or the corner table she arranged at the hottest restaurant, but it was all an act for their benefit because if I really wanted to change my work habits, I could have.

I could easily have quit and lived off what I already had in the bank.

The truth was I needed to keep busy. I liked the routines and consistency of my days, I liked the unique challenges each acquisition presented, and I liked the rewards in terms of seeing my name in the newspapers and my ever-growing percentage of the firm's profits.

I did ask two more women to marry me. One when I was forty-eight and another ten years later. They were both close to saying yes, but they were much younger than me and ultimately the money and the lifestyle I offered was not enough. They knew I was not going to change my work habits or my attitude, and I am sure they had no trouble finding someone younger and more compatible, someone not so set in his ways.

Money didn't seem as hard to find in those years as opposed to when I first began my career. There were rich, younger entrepreneurs everywhere making fortunes in startups, hedge funds, commodities, and the stock market.

It wasn't until I blew past sixty that I decided it was too late to fill in that missing piece of my life. By then I was the head of corporate litigation worldwide and had over five hundred attorneys directly or indirectly reporting to me. I had reached the pinnacle of my profession and like all the other successful people I knew whether they were clients or other partners, I had made the sacrifices willingly. No one held a gun to my head.

Habits get set in stone over time, particularly when they result in great success according to society's most visible and accepted measures.

Even after I stopped practicing law and had enough free time to spend an hour or two every day building houses out of cards, I stuck close to my Florida retirement home having grown accustomed over the years to keeping my own company. I went out on rare occasions with one of the widows in the community who talked me up at the clubhouse, mostly because I was still addicted to fancy restaurants and preferred not to eat at them alone, but I wasn't planning on sharing what was left of my life with anyone else.

Whenever Harmony brought it up—she didn't think it was ever too late to find love— I responded with the same answer I have relied on for years . . . *not every life is about love*. I liked to joke that people cannot live without oxygen and food, but they can without love. Despite what her father believed, not every life was about change either and not all choices remain available forever.

I remember when Harmony called to talk about this man that she had met who she really liked and would eventually become her husband. She seemed more afraid than unsure about where to take it next. I advised her not to let fear make the decision for her. It was ironic for me to give that kind of advice considering how afraid I had been for so long of following in Jack's footsteps by committing my life to someone else and selling out my dreams and opportunities.

It is true, you should never let fear make your choices for you, and you should always be open to change. I came to understand that a little too late. They should teach life skills like that in high school. Perhaps if I had read more novels on my own the way Jack did back then or taken the ones that I did read more seriously, I wouldn't have the regrets I do now.

I remember something Jack wrote in one of his letters. I looked for the letter but couldn't find it. Some of Jack's letters have disappeared. I was less diligent than I should have been in terms of saving all of them, probably because I was never very sentimental about things like that, not until recently.

Jack wrote that life was more than just following your heart sometimes and your head at other times and being wise enough to know which to listen to and when. He said you had to listen to the music of the universe as well, to the spirit voices that spoke in whispers, and connected you to everything and everyone from the long past to the distant future.

I remember chuckling when I first read that thinking it was more of Jack's psychedelic, hippie ramblings. Although sometimes late at night when I can't sleep, I feel as if I can hear the whispers and I can't decide whether it's the music of the universe or my imagination.

I'm not talking about ancestor worship. I don't believe that there are family spirits up there somewhere, disembodied consciousnesses looking out for me and seeking to influence my fortunes by interceding with the universe. But sometimes I do feel as if we are all connected to something greater than ourselves, to moments past, present and future, and what I am hearing—feeling is probably a better word—transcends anything I have ever experienced or believed before.

What this means in terms of what comes next, I don't know. I don't have Jack's confidence in the answer.

Jack believed that at the very beginning the cosmos was a single ball of matter of infinite density and heat, and we all started together as part of that single ball. I've done some reading about it online; it's called the Singularity. It's the big bang that started time and space and begot everything and everyone by scattering the matter we are all made of—every living creature, every rock, every planet, every galaxy—and creating the universe.

Every moment of time and every life comes from that one spark of creation. Those same atoms and energy reverberate in each of us and connect us to each other and the space-time continuum to borrow a line from Star Trek.

Sometimes when I lie awake in the early morning hours, I can almost feel my boundaries begin to dissolve—as if my skin were melting away—leaving nothing to separate me from the cosmos. I listen to my breathing and it's almost as if it's no longer mine alone, it's as if I am breathing in and out with the Earth, with my ancestors and descendants, with the galaxies and stars that exist beyond the reaches of my imagination, and with the endless flow of time.

It's not the least bit scary to feel part of something much bigger than yourself. I think Jack was lucky to have found that feeling when he did, instead of having to wait until the end, although I'm thankful to feel connected, even if it's just for a few minutes late at night and possibly—even likely—an old man's hopeful delusion.

I find it calming and reassuring nevertheless, especially for someone who has never embraced or been embraced by the kind of love Jack found because I think love does indeed help you hear the music of the universe.

The death of Jack's parents and our telephone conversation after their funeral, as well as my inability to find a companion, made me less eager again to write him back, and his letter sat in my drawer for the longest time. I can't tell you what I was thinking or why because I don't remember.

I know I was angry at him for not attending his own parents' funeral, and back then I spent a lot of time angry whether it was at my adversaries, my clients when they refused to follow my advice, the judges who did not appreciate my logic and ruled against me, or the women who could not see me the way I saw myself.

Anger is never productive; it is easy to see that looking back on it now. Anger will never help you understand yourself better or the person you're angry at. Jack once wrote that holding onto anger was like drinking poison and expecting the other person to die. I think he got that from the Buddha.

I did write Jack back eventually, but I can't find a copy of it. We exchanged a few short letters which have also disappeared. I remember offering to buy Jack a house in our old neighborhood if he wanted to move back and to pay his tuition if he wanted to attend one of the local colleges to get a teaching degree in math.

I still had to be angry to have made an offer like that and I remember Jack's response almost word for word. It was short and quick.

> *People are not commodities to be bought and sold like companies. Your offer is demeaning to me, but not nearly as demeaning as it is to you.*

I remember he signed his name at the end with no closing salutation.

It made me even angrier that Jack could not appreciate my good intentions. I kept telling myself I was doing it for Jack and his family. In truth, he was right, I was doing it for myself, and I used my anger to cover up my embarrassment.

No human being should be treated as if their principles, their way of life, and their dignity are for sale.

A period of silence—and darkness—descended upon our relationship.

Another five years went by, four or five girlfriends as well, and my partnership share blew past seven figures by the time I decided to write to Jack and apologize.

> *Hi Jack aka Bodhi,*
>
> *It's been a while.*
>
> *I don't know if I ever did say how sorry I was about your parents. Your call caught me off guard and to be honest I found our conversation a bit disheartening. I was angry and you know me with anger, I can hold onto it for dear life. Anyway, I think that's what eventually led to my thoughtless offer. I was offering you an escape valve in case you wanted one.*
>
> *I suppose it's that old refrain "I meant well."*
>
> *As you know, my mindset is a lot closer to our parents than to yours.*
>
> *No excuse, I realize that, but you remember how I used to blurt out my thoughts in class without giving them a moment to rattle around inside my brain. Fortunately, they were always funny. You'd think lawyering would have slowed me down and made me think more before speaking. It does when it comes to business and in court, personally not so much, which might explain why I haven't found the right woman, or should I say any woman willing to put up with me beyond a season or two of expensive dinners and spa weekends.*
>
> *Unfortunately, I'm not that funny anymore.*

Going back to that call after your parent's funeral, I think I was more disappointed than anything else because I was sure you'd be there, and I was looking forward to seeing you again. I'm a traditionalist as you well know, and it's hard for me to buy into this new age philosophy about the body being meaningless and a funeral just as meaningful if you hold it in your head—or in the forest—a hundred miles away.

When it's my time to go and with the way I work I'm sure it will be long before you, I hope you'll make the pilgrimage to my gravesite to say goodbye in person. That's where I'll be waiting and watching whether from above or below. If you don't come, I swear I'll haunt you for the rest of eternity which would appear possible in your cosmic view of our endless interconnectedness.

Okay, I've made my joke and made my apology so let's move on.

Best,

Ry

TIME FLIES
CHAPTER SEVEN

Jack and Kai both died in their sixties, way too young, both from lung cancer. While Kai had Parkinson's first, it didn't kill her. Neither one of them ever smoked cigarettes, but they smoked joints constantly and were smoking them right up to the end. I learned about Kai's death in a call from Harmony. I got a heads up from her as well when Jack's was near the end so I could travel up there to say goodbye. It was my first-time visiting Woodstock and seeing the cabin he and Kai had built.

There was no funeral for Jack or Kai. Both were cremated and their remains scattered in the woods behind the cabin. Jack's wasn't a service as much as a picnic. There was food and drink, joints as well, and everyone told stories while various children, mostly grandchildren, climbed trees and looked for salamanders.

Harmony kept the cabin. She doesn't live there but says she will never sell it. She keeps it as a retreat for her family and as a place to go to write poetry when she needs to be alone. She says she feels closer to everything in the cabin, everything being more than just nature; it includes everyone.

Harmony reminds me a lot of Jack. She talks about the "arrow of time" having two-heads, one connecting us to the past and the other to the future, much the way our atoms, once clustered together before the big bang, remain connected through space no matter how far apart they drift. There is no distance that cannot be bridged in an instant, a vibration in an atom on one side of the universe instantly felt by an atom on the other side.

It seems like a more hi-tech connection to the cosmos than Jack's, but I suppose that's the way the younger generation thinks these days.

Harmony believes in reincarnation for the same reason Jack did because she says we are all made up of the same stardust. She believes just as Jack did that the universe wastes nothing and recycles everything.

"Incorporeal and corporeal things," she told me after Jack's funeral, "everything."

That includes consciousness.

We do not discuss those transformations in depth or very often. Discussions that personal seem more appropriate between people my own age like Jack and I, but I do find a lot of what she believes in her poetry. I wish I had copies of Jack's old poems to compare them to.

Harmony does not have any poems by Jack either. Apparently, he only wrote them in high school, probably because he was too busy living after that; his old poems must have been tossed by his sister when she cleaned out their parents' house to ready it for sale.

I cannot find Jack's response to my apology letter, but I remember all was fine afterwards. Bodhi was not one to hold onto anger. The art of letting go meant being ready to forgive others as well as yourself.

I think Jack brought Harmony to the city to see me and visit the Museum of Natural History shortly after that letter. I could be wrong. Time no longer seems so linear when you look back at it from a great distance. It's hard to tell when something happened or in what order.

Hi Jack,

I hope you and Kai are well. I imagine Harmony is about ready to graduate high school. She is a beautiful girl, and I don't mean it in terms of appearance, although she is that too. She has a way about her, a genuine smile, and ease with conversation that draws you to her. She's much better at it than you ever were. I know she got that from Kai.

She is a good listener like you were, except her feelings are clearly written on her face. When we were growing up, I could never tell what you were thinking or feeling, not until you spoke. Sometimes not even then. Harmony doesn't hide anything which is refreshing for a lawyer who spends every waking moment playing hi-stakes poker and trying to figure out who is bluffing and who is not.

She is way too honest to ever become a lawyer or a bureaucrat, so you don't have to worry about that.

Yes, another bad joke.

It's hard for me to believe she is the same age we were when we sat around dreaming about college and our future.

I can barely remember who we were and what we used to think about back then. It's easier for me to remember the things we did when we were younger. Remember, the forts, the pond, and the races. I wish I could recall what I used to think about back then as I lay in bed waiting for sleep to catch hold of me, which it did so easily. I know it was very different from the things on my mind now.

I am enclosing a check for Harmony for college, assuming she decides to go. Yes, it's a little large, but I don't have much else to spend my money on these days. It's for her, not you, and it should be up to her whether to accept it or not. I am sure you and Kai let her make her own decisions about things like this.

I was right about that because the check was cashed. Harmony told me later that the money came in handy for the things she needed for college since she did not have enough clothes, not the kind she wanted, and needed a lot of stuff to set up her dorm room. The first thing she bought was a computer.

As for me, I've fully achieved my dream. I've moved into the ranks of senior partner. I'm the one the big corporations call now when they have doubts about whether what they want to do is legal or when they've discovered another fish to fry. I'm the one in the first chair in court and I won't tell you how much I earn because I'm sure you would have a few choice words for me in your next letter.

Suffice it to say that it's more than we used to dream about back in our pre-Woodstock days, exponentially to put it in terms you will certainly understand.

I have a large apartment looking out on Central Park with a view of both the Hudson and the East River. It even has a small apartment off the kitchen for the household help. I have never used it, but I do have a housekeeper who comes in twice a week to help straighten things out and do the laundry. She also gets it ready for my return when I've been away fighting for American capitalism.

Still funny after all these years.

I take a car service to work and home every day and I must have ten times as many suits as my father ever owned. He's retired now, he had to retire because of problems with the blood circulation in his legs and groin. It comes from being overweight and diabetic, as well as

*his endless years of smoking. If not for that, I'm sure he
would have preferred dying at his desk, as do I.*

My father would have two bypasses in his legs and one by his
heart. He'd die soon after the last one. My mother eventually
moved down to Florida and while I did not visit much—I never
had the time—my secretary made sure I called regularly. When
she died, she left everything to my sister. I knew she would
because she had called years earlier to ask if I minded. I told her
not in the least. My sister was solid middle class with two kids
and lots of expenses. My mother knew I didn't need her money
and I arranged for someone in the firm's Miami office to prepare
her will and supervise its execution.

She left me my father's watch, a Longines, which is in my
sock drawer. It's an old-fashion wind-up watch, but it did work
when I last checked, which was the day that I received it. I already
had half a dozen Rolexes by then and I always wore one to work.
It was part of my image.

I never became close to my sister and her kids the way I
should have, especially after she moved away. Once I was elected
to the firm's governing board responsible for supervising over two
thousand attorneys in twenty offices around the world, I barely had
time for dinner most nights, let alone calls and visits.

*Tell me what's going on with you and Kai. It's been
a long time since you sent me a newsy letter. I'm hoping
you have entered the computer age. Most legal research
these days is done on the computer. I can't remember the
last time I opened a law book.*

*The kids these days—even the young lawyers—play
video games and I suppose that's better than the silly
sitcoms we used to watch like that one about a guy whose
mother dies and returns as a car. I suppose I should say I
watched it because you were never into television,*

although I'm sure I told you about the show. Maybe that planted the seed for your ideas about reincarnation.

Another bad joke, sorry.

Anyway, have you watched any television shows in the last thirty years? I wouldn't be surprised if the answer was no. Would you mind if I sent a television to Harmony next Christmas? No joke. Or a nice stereo, let me know. She should know more about the world and the different paths it offers, this way she can make an informed choice just as you did.

You can't hide anything from the kids these days, particularly after they go off to college. Anyway, everything in the world is out there on the internet, so I can't imagine a television will make any difference.

Wouldn't it be funny if she decided to become a computer geek and helped create the first mass produced android robot? One you can buy on sale at Home Depot.

I'm sure you're not laughing, but I am.

Regards,

Ry

One advantage of the ethernet was that I could easily do research on people and businesses. I discovered that Community Center was still going strong, and that Kai had opened a little bakery inside it. The reviews were all four and five stars and her cookies and pies sold out most days by noon.

I found Jack and Larry, which I assumed was Bear's real name, identified as the proprietors of a home renovation business in Woodstock and I even found a picture of the two of them with tool belts hanging down from their waists. Larry was indeed large, round, and hairy, and did remind me of a bear.

Jack was not nearly as thin as he was growing up when I used to joke that he looked like a lollipop on two sticks, but he wasn't nearly as heavy as me. He had long hair and a full beard that looked as if it had been splattered with white paint. His smile in the photo was genuine and larger than any I could recall ever seeing when we were growing up.

Jack's next letter came about a year later. I had been in Chicago for a month fighting a tender offer and it was waiting for me when I got home. The apartment always felt cold and empty when I returned from a long legal fight, notwithstanding that I had the housekeeper stock the fridge and turn down the bed. At that point in my career, it didn't bother me very much, it was enough if my apartment felt like one of the hotel rooms where I spent much of my time.

> *Hi Ry,*
> *I've been thinking about our recent exchange of letters regarding anger and forgiveness.*

I had to chuckle at his use of the word "recent". Those letters had to be five years earlier. Only Jack could consider that recent.

> *Embracing forgiveness is important. Kai taught me that. I have found that as soon as I forgive—whether it's me or someone else—peace, hope, gratitude, and joy flow back into my heart.*
> *Holding onto negative emotions, as I often say to Harmony and yes, remind myself from time to time, cloud your thinking and prevent you from putting things in their proper perspective. Anger can spoil a beautiful sunset, reason enough to let it go. When you hold too tight to a negative emotion, it's impossible to see world the way it is, you can only see it the way you are.*
> *A recent Buddhist speaker I heard said that holding onto anger was like picking up a burning piece of coal to throw at the person you're angry with. You're the one*

who gets burned. You can add that to the earlier one about drinking poison and hoping the other person dies.

Kai likes to say that anger is one letter away from danger and the added d stands for dumb. She says there's a numerical reason for that, but I forget what it is. I don't love math the way I used to. Kai says the numerical value of letters in words and names is just as useful as astrology in understanding our place in the universe. The funny thing is that numerology can be found in science as well.

Mathematicians have always looked for sets and patterns as part of their scientific observations. Over the years, scientists and mathematicians have been intrigued by the coincidental resemblance of certain large numbers. I'm referring to the ratio of the age of the universe to the atomic unit of time, the number of electrons in the universe, and the difference in strengths between gravity and the electric force for electrons and protons.

Despite Jack's statement to the contrary, it was obvious to me that he still loved math. I suppose it's easier to keep on loving something you never expect to love you back.

I couldn't understand a word Jack had written about those large numbers, but I didn't care because I got the gist of it. While I always made the effort necessary to understand every legal argument and every ruling by the court, I couldn't be bothered when it came to subjects that didn't pique my interest or figure in my life.

I had heard that "burning coal" line about anger before, except it was attributed to Alcoholics Anonymous. Jack sounded a little less strident in his letters now, less revolutionary, perhaps even a little reactionary. I assumed growing older and being the father of a child the same age as he was when he ran away might be pushing him more into the mainstream. Maybe he was even paying income taxes, voting in elections, and considering a run for local office on the "legalize marijuana platform."

> *Harmony remains a joy. She's curious, energetic and in some ways more like you than me . . . meaning she's gregarious and competitive. She's not the least bit self-conscious which is Kai, although Kai never had as many friends and beaus as Harmony does. Me neither. As you know, I had only one real friend growing up, the one who went on to become a rich lawyer devoted to helping big businesses get bigger and more profitable, but unfortunately leaving himself very little time to enjoy the fruits of his labor.*
> *Sounds like a moral there somewhere.*

I disagreed with Jack about that. I was enjoying the fruits of my labor. I liked eating out at fine restaurants around the country and staying in five-star hotels. I was never at a loss for female companionship at home or during my stays in other cities and I liked coming home to a beautiful old apartment in New York City, even if it was empty and often late at night.

I also liked taking vacations, as infrequent as they might be, to Europe and the Caribbean. I liked buying whatever I wanted, whether it was another Faberge Egg for my collection or another Rolex, and never worrying about the cost of anything or whether I needed it or not.

You can't have everything in life, at least not when it comes to the non-material things, but you can get all the material rewards you want if you do well enough, and I had more than ninety-nine-point-nine percent of the rest of the world when it came to those creature comforts. With respect to those non-material things, I had my share. I had lots of acquaintances, love affairs, and lawyer friends always eager to join me for a night out on the town.

Would I trade some of it for love—the kind that lasts forever—and a family? It's a rhetorical question. What's the point of thinking about it now? When anyone asks, I still fall back on my tried-and-true response—*not every life is about love*—although it doesn't sound nearly as convincing or reassuring as it once did, particularly when I say it to myself.

Many of the words and ideas we rely on when we are younger lose their potency as we get older.

> *The restoration business I started with Bear is doing nicely, as is the store. However, Woodstock is gentrifying, and the visitors these days have little interest in crystals and small handicrafts. They want one-of-a-kind jewelry that none of their friends have, and museum quality arts and crafts.*
>
> *City people are buying houses up here and rather than fixing them up, they are knocking them down and building new ones twice the size that look more like spas than homes. We won't work on anything like that, even though we've been asked. Bear and I will only do restorations. Fortunately, there are always buyers who appreciate the good bones of a house, so there's still plenty of work to go around.*
>
> *Did I mention that we put a deck at the back of the house? Now I finally consider it finished. Harmony likes to say it's more a cabin than a house, but it's plenty big enough for three and yes, Mr. City Slicker, it does have electricity and indoor plumbing. No air conditioning, but we hardly ever need it up here. The mountains and forests are the best natural air conditioners there are.*
>
> *I have exchanged a few letters with my sister. She's doing well out west. Harmony wants to see her cousins, since they're the only first cousins she has. That will be up to her when the opportunity presents itself.*

Harmony does get to know Jack's sister and her cousins. They stay in touch, although they don't have a lot in common other than their DNA. As Harmony often tells me, she considers me the closest family she has after her children and husband. The dogs I suppose as well.

I never told you that Kai's brother disappeared about fifteen years ago and has never been heard from. He was getting deeper and deeper into drug sales, and not just pot. We're pretty sure he crossed one of his suppliers or customers, or perhaps the wrong competitor.

After my sister sold our parents' house, I told her to keep all the money because I didn't want any of it. She sent me a few things including that framed picture my mother used to keep in the den of the two of us after we built that cardboard fort in my backyard. Remember, it took the entire weekend, and I insisted on painting it after we were done to protect it from the rain. It came out great and lasted over a month.

I remember getting frustrated at Jack's methodical approach to it. He insisted that it have a cardboard floor instead of grass, cut out windows on three sides, and a door that opened and closed. When that was all done, we still couldn't play in it until we painted the outside walls brown with black lines to make it look as if it were made of logs and protected the roof with some tar paper Jacko found in his garage.

It was his house and his father's box, so it was up to Jack. That was the rule back then—your house, your way. All I wanted to do was play cowboys and Indians and wreck the fort as part of the game. I would have preferred to burn it down the way they did in the movies but tearing it apart would have been just as much fun.

Jack wanted it to be a fort, a safe place where we could never be harmed. In the end, I was glad we did it Jack's way because it lasted through a month of sun and rain, and we won a lot of battles before it got too soggy and collapsed.

Perhaps I should have noticed the builder in Jack back then.

She also sent me a photo of that assembly in sixth grade, the one where we were both on the homework debate panel. You were arguing for less and I was arguing for more. If I had it to do all over again, I'd have argued for less or at least homework that was more creative and not all repetition and memorization. Not that we had a choice since we were randomly assigned our positions.

My sister says she might be moving again, this time to the Dallas area. She can teach anywhere, but her husband has a job offer at some big energy company, perhaps one you might take over someday. She says she doesn't want to move, but the salary is too good to pass up and it comes with a bonus. It's a shame to make decisions like that based on money, even though most of the world does . . . as you well know.

I was happy to hear another dig. It felt as if we were completely back to normal.

You don't get to pick your birth family, but you do get to pick your friends and lovers who become your adult family. That's what I told Harmony. She will get it when her time comes to move on. My letters with my sister will peter out. We never had a lot in common growing up and even less now.

She will contact me when there is a milestone event but that's the way it is for most of the world. They do what they're supposed to, what's expected of them, without feeling much of anything or knowing why. You and I have always been family by choice, friends who remained connected despite our divergent paths because we wanted to . . . and needed to, in part, no doubt, because of our cosmic connection. With a connection like ours, correspondence works just fine. Proximity and the passing of time are irrelevant.

That might be the way Jack looked at it, but not me. I thought we should have gotten together on a regular basis, at least once or twice a year.

The other night I was thinking about the King in terms of the cosmos and karma. I believe that my life—yours as well—have found their purpose, notwithstanding what we did that day because it was unintentional. It was an accident and like most accidents it was due to carelessness and lack of thought. We were a couple of young boys who did something stupid without thinking it through.

I couldn't believe Jack was still thinking about the frog's death after all this time. It hadn't crossed my mind in years.

It got me thinking about something you and I have never talked much about. You know what I mean.

I knew exactly what Jack was referring to. It was something I did think about from time to time and dreamt about on more than one occasion.

It was a warm summer day. We were fifteen and my father had dropped us off at Yankee Stadium to see an afternoon game. It was a Wednesday, and he had a doctor's appointment in the morning, so he was able to drop us off around noon when the gates opened and pick us up after the game.

It was the mid-sixties and for the first time in generations the Yankee were awful. They were at the beginning of a long dry spell that would keep them mired at the bottom of the standings over the next decade. Still, I was a die-hard Yankee fan like my father and remained loyal. Jacko pretended to care to support me.

The game was a blowout. We sat in the bleachers watching the Yankee lose eight to one. The game was over quickly and since it was an hour before we were supposed to meet my father in front of the courthouse on the Grand Concourse, we decided to explore the neighborhood.

Jerome Avenue was lined with pre-war buildings with stores at the bottom and apartments on top. There were stores for everything, many of the ones across from the stadium sold Yankee jerseys and hats, the others sold sandwiches and had bars for drinking. On the next block there was a small grocery store, different from the big supermarkets we had in the suburbs. The store next to it sold beds and the one after that sold baby furniture and clothes. Further down was a hardware store, a candy store, and a store that specialized in lamps and light fixtures.

There was even a shop that sold nothing but pickles in barrels, the pickle-maker had to roll them out every morning and back in every evening. Along with eight barrels of pickles, each a different grade of sour, there were two filled with green tomatoes, one half-sour and one full-sour, and a barrel devoted to sauerkraut.

Jacko and I were meandering down Jerome Avenue taking a roundabout route to the Grand Concourse when we decided to stop for some Italian ices, the authentic homemade kind we couldn't find in the suburbs. We sat down on a bench in the park across the street to eat them. It was across from an apartment building that looked like it pre-dated World War I.

Back then the apartment buildings in the Bronx were not very tall, not like in Manhattan. Some of them were six stories, the rest four or five. The one directly across the street from our bench was five. We watched mothers pushing carriages up and down the street, men with hand trucks piled high with cartons making deliveries, older kids running errands, and men in suits hurrying somewhere.

"Everyone in the city is always in a hurry," Jacko said.

"Because they have to walk everywhere, they can't just get into a car and drive."

"They could leave a little earlier and walk slower," Jacko said, as if he were doing the math in his head.

"There's a lot of things to do when you live in the city and never enough time to do them."

I thought that sounded wise and mature. It was based on a line I had heard recently on one of the sitcoms.

"Why would there be more things to do in the city than the suburbs, and why would there be less time to do them?"

"Because there are so many more people around which mean more lines."

Jacko nodded, appealing to his mathematical mind always worked.

We stopped talking while we watched a young mother practically pull her son's arm out of his socket as she tried to keep him walking. He wanted to stop to stare into the candy store window at the corner. We could hear him whining about it from across the street.

We both finished our ice and pretended to toss the crushed cups like basketballs into the garbage can by the bench. I was about to stand up and suggest we head toward the Grand Concourse when Jacko started talking again. I wonder if his life might have turned out differently if he hadn't.

"I could never live in the city," Jacko said.

"Not as a kid maybe but wait until you're older."

"I don't think it'll make a difference. There's just too much noise and not nearly enough open space and trees."

"Ever hear of Central Park?"

"The city always seems so grey and lonely."

"It's full of people," I said, with a chuckle.

"Living alone together."

"Okay, that's depressing. I think we should get going."

"It feels like a spiderweb," Jacko added.

"You are nuts, you know that. I'm moving into Manhattan the day after I graduate law school."

Jacko shrugged and looked back up at the building across from us. That's when he noticed the woman on the fifth floor wiggling out onto a narrow windowsill with a sponge and a rag.

"That's another reason not to live in the city," Jacko said, pointing her out.

A shiver ran up his spine. He was afraid of heights, had been since we were kids. Even the top of the monkey bars made him anxious.

"You wouldn't look out of a window that high," I said, "if I nailed your feet to the floor."

Jacko's second-floor bedroom window was no more than ten feet from the ground, but he refused to lean out of it.

"That sill is really narrow," Jacko said, "way too small for her to sit on."

"They do that sort of thing all the time."

"Who?"

"Housewives. How else can they clean the windows?"

"Let the rain do it."

"You're a wimp."

I was not afraid of heights and loved to climb trees and tease Jacko, but I did get the willies watching that woman wiggle further out on a windowsill five stories above the sidewalk.

"It's not worth it," Jacko said.

It didn't seem worth it to me either. I had never seen my mother clean any of our windows from the outside, only the inside, even though the windows on the first floor of our house were easy to reach.   She could have cleaned them standing on a small stepstool. Maybe she did when I was in school, although I doubted it because I had never heard my father complain about the windows needing to be cleaned and he was quick to complain when anything around the house was dirty or out of place.

I looked over at Jacko, he couldn't take his eyes off her. He winced every time she reached up to wipe one of the windowpanes while holding onto the windowsill with her other hand to help keep her balance.

"When it's your time to go," I said, trying to sound mature and brave, "there's not much you can do about it. Look at Mike Mench's father, he died sitting on the couch watching TV."

"He had a heart attack."

"Not much you can do about it when your time's up."

I had heard that line recently about a private on *Combat* who was hit by a stray bullet fired by some drunken German soldier on the other side of the front line that somehow found its way to his chest even although he was asleep in an old barn.

I liked how tough and brave the sergeant sounded when he said it.

We both watched as the woman wiggled out a little further so she could reach the upper two panes. A good part of her butt was now hanging off the sill.

"She's nuts," Jacko whispered.

"Her husband must like clean windows. I'm sure she's done it a hundred times."

At that moment we both watched as the rag slip from her hand. She reached out to catch it but missed. The rag kept falling and having lost her balance trying to catch it, she and the sponge came tumbling down after it.

Neither Jacko nor I could move. I know I stopped breathing. Maybe if there was a policeman or adult standing on the sidewalk who had noticed her as well, he might have rushed over to try to catch her or at least break her fall, but what could Jacko and I do, we were just a couple of kids sitting in a park across the street.

I suppose we could have screamed and called for help, but it happened so fast, and we were both too shocked—horrified really—to make a sound. We just sat paralyzed watching her fall. I remember she spun around like one of those Olympic divers, except instead of extending her arms over her head for a smooth headfirst entry, they were flapping about as if she were trying to fly.

Somehow, I knew she was going to land flat on her back.

It seemed to take forever for her to reach the sidewalk, as if it were a movie and the director decided to show this part in slow motion. The splat she made when she hit it was unlike any sound I had ever heard before or since. It was more than a thud; it was a thud, a slap, a clap, and a crack all at once, followed by a loud pop—almost like a gunshot on TV—that echoed all around us as she lay motionless on her back like something that had never been alive.

The soft splat that followed was the sponge landing closer to the building entrance.

Even from across the street we could see the blood oozing from her head onto the sidewalk, slowly and silently making its way to the gutter like it was a horror movie. A moment later our view was blocked by the adults who swarmed around her. There was a lot of commotion, mothers shielding the eyes of their children as they hurried past and storekeepers coming out and covering their mouths with their hands.

We sat transfixed as the paramedics loaded her into the back of the ambulance keeping her head covered as they did. Jacko and I had seen enough movies to know what that meant.

We didn't move or speak for the longest time. What was there to say? We sat there listening to the crowd murmuring as they watched the ambulance drive away before turning back to stare down at the rivulets of blood still running toward the gutter.

The sound of my breathing drowned out my thoughts.

After what seemed like an hour but couldn't have been more than five minutes one of the nearby store owners came out with a hose and started washing down the sidewalk. The crowd dispersed.

"We have to get going," I finally said after looking at my watch.

Jacko didn't respond, he just stood up, and we started walking toward the Grand Concourse.

"How was the game boys?" my father asked after we climbed into the car.

Neither of us responded.

"I know, I know, I heard the score over the radio. Another blowout. Those Yankees have really hit bottom, haven't they?"

I winced at the way he put it and turned to Jacko who had his eyes closed. He looked as if he was reliving the only fall that mattered now. I don't remember any more of the conversation, or if there was any, but I do remember closing my eyes and leaning my head back against the seat because I suddenly felt exhausted and wanted to sleep. A car ride was usually good at taking care of that, but not this time.

I do know that neither one of us told my father what we had just witnessed. I didn't mention a word about it to my mother after we got home, and Jacko said he didn't tell his parents either. It seemed like the kind of thing that belonged in the pledge box. We talked about what had happened the next night over the telephone. We talked for over an hour. I think it was the longest telephone conversation we ever had.

"I wonder if she had any kids?" Jacko asked.

"I'm sure she did. Everyone who lives in a neighborhood like that has kids. Otherwise, they'd live in Manhattan."

There was a long pause while Jacko thought it over.

"Do you think it could have been our fault?"

I started choking on my own saliva in response to that question for so long that my mother called out from the kitchen to make sure I was alright.

"What are you talking about?" I whispered, closing the den door for more privacy.

"We were looking up at her," Jacko said, "and talking about her. I even pointed at her."

"She was cleaning a window, Jacko. She wasn't looking down at us and she certainly couldn't hear us."

"What if she noticed me out of the corner of her eye when I pointed up and lost the rag when she glanced down?"

"You're nuts."

"What if she somehow sensed my fear."

"Your fear of heights?"

"For her. Maybe she was trying to climb back in when the rag fell, and she lost her balance?"

I was too shocked to argue. I thought Jacko, the mathematician, was more logical than that. In my mind, he was always Spock to my Captain Kirk.

"I think I knew she was going to fall," he whispered, "that's why I couldn't take my eyes off her."

Maybe I should have recognized back then that Jacko was developing this cosmic view of life that connected everyone who shared a moment—a view that didn't have to be the least bit logical—as if a person's future could somehow be sensed or influenced by a stranger five stories below.

I repeated my earlier response, "You sound nutty, you know that. You're not a fortune teller or a psychic, and I've known you long enough to be sure."

When the silence continued for too long, I decided it was up to me to get Jacko past his imaginary guilt and bring him back to reality.

"What if someone inside pushed her," I said. "Maybe one of her little kids trying to get her attention because he wanted a snack and was too young to understand."

Jacko dismissed that idea with a snort.

"Okay, what if her husband had a girlfriend and was thinking about getting a divorce and when he saw her sitting out on the windowsill acted on the spur of the moment? Not something he planned or even thought about, you know, one of those impulse murders."

"You've been watching too much television," Jacko said. "It's more likely she let herself fall than she got pushed."

"If that were the case, she would have let herself fall right away. Why clean the window first?"

"Finishing up her chores to leave everything in order before going."

Now it was my turn to snort.

"Or maybe it was an impulsive suicide," Jacko said. "What if she was feeling a little depressed? I read somewhere that women sometimes get like that after they have a baby. What if it was her first and the baby was a hard one, you know, crying all the time, and sitting out on the windowsill suddenly put this idea in her head and she made up her mind in an instant without thinking about it. It's not the kind of decision you get to take back."

"Then why drop the rag and try to catch it?"

Jacko thought it over.

"What if the rag slipping out of her hand was an accident which is when the idea of killing herself popped into her head and overwhelmed her."

"You've been reading too many weird books."

"People do strange things when they spend too much time thinking about their own life . . . and death."

That sent a shudder down my spine. It was way too heavy a conversation for me, although the fact that it wasn't for Jacko should have told me something. I did not like talking about death back then. Don't much like talking about it now.

At that point I changed the conversation. I suggested that Jacko write a story about it, one that left the reader guessing what really happened. If he ever did, he never showed it to me.

We didn't talk about her again, not that I can recall.

I tried not to think too much about her over the years. I dreamt about her two or three times a year when I was in high school and less often in college. In some of the dreams I tried to warn her, but when she looked down to see who was yelling at her, she lost her balance and fell sooner. In the other dreams, I was the one falling from the windowsill.

The dreams stopped after law school as her fall got buried under a thousand new memories. I'd gotten better by then at putting uncomfortable thoughts out of my head, lawyers must learn to do that particularly after they lose a case or hear something from a client they don't want to know, which happens more often than any of us would like to admit.

Without the 24/7 demands of my practice, I have way too much free time to sit around and look back. It becomes harder to ignore your memories when your days are no longer scheduled months in advance. The quiet and stillness of old age brings up whispers, maybe some of them are from the cosmos, but most of them are from the past—the what-once-was past, as well as the what-could-have-been past.

If every life is made up of past experiences and the present moment, a definition Jack was fond of, and my present moment is always pretty much the same, it's no surprise that the past takes up more of the oxygen.

A fall, a jump, a push, it seems like it could have been any one of them when I look back on it now. I often wished we had gone across the street to find out her name. When you share a moment like that with someone on their journey, even if it's only their last breath, it means there's a meaningful cosmic connection between the two of you or in this case between the three of us.

Connections like that are subatomic, they are in our atoms, part of the vibrations that can be subconsciously felt over great distances in time and space. Those connections stretch back to the very beginning, to the big bang when our electrons and protons—hers, mine, and yours—were side by side awaiting creation.

Those kinds of connections never end.

A nice belief to hold onto if you can. Not easy for most of us who keep our feet planted in the observable world.

I did some research on the internet at the library. I recalled the exact date and location and strangely enough it came up in an obituary. Her name was Jacqueline, and she was the wife of a Korean War vet. She had two children, a little boy, and a baby girl, and she had just turned twenty-five. The obituary said she lost her balance while cleaning her kitchen window and died instantly. She grew up in New Jersey, just over the border from where you and I grew up, less than ten miles away.

I'm sure you don't feel the connection or believe in it, but I do. Think about it, Jacqueline is the female version of Jack. I was meant to bear witness to her transformation. I feel that connection even now, as strongly as I did that afternoon when we sat across the street on the bench watching her, although I couldn't articulate it at the time.

The only connection I felt was to that moment, the one I shared with Jack, not Jacqueline. I didn't feel any connection to her on a subatomic level or otherwise. I didn't see how memories and connections could attach to protons and electrons, or how vibrations could reach across space in an instant and communicate anything.

Of course, I hadn't thought about it over the years the way Jack had, and I certainly wasn't tuned into the cosmos the way he was

Until Woodstock, I had this recurring dream about falling from a window on the top floor of this enormous building, a building so high that it was above the clouds. I didn't fall as much as lean out and jump because there was something below that I wanted to see that was on the ground waiting for me. And I knew I would enjoy the sensation, which I did. It felt as if I was flying toward my destiny.

I always fell slowly in the dream, facing down, not turning around the way she did. When I passed through the clouds, I could see a circle of boys with their arms outstretched ready to catch me, and I wasn't the least bit afraid.

Once I got close enough to see their faces, I realized that the boys were all me at different ages and different times—prehistoric times, medieval times, modern times, and future times. They were all the boys I had once been and would be in the lives to come. I always woke up before I reached them, and I always woke up disappointed because there were so many things that I wanted to ask.

There had to be a reason you and I were in that spot at that exact moment to witness her fall. I think I felt it back then, though I wasn't sure what it was, and I couldn't find the right words. Remember, we started

talking about it the next night over the phone, but it made you uncomfortable and I stopped.

I knew how much you hated talking about endings, and things you couldn't see or know with absolute certainty. I was the mathematical one devoted to logic and deduction, you were the dreamer and the fantasy fan, yet you were never comfortable letting your imagination wander too far off the beaten track.

I suppose you were already a bit of a lawyer back then.

I think that moment was meant to be a lesson for us that life is a free fall, which is why it didn't make much sense putting off living it to chase some distant dream. Time is too precious to waste, which is why it's important to live every moment as if it were a lifetime, and to be open to connect to those people we have shared prior lifetimes and moments with.

I know you don't believe any of this, but I saw an aura around Astra when she first sat down at Woodstock. Astra did as well. Love at first sight is the instant recognition of that cosmic connection. Falling in love over time is a more gradual recognition of that connection. The result in either case is the same . . . true love.

There is no greater joy than finding and living that cosmic connection in this life.

I had that falling dream the first night I slept with Astra in our tent at Woodstock. This time I did reach the ground, gracefully landing at the center of the circle of boys as if I was wearing a parachute, but now Astra was at the center. I had never noticed her before because I was always too focused on the circle of me.

It was the last time I had that dream.

Jacqueline and Astra are all part of my cosmic circle, just as you are. If you had been more open to those cosmic connections, as opposed to focusing so intently on your work and net worth, you might have found the center of your circle as well . . . your bashert, a Yiddish word for true love—that cosmic connection— someone who would have completed you and helped you move closer to nirvana.

As it stands now, you will need to live additional lives and learn more before that can happen, but that's okay, most people do.

What I took from Jack's letter was that his rejection of college and the path we had talked about following for years was not just caused by Vietnam, his cousin, his uncle, his parents, me, Woodstock, Astra, and the King's accidental death, it was also partly the result of Jacqueline's fall. It took all of them to convince Jack, at least subconsciously, that he needed to follow the moments instead of his dreams.

Instead of convincing me that there was some sort of cosmic thread guiding our steps, Jack's words convinced me that life was all about timing and luck. If we had left the Frog King alone, had not stopped for ices after the game and not made it to Woodstock, Jack might have gone on to college and grad school, built the android robot he had dreamed about, and become one of those hi-tech computer success stories.

I lost my fear of heights after that dream at Woodstock. It's true, I can work on the roofs of the tallest houses now without the least bit of anxiety. I no longer fear the ground or what it represents. I know it's coming; it comes for all of us, and I know it's not the end. I no longer feel badly for Jacqueline because I know we will meet again, just as we have many times before.

It's a wonderful way to live, welcoming time as a friend, a conduit to a better and more everlasting experience, knowing there are no ends, just another turn of the wheel in our endless journey of discovery and change.

Money means nothing when you realize we all come from the stars and return to them again. Life is not a race. There is no finish line. It's not about who comes in first, who runs the furthest, or who accumulates the most. It's about enjoying the ride and learning from it.

Hopefully you will come to realize that during the next turn of your circle.

Your friend for all eternity,
Bodhi

Jack lived up to his principles. He had recently turned sixty-seven when Harmony called to tell me he was sick. Harmony and I spoke regularly by then. She had called me during her first term at NYU to say hello and thank me for my graduation gift and I took her out to lunch. The calls after that became a monthly thing and the lunches almost as often.

She told her parents; she kept nothing secret, and I really did come to feel like her uncle.

"My father's dying," she said tearfully. This was long after she had graduated and moved back to Woodstock. She was already married with two children.

I was too choked up to respond.

"He's got lung cancer."

"That damn smoking."

It had been responsible for the death over the years of a lot of people I knew. Lawyers were notorious smokers. If it wasn't lung cancer, it was a heart attack. Lawyers were usually out of shape, me included.

"Not cigarettes," Harmony said with a soft chuckle.

She thought of life and death much the way Jack and Kai did. Maybe the belief that death is just another beginning, another a turn of the circle, should be taught in Sunday School, alongside heaven and hell, so we all have a choice. Unfortunately, some seeds have trouble taking root no matter how early you plant them. You need to be lucky like Jack, Kai, and Harmony to be born with a fertile enough heart and an open enough mind to allow a cosmic seed like that to germinate and grow.

I learned a lot from Jack's letters over the years, yet it is still difficult for me to accept the circularity of being and the endless and instant connections we make and maintain through the infinity of time, at least not deep in my gut the way he did.

"How long?" I asked Harmony.

"A year or so."

"Was he okay with you telling me?"

"I didn't have to ask, he won't mind."

Then I asked a typical lawyer's question because I couldn't think of anything else to say; does he have a will?

Harmony didn't know, but she doubted it.

Kai had died about three years earlier. She had Parkinson's for a long time, although it was lung cancer that did her in as well. Cancer had its place in the fresh mountain air of the Catskills, the same as it does in the polluted city.

I assured Harmony it didn't matter whether Jack had a will or not since the intestacy laws would give everything to her.

She clearly hadn't given it any thought.

After she told Jack about our call, she asked him when I could come for a visit. He told her when he was ready to move on.

I asked her how he would know when that was.

"He'll know . . . he's not taking any treatments to slow it down. No chemo or radiation, no drugs of any kind."

I urged her to convince him to try and made a half dozen lawyerly arguments about why that made sense.

"Your father was always a man of math and science. They're making new discoveries every day. Accepting that there are lives to live afterward doesn't mean you're supposed to give up on the one you have now, not without a fight. You know what they say, do not go gentle into that good night."

"It's not night, that's not what he believes . . . or what I believe," Harmony said very sweetly, getting my poetic reference to Dylan Thomas but making it clear she disagreed with it.

"There is nothing they can do for him," she added. "The doctor made that clear. Treatment might buy him some time, but it would also ruin what time he has left. It's not the way my father wants to leave. Accepting what comes next is part of life."

At that moment, I wished I had known Kai better. Any woman who could raise a girl like Harmony would have been a wonderful friend to have.

Harmony kept me regularly apprised of Jack's condition while he and I continued to exchange letters as we had been doing for almost fifty years.

> *Hi Ry,*
>
> *Harmony told you the news. I'm glad. If I had it to do all over again, I wouldn't change a thing, not even the smoking. I love the way the world looks when I'm stoned, and how connected I feel to the cosmos.*
>
> *What's coming is just another turn of the wheel. I know you have your doubts, I don't.*
>
> *And I won't stop smoking marijuana, not until I become a whiff of smoke myself.*
>
> *Anyway, I don't feel sick, not really. It's not like I can feel this mass in my lungs gorging itself on my body, as if it has a life of its own. In truth, it is simply opening a door for me.*
>
> *I do cough more for sure, and sometimes I get tired doing things that never tired me before, but that's natural*

as the body grows old and gets ready to return to the stars. As you have heard me say many times before, the universe recycles everything, and everything includes more than just the physical manifestation of who we are.

Hard to believe we are a stone's throw away from seventy. It seems like yesterday we were skipping stones across the pond and marveling at the moon landing, and a day before that we were sharing our seventh birthday party. Remember that one? You ran through the screen door at the back of your house and was your father ever mad.

I suppose it's not surprising that those moments seem so close at hand since the past, present, and future merge into one as the wheel of life turns to a new beginning. It's almost like a temporal whirlpool.

Jack often wrote about time. He once said that there are two kinds of people in the world, those who see time as a circle and those who see it as a straight line. People connected to the cosmos, spiritual people, creative people, and farmers—I remember thinking at first that Jack was joking when he included farmers—realize how time returns everything back to the beginning, endlessly repeating the process of maturation, death, and rebirth.

Lawyers, businesspeople, politicians, and those who see themselves as travelers on a journey most often live in linear time. They see time as a measure of their progress toward a goal or a destination. They believe that the past is lost forever because they consider every moment unique and never to be repeated.

Jack thought that the greatest evils in the world were committed by followers of linear time. Believers in circular time lived with a greater moral imperative since they lived in the circle of life and realized that there was no escaping the consequences of their actions.

As Jack wrote in one of his later letters, which I didn't really appreciate as much as I do now: *If you can accept that time is infinite like space, which most people can, then our existence, who we are this very moment, will recur again and again ad infinitum in the endless river of time. It's just math if you think about it.*

According to Jack, the ancients recognized eternal recurrence and eternal return long before there were organized religions. He cited the Stoics in ancient Greece as an example, writing that they believed the universe was a wheel endlessly repeating the stages of transformation.

Even Fredrich Nietzsche, Jack wrote, one of the darkest philosophers of all time and a fervent nihilist, called eternal recurrence a joyful truth that should be embraced by anyone who wants to live life to the fullest.

Jack was smart and well-read even though he never earned a college degree.

I do believe that time and space is forever and infinite, and I do believe in the eternal play of repetition as I once read it called, but the conclusion Jack reached to make us—our very being and consciousness—part of that eternal return is where I have difficulty keeping up.

Jack considered eternal recurrence a mathematical certainty— as obvious as addition and subtraction and as inevitable as the solstice and equinox—which means somewhat ironically that math nerds like Jack feel much less troubled than the rest of us by the great unknown.

Some nights I can almost feel it—the circularity of time—and can embrace for that moment the concept of the past, present, and future as one with our atoms, a recurring lifeforce ready to return on the next turn of the wheel. It's a comfort when that feeling hits and sleep is always a lot easier to find.

Otherwise, things are good. I'm out most mornings splitting wood or doing something around the house. I see Harmony and the kids almost every day. We have closed the restoration business, but the Community Center continues to do well. It practically runs itself.

Maybe I'll come back—a thousand years from now—as a customer to see how it's doing.

Yes, it's a joke, although not entirely.

Heard you're retiring and moving down to Florida. Harmony keeps me informed. How strange does that sound—retired in Florida—when just yesterday we were catching frogs at Hopping Pond, running cross country, and comparing grades.

I should have let you beat me in something, but would you have been happy winning that way? I doubt it. You would have been able to tell if I was dogging it because I was never very good at lying. You certainly won in terms of accumulating the most money and things during this lap around the track, although if that was a race, you were running it by yourself.

I'm beginning to sound a bit maudlin, so let me conclude by saying I am truly excited to see what comes next, excited to rejoin the cosmos. I'll let you know when that moment is near. I'm not worried about you getting overly sentimental, unless age has changed that, but if you show up in a suit and tie, I'll tell Harmony not to let you in. You must have a pair of jeans somewhere in your closet. If not, buy a pair at the Community Center on your way over. Get a pair embroidered with stars.

In the Buddhist tradition, so much of what happens at the end of this life revolves around two questions: Am I loved, and did I love well? I know how I will answer. How about you? There's still time, my friend. You are never too old. Florida is filled with women your age who can still love and be loved.

> *Just don't tell them about your money first.   This*
> *way you'll get an honest answer.*
> *Just a joke.*
> *Best,*
> *Bodhi/Jack*

It was too late for that; I'd been alone too long to change. Jack often wrote that change is life and life is change. I disagreed back when he wrote it, and I disagree now. Some lives, my life, were more about routines and those little consistencies that kept it moving forward.

Not every life has to be about change, any more than it has to be about love.

I can't find a copy of the letter I wrote back in response to Jack's "maudlin" one. I'm sure I blabbered on about how unfair it seemed and how much I would miss him, and that he should fight hard to hang on. I'm sure I added a page of trivialities to take his mind off it, telling him about the new Rolex I got from the firm when I retired or the home that I was thinking of buying in Florida that was 8,000 square feet and had a dock on the harbor waterway that was a stone's throw from the ocean.

Ultimately, I bought something much smaller on a large manmade lake in an exclusive walled off community. I wasn't buying a boat at this stage of my life or looking to entertain or be entertained by nosy neighbors. There was no one I wanted to impress, and I figured a smaller place away from the beach with a panoramic view of the Gulf would be nice enough and much more private.

Maybe I told Jack about the vintage Porsche convertible I was planning to buy to ride around in on sunny days or the substantial donation I was going to make in his name to the Woodstock Library and the Woodstock Nature Conservatory. Harmony liked both charities, but I doubt I would have mentioned it since it is not the kind of thing you mention when someone is still alive.

I wish I could find it or remember what I wrote. It's harder to recall the recent past when you're in your eighth decade than it is the distant past.

I did get another letter from Jack a few months later. He wrote back a lot quicker at this point.

Hi Ry,

Ready for my latest thoughts about life and death. Obviously, I've been thinking a lot about it. I find it a pleasant diversion from the exhaustion and occasional discomfort. Buddhism teaches that you reach the highest level of meditation when you contemplate the last moments in this life and the next one to come.

Everything in this life is impermanent and constantly changing; I know I've said that many times before. Living is passing from one moment to the next . . . from one experience to another. Death is the final moment we all experience before we metamorphosize into our next form. Finding the compassion and acceptance necessary to embrace change, even this one, is what mindfulness is all about.

Death represents a renewal, a regeneration, and, without question, a continuity. Contemplating it in this cosmic light imbues it with a wonderful transformative quality. If you can find that universal compassion, it's easy to meet death the same way you first met life with curiosity and excitement and with no clue as what it was and how it would turn out.

Life is a gift and death simply another part of that gift; together with life it makes existence whole, complete, and meaningful.

I believe in the continuity of what one teacher I knew called the subtle mind and the subtle energy. It's what carries us into the next life and the one after that and so on. The subtle mind and the subtle energy are eternal, the glue that holds our atoms in place; it once knew creation—way, way back—and now knows endless energy and change. Creation never ends.

How could it?

It's part of you as well, my eternal friend, don't worry, even if you haven't fully embraced it yet. Hopefully you will before your time comes, but if you don't it won't matter because it's the way of the cosmos, the way of all existence . . . whether you accept it or not.

Eternally yours,

Bodhi

I found a copy of the letter I wrote back to Jack in response to that one which unfortunately was his last.

Dear Bodhi/Jack/Jacko,

If that subtle mind and subtle energy you speak of knows creation without end and is the same now as when we first met, I feel comfortable calling you—or it—Jacko again.

Funny, huh?

The question is this, since I know your subtleties so well and have known them for so long—since the big bang I suppose—will I be able recognize them after you transform? Will you be able to recognize my subtle mind and subtle energy after I move on? If you were to ask any of my former colleagues and adversaries, they would laugh at the use of subtle to describe anything about me.

I hope we do recognize each other again, at least on that subatomic level you're so fond of writing about, although I would prefer that it was more organic, more holistic if you prefer, so I could make a few wisecracks the way I used to in class.

Shouldn't humor be one of those subatomic things that travel along with the subtle mind and subtle energy? Humor should never end. Every life needs humor, no matter how many of them you have. Perhaps we need humor as much as we do love and change.

Okay, enough of my little joke.

I hope this letter finds you feeling alright. Harmony tells me that you are not in much pain which is good, although she says you've made it clear that you will not wait around when you are and plan to speed up the process. I don't have to remind you that is illegal in this part of the universe, although I do understand. You always had to cross the finish line first . . . in this case ahead of the Dark Angel.

Please let me know if you start thinking along those lines so I can come up to see you before you do. I'll even bring you a little surprise gift.

The surprise I had found on the internet was an original Woodstock T-shirt. The ones they had given out to the staff to wear. I figured Jack might like to wear it to his cremation.

The new house in Florida is nice. The best part is the sunsets over the Gulf. They are spectacular and no two are alike. While I'm just beginning to set up my new routines, I spend most of the day watching the clouds and birds the way we used to when we were kids. There's a full circle for you. In the city, the clouds were obscured by the skyscrapers and the pigeons ruled. I never watched them except to make sure I didn't step on one.

The restaurants aren't as good down here, but it doesn't matter because I'm doing mostly takeout. It's a lot easier.

I told Harmony she is more than welcome to visit with the family anytime she wants.   The house is big enough that we could go a week or two without bumping into each other.

Harmony never took me up on my offer. She is not a big fan of Florida or traveling, much like her parents. She thought it would be a better idea if I bought a little house in Woodstock and spent the summer months up there so I could enjoy the mountain air and spend more time with her and her family.

"The summer up here," she said, "has got to be a lot nicer than the humidity down there."

It was a generous offer and I resisted it at first because I was so accustomed to keeping my own company. I didn't know if I could handle the attention and demands of being part of a family again. But I gave in after Jack's death because Florida didn't feel the same when I returned.   I couldn't stop noticing how old everyone was, whether they were my neighbors, the people in the aisles at the supermarket, or the strollers walking along the beach.

Sometimes the clubhouse reminded me of the waiting room at the geriatrician's office. It felt as if they were all waiting around for bad news.

The heat and humidity can be unbearable at times in Florida and not just during the summer when it can be like going from the refrigerator to a pizza oven as soon as you leave the house.

I needed more young people around to average down my life, and I needed seasons, four real seasons. I missed the snow and the autumn leaves. I missed the transitions from winter to spring, from spring to summer, from summer to fall, even from fall to winter.

I missed the Northeast.

Using the internet and a realtor, I took a virtual tour of a lovely house on the outskirts of Woodstock owned by a former rock musician, and I put a bid on it, a high bid to make sure I got it.

I remember how reluctant I was to close this letter to Jack, perhaps because I knew it would be the last.

You know what I've been thinking a lot about lately? I'm sure you couldn't guess in a million years. It's something that happened when we were teenagers. It's not the King, or the Yankee Game, or me tightrope-walking the bridge railing across the parkway while you followed alongside calling me an idiot.

It's not the prom or any of the races we ran in school where you snuck ahead of me at the finish line . . . okay, I faded, you didn't. It's not graduation where the principal gutted your valedictory while praising my speech, although I did enjoy that a bit. It's not those weird and crazy meals your mother used to make some of which I liked, but most of which still make me shudder even now when I think of them—remember the one with the grasshoppers and other assorted insects she said were high in protein that she cooked with rice noodles in some kinds of green sauce.

I had a dream about that one the other night, except it wasn't bugs she used but small body parts—eyeballs, earlobes, fingers, and toes. I didn't much care for those either, at least not in my dream.

Pretty funny when you think about it.

It's not our arguments over Cassius Clay, fishing, or the Vietnam War. It's not racing up the monkey bars, jumping off the swings or watching your father carve birds and paint them with those tiny brushes. It wasn't his magic tricks or you trying to teach me to juggle or your terrible voice when you played the guitar, although I will admit now under penalty of perjury that you played it better than I did.

It's a shame you didn't continue. I wish I had. It would be more fun now than building houses out of cards.

What I have been thinking about is nothing special, a moment I've often thought about over the years that I wonder if you even remember. It was the first day of ninth grade. You were waiting for me in the hall when I arrived. You were excited, you always were about the first day because you liked school much more than I did.

I was bummed out. I loved the summer, the freedom to wander, the absence of homework, and the days and weeks without plans or structure. You always needed structure back then. The funny thing is that you rejected structure after Woodstock, while I embraced it.

Anyway, I walked up to you, and you could see it on my face and asked me, "why so morose?"

You liked to use your writer's words back then. Morose, that was an odd one; I suppose you were imagining me as a character in one of your stories.

"Do I really have to tell you why?"

You stared blankly back like I did.

"The summer's over, Jacko. The whole school year is ahead . . . the long, slow school year. Our next real vacation is four months away."

I remember you rubbing your chin like you hadn't thought about it that way and needed to process what I had said. You used to do that all the time, you remember, rub your chin when you were puzzled about something, as if you were hoping a genie might pop into your head with the answer. Then you lowered your hand and snapped you fingers like it couldn't have been more obvious.

"Let me say this," you said, "you should enjoy every day of ninth grade because next summer will be here in a flash and a moment later, we'll be graduating and a moment after that you and I will be old men complaining

about our aches and pains. Life is like a ball rolling downhill, it just keeps going faster and faster."

You didn't sound like my friend at that moment, but more like an old man, an old soul channeling a cosmic connection that you didn't even realize you had. My jaw fell open in response. It was not the answer I was expecting because I didn't think like that back then.

"What the hell are you talking about?" Those were my exact words. "Is that supposed to cheer me up?"

I remember being a little angry because all I wanted was some commiseration or a nod in agreement. A two-word acknowledgement—I agree—would have been enough. I would have bet you anything that every other ninth grader walking into school that day felt the same way I did.

Do you recall that day and what you said in response?

"I'm not trying to cheer you up," you said. "You asked me what I thought and how I felt about the first day of ninth grade and I'm telling you. I'm glad it's here, I'm looking forward to it, and I want to enjoy every minute of it. I want to enjoy every day of ninth grade and I'm not going to complain about it or wish it away or pray for summer again. It'll be here soon enough whether I want it to be or not. Would you prefer I lie?"

I think that might have been the first time you started talking crazy about time. We had discussions that past summer about fish feeling pain and the Vietnam War, but this was different. This was more cosmic, as you like to put it, and way too philosophical for the first day of high school.

It was a part of your DNA I hadn't noticed before.

I remember standing there with my hands on my hips and shaking my head from side to side while I wondered who you were and what had happened to my old friend Jacko. I think I snorted in response, I'm not sure, but that didn't stop you from continuing.

"Haven't you noticed how quickly someday becomes today and today becomes last year. The days are no different than the months and the months are no different than the years. They never stop moving and we never stop moving with them. It's like we're caught in their current and there's nothing we can do about it. What's the point of getting upset or feeling morose? Ninth grade is here and feeling sorry for yourself won't change that. It just ruins the day. Enjoy it because tomorrow you'll be an old man wishing you were back here starting ninth grade again."

I may not have been as deep as you were back then, I may have been more interested in watching Samantha on Bewitched than sitting in my room trying to understand the world or the nature of time, but I understood what you were getting at. I think you frightened me a little bit because I recognized the truth of what you were saying, even if it was subconsciously, even as I shook my head and refused to think any more about it.

"Enjoy today," you added, "because it won't be here for long."

"Not likely," I snapped back before shaking my head again and walking off.

I have often thought about that morning and that conversation. I remember thinking about it at the end of ninth grade when I couldn't believe how fast the year had gone, and the night before graduation when I marveled at how much faster tenth, eleventh, and twelve went by. I thought about it the night before I started law school when I no longer felt like someone's child, and the night after they made me a partner and I realized how much money I already had in the bank and how much more I would be making.

I thought about it when you told me you were having a daughter and the day I retired, as well as many days in between.

I think about it often now. Maybe that's what Faulkner really meant when he said, "The past is never dead. It's not even past."

I know you believe that time is a circle inside of which is the past, the present and the future, and that life is a collection of experiences, not the passing of time. I wish I could embrace that philosophy the way you do. I wonder if there ever was a culture without the concept of time, a culture that didn't count it or feel it passing.

It's amazing to me sometimes how time can make the strangest things seem ordinary and the most ordinary things seem strange.

It's like this Dr. Seuss poem I read in a magazine the other day—yes, I do read poetry on occasion although I try to stick to the kind I can easily understand. He was wondering how it got so late so soon.

Sounds like something Yogi Berra might have said.

His poem described life as all memory, except for the present moment. Just like you always have. He concluded that there were only two places to live, either in the present moment or in your memories. Like you, he chose the present.

I wish I had spent as much time as you trying to understand time and the circle of life. I wish I had spent more of my past in the present, if that makes sense, as I try to do now, although there are a lot of days that I can't help staring back and glancing ahead.

Of course, I was writing all this to Jack on his deathbed. I wanted to make his transition easier, whatever that would be. I did believe him in part when it came to the circle, at least at times I did, but if believing requires a threshold, say greater than fifty percent certainty to become a true belief, I was stuck in the low forties. Not bad for a lawyer-type like me, but still short of the level required for a jury verdict.

I suppose there's a little bit of the Buddha in all of us, Jacko. Wishful for some, more fervent for others. I think yours started rising to the surface that first day of ninth grade and grew quietly until it was ready to break free when the right moment presented itself at Woodstock.
You were very lucky.
See you soon.
Love,
Bry

CROSSING OVER
CHAPTER EIGHT

When the time came, Harmony called me. I wasn't doing anything special, pretty much what I did most days since moving down to Florida, sitting in my back yard sipping a single malt scotch while watching the sunset. They are all nice here and pleasant companions to drink with.

I was on a plane early the next morning.

When I got to Woodstock, I stayed in a nice B&B Harmony had reserved for me which Jack and Bear had restored about fifteen years earlier. I went straight to the cabin after checking in and it was pretty much the way I had imagined it. It was in the middle of nowhere, dwarfed by the forest and mountain that embraced it; a log cabin that blended in with nature, as if it had been there since the beginning of time and would remain there forever.

It was the middle of summer, and the cabin was surrounded by milkweed, clover, daisies, and mountain laurel, Harmony identified them for me. In my mind's eye I could see back to the earlier seasons, almost as if I were looking at a series of postcards. I saw the red, orange, and yellow leaves of autumn providing a canopy and a blanket, the pure white winter snow embracing the cabin with soft grey wisps of smoke hovering above the chimney, and patches of wild spring strawberries, spotted geraniums, dandelions, violets, and buttercups waking Jack and Kai up to the spring.

I couldn't help feeling jealous.

Jack was propped up in bed. I hadn't seen him since the day he brought Harmony to NYC to begin college. Of course, he looked older, old really, a fatal illness will do that to you, but it was not as if the circle had completely turned yet because I could still see my high school buddy in his curious, unfaded eyes. It brought me back for an instant to that first day of ninth grade and I could feel the connection—the nearness—between that moment and this one.

Everything else about Jack looked frail. His hair was sparse and as white as the snow I had just imagined blanketing the cabin. His face was deeply lined as if a woodcarver had taken a chisel to it, and his eyelids were heavy as if he was on the verge of a long sleep.

His looks were deceiving since Jack was alert and happy to see me. He smiled and called out in a strong, youthful voice, "You made it, Bry, and it only took half a century for you to get here."

"Because I couldn't find the address," I responded, and we both laughed.

Jack's smile was not half-hearted, it was genuine, bigger than it had ever been in high school, and it was filled with affection and good cheer; unexpected for a man enjoying those feelings for the last time, at least to my mind. Even though he was going on to another place, a supposedly better place, he was still taking leave of the form he had enjoyed for almost seventy years.

I watched the tremor in his hand as he raised it to his chin.

I looked at Harmony who smiled back at me and then at Jack.

Jack chuckled.

"What's so funny?" I asked, trying to sound the way I might have sixty years earlier in the woods or on our bicycles.

When he didn't answer right away, I added "thinking about ninth grade?"

Jack shook his head no.

"Do you know that the earliest memory I have is not of my parents, it's of you."

"Me too," I said. "Mine is that day on the monkey bars when I was climbing after you and hit my chin, do you remember it?"

Jack nodded, "yes, we weren't even five yet."

I reached under my chin.

"I can still feel the scar."

"Your mother had to take you to the doctor because it wouldn't stop bleeding." Jack smiled. "I remember feeling responsible."

"Because you were in front of me?"

"Because you grabbed my foot instead of the bar and lost your balance.

"That's not the way I remember it. I remember my foot slipping and my chin hitting the bar."

"That's not my first memory," Jack said.

"What is it?"

"It was a playdate at your house. You couldn't wait to show me your room because you had this big mobile of the solar system and when I named the planets in order, I had memorized it from a Golden Book, you made me teach it to you. Do you remember that?"

I closed my eyes and tried, but without any luck.

"No, but I remember that mobile. It hung there until I was in second or third grade."

Jack closed his eyes for a moment as if he were trying to go back there as well.

"I thought I taught myself the planets," I said to Harmony as much as to Jack.

"That sounds like the Bry I remember," Jack said, opening his eyes, "always taking credit."

We both laughed.

"I think it's appropriate in terms of closing this circle that you be part of my last memory."

I nodded and Jack nodded back. He took a long, slow breath with effort this time and let it out slowly.

Harmony, who had been sitting at the foot of the bed, leaned forward, and asked her father if he needed to rest.

"No, why don't you bring us some of mom's special tea."

She gave both of us a warm smile before leaving. Clearly, Jack wanted some alone time with me.

"And some of her cookies," Jack called out, his voice as strong and familiar as ever.

Harmony closed the door softly behind her.

"She has all of Kai's recipes," Jack said. "Between you and me, she does a good job, but they don't taste quite the same. Harmony doesn't like baking as much as Kai did and you can tell. More goes into a cookie than just the ingredients."

I smiled. I wanted to laugh but I couldn't under the circumstances. It might be as true as anything else Jack believed, but I didn't have the experience to know that for sure since no one had ever baked cookies for me, not even my mother. It was always store bought when I was growing up and the pastry chef at whatever restaurant was my favorite at the time.

"Well, Bry, looks like this is it." Jack spoke with the same easy confidence he had when we stood at the gym door waiting to lead the class to graduation.

"*It* being what?" I replied with the best smile I could manage. I was not nearly as good at smiling as I had been as a kid. The kind of law I practiced for all those years hardly required a plethora of smiles. The ones I did pass out during introductions like business cards took very little effort because they were fleeting and meaningless.

"*It*, old man, is my return to the cosmos to continue my journey . . . and to reunite with Kai."

I nodded since I didn't know what to say in response.

We talked all afternoon and long into the night. Harmony brought in the tea and cookies, both of which were delicious. She wasn't the least bit teary. She was clearly prepared for what was coming.

"Don't worry, Uncle Ry," she whispered at one point when I stepped out to use the bathroom, "take all the time you want. I've already had my talk with Dad. We all have."

Jack and I talked about all kinds of things from old memories to the new ones he expected to be making soon, the cosmic kind that would get stored up in that subtle energy and subtle consciousness of his and carried into the next life. The way Jack explained it, memories are never lost, they get locked away behind a closed door inside of us that doesn't open again until we enter the period between lives.

We talked about King Frog and Jacqueline. We talked about math and Woodstock. Jack reassured me it was all good, all part of learning and growing from one life to the next. While transitions are not always easy, he added, we always come out on the   other   side.

"Birth and death are no different."

Jack's last words before he whispered it was time for me to leave and to ask Harmony to come back in was that I should not be the least bit sad because, "we will be together soon enough among the stars."

"I certainly hope so."

"Remember this," Jack said, "living is finite, but life is infinite."

Some nights, I close my eyes and go back to that moment. Maybe it's just my imagination or Jack was the best actor in the world, but he seemed genuinely excited about what was coming next. If it can be said that a light shined from someone's countenance at the end, as I've read in many novels, it certainly did from Jack.

He looked angelic when I turned back at the door to wave goodbye. Thin, wrinkled, and ill, but peaceful and content.

Unfortunately, I know it's impossible for me to believe the way Jack did, certainly not after spending most of my life disbelieving.

When my mother died, I watched her body being lowered into the ground and I whispered to my sister that she was going to a better place, although it wasn't with nearly the same conviction I had when arguing my client's position in court. I didn't feel as if she was still with us watching from above, I mostly felt as if I was next in line and had taken a giant step closer to the abyss.

The best I can do now, despite my efforts to replay Jack's words, as well as to read some of the books he recommended about the Buddha and the circle of life, is to admit that I don't know for sure. No one does. Which means Jack and a billion other people could be right. Why not? Admitting your ignorance is the first step to believing in something greater than yourself.

I didn't raise my doubts with Jack at the end, although he knew me well enough to know they were there. I don't talk about them with Harmony either. I don't talk about things like that with her or anyone else. At my age, there are some things you need to figure out on your own. The gap between the mind, where the intellect resides, and the heart, the seat of belief, can seem enormous at times. Yet sometimes it seems as if there's hardly any space between them.

There was no funeral for Jack, just a lunch with his friends, neighbors, and family. It was joyous and ceremonial—as if it were part of some ancient rite—especially when his ashes were scattered at the same spots in the forest and in the stream where Kai's ashes had been spread.

In response to my questions, Harmony confirmed that Jack did not have a will. He had no bank account; just cash he kept in a fireproof box in his closet. The only things registered with the state were his truck and the cabin, both of which he had transferred to Harmony long before he died.

Harmony and her husband lived with their two kids in a beautiful old house closer to town. She planned on keeping the cabin as a sort of vacation home, a place to go with Barry and the kids, Dan, and Janice, when they needed to do some hiking and fishing. I never asked her why her kids had such normal names, but their names always make me smile, and I didn't ask how her father felt about their fishing because I knew. Harmony had her own path to follow, and Jack had no problem with that.

What Harmony doesn't know is that she will inherit a sizeable portion of my estate which includes an empty apartment on Central Park, a house in Naples with a view of the Gulf of Mexico, my home outside Woodstock, and a lot of stocks and bonds. My sister and her kids will get their share, I can't be that cavalier about family, and the rest will go to charity.

I spent most of my life feeling badly that Jack had abandoned his dream about earning a doctorate in math and being there for the birth of the computer age, and for throwing it all away after Woodstock for a woman and a lifestyle. Yet, if I had it to do all over again, I might consider taking the bus with him back to Woodstock and finding my own Kai or moving up there after law school and becoming the small-town lawyer he once suggested.

Perhaps my first real love, the only one to my thinking, Michie, my fabric designer, would have stayed and come with me if that had been my plan. What more beautiful place than the Catskills to inspire an artist?

My final moment can't be far off, and I know that when I'm lying there waiting, Harmony will be at my side, although any smile I put on will probably feel fake no matter how much better I've gotten at it. I missed too much in this earthly life to be satisfied with the way I lived it.

If life is indeed a circle, then I will try to make sure my next one is all about love and filled with change.

www.ingramcontent.com/pod-product-compliance
Lightning Source LLC
Chambersburg PA
CBHW031149160726
47991CB00004B/1600

9 798986 428444